ONCE
TWO
SISTERS

ONCE TWO SISTERS

A NOVEL

SARAH WARBURTON

CROOKED
LANE

NEW YORK

Published in the United States by Crooked Lane Books, an imprint of The Quick Brown Fox & Company LLC.

Crooked Lane Books and its logo are trademarks of The Quick Brown Fox & Company LLC.

Library of Congress Catalog-in-Publication data available upon request.

ISBN (hardcover): 978-1-64385-525-7
ISBN (ebook): 978-1-64385-526-4

Cover design by Melanie Sun

Printed in the United States.

www.crookedlanebooks.com

Crooked Lane Books
34 West 27th St., 10th Floor
New York, NY 10001

First Edition: September 2020

10 9 8 7 6 5 4 3 2 1

For my whole family, especially Tim.

CHAPTER

1

I'VE BEEN KILLED and incarcerated, tortured and
seduced, stalked and obsessed. I've been the murderer
and the victim, the detective and the fugitive, the hero
and the villain. I've died over and over again. In the
swamps of Louisiana, on the streets of Chicago, in a
small suburban town where nothing ever happens. I've
been a housewife, a call girl, a forensic anthropologist, a
secretary, an assassin, a nun. And whether I am angel or
demon, innocent or damned, only one person is to blame:
my sister, Ava Hallett.

Everyone in America has read my story in her books,
seen her on the talk-show circuit, eaten popcorn while I
weep and bleed on the silver screen. The only reason she
doesn't have a television series is her apparent inability to
write a series. One stand-alone best seller after another,
and I'm the common denominator.

Ava is older than I am, and she laid claim to writing
as casually as calling dibs on riding shotgun. And she
didn't stop there. Every job, every hobby, every boyfriend

or passion or goddamn private thought I've ever had, she's jammed into a novel. She takes my life and murders it, over and over again.

I wish I were more zen, a person who could let this shit go. I should have joined the Peace Corps or back-packed through Thailand. Without her, maybe I would have been ordinary, the kind of girl who goes to college in her hometown and marries the boy next door.

Instead, I ditched everything—my life in Northern Virginia, my relationship with my dysfunctional family, and the girl I used to be. Because of Ava, I'm living over fifteen hundred miles away in the suburbs of Houston, under an assumed name.

Now I sit, anonymous, with two other moms—Bethany and Felicia—at the edge of a playground, pretending to watch all the kids going up and down the slides. And I feel as if my happily-ever-after days in Texas must be numbered. This happiness is too easy. There's no way I can hold on to it.

The three of us watch our kids, parallel-playing in separate areas. In sync but apart. Bethany's son is hang-ing by his knees from the climbing frame, Felicia's son spins around and around with his arms flung wide, and my stepdaughter Emma is digging through the mulch with a stick.

Bethany sits next to me in the shade. She's heavily pregnant, and sweat beads lightly under her bangs. Although she's pushing forty, her blonde hair is up in a ponytail and she wears denim cutoffs like a teenager. She's been talking at a brisk clip around the wad of gum in her mouth, words pouring out of her.

"Dan was in oil, so he spent years traveling overseas, working for the money. He banked every dollar he made.

Then he had a layover in Atlanta, went to a Waffle House, and I was his waitress. I tell you what, his family was not thrilled that he'd found himself a divorced single mom with a teenager, a toddler, and a crazy ex, but now that we've got a boy of our own on the way, they've got nothing to say." Bethany pats her stomach complacently.

I glance over at Felicia, and sure enough, she's not even suppressing her smirk. The beautiful thing about Bethany is that she gives you all the gossip you'd ever want to know about her, right to your face. She's not ashamed of anything.

Felicia and I, we like to know what's going on with people, their stories. Felicia used to work behind the scenes in television, something about scripts and layout, which I always thought was just for magazines. She's very visual, and I know she's loving the picture Bethany makes as she tilts her head back and takes a swig from her Diet Pepsi.

You'd think someone with secrets like mine couldn't be friends with someone like Felicia, wouldn't you? But the key to covering up your past is to layer in a story that's good enough to be a distraction. My personal smoke screen is the way I met my husband, Andrew, on FindMyMatch.com.

In a way, our story is the inverse of Bethany's. He was the single parent, I was the self-sufficient stranger— although I wasn't rich, and I was on the run. Not that Andrew knew that. For him, my smoke screen had to be that I was an only child, in mourning for my parents, who'd died together in a car crash. I almost backpedaled when I learned his wife had died in childbirth. But in the end I just added that guilt to the pile I'd already accumulated.

Andrew was calm, smart, and patient, and Emma seemed like the one thing I'd been waiting for my whole life. I fell hard for them both, but I didn't kid myself that I deserved them. All I could hope was that starting over as a new person with a loving family would give me a chance to earn it for real.

When I told the story to Felicia, I spun a dozen tales of online dating nightmares. I could get laughs for the imaginary guy with the foot fetish, the one whose wife crashed our date, the one who referred to himself in the third person. "We are so lucky," I told her. "We've got great guys. The world is full of crazies."

Not like me. I'm only crazy on paper. Once I shed my name, I left all the madness behind. Maybe I am lying about my past, but I'm being honest here in the present. I love the feel of the sun on my face, my friends beside me, the happy shrieks of children. I'm not lying about anything that really matters.

"Lizzie!" Emma comes running over to me with something clenched in her hand. "Look what I found!"

I brace myself as she sticks her hand uncomfortably close to my face. This discovery could be anything from a beetle to a used eraser. She unfolds her chubby fingers to reveal a rhinestone pendant with the top loop broken off. The letter is *L*.

"It's real diamonds, and *L* is for Lizzie." Eagerly she presses it into my hand and takes off again, mulch flying under her feet. I curl my fingers over the trinket, wishing Lizzie had always been my real name or anywhere close to it.

"Sweet," Felicia says, and I can see she's glad she isn't holding somebody else's discarded junk. Her turn will come around again. I still remember when her son started collecting leaves—everything that came out of Felicia's purse for weeks was powdered with dried brown leaf fragments.

"Want a piece of gum?" Bethany asks, adding another stick to the bulge in her cheek.

I shake my head as Felicia's phone buzzes. She pulls it out, then looks up at us. "Getting together a carpool for book club. You going?"

Bethany shrugs. We all know she isn't interested. Even at the pool, she never pulls so much as a magazine out of her bag. I have been a regular at the book club, even though I tell myself it's a mistake every single month. And when this month's book was nominated, I tried to trash it. I said I'd heard it was derivative and slow, with nothing to discuss. But it didn't work. Ava's books are always best sellers. Even a book club with a taste for literary fiction couldn't overlook a thriller for women, about women, and by a woman. By everyone's favorite author—everyone's but mine.

"I can't make it this month," I lie.

Felicia won't let it alone. "If Andrew's out of town, just get a sitter. My neighbor's daughter needs pocket money."

"We'll see." I try to be noncommittal, but she shoots me a look that says *I see right through you. Liar.*

"Bring Emma over to my place. Tom won't mind watching one extra."

"I'll let you know."

While normally I crave the feeling of being wanted and valued, I can't handle three hours of discussing my sister's latest, *Bloody Heart, Wild Woods.* It's the only one I haven't read, the one she wrote after I went off the grid. The book club provided a little description of the story, set off the coast of New England, and it didn't sound like my life, but I've been fooled into complacency before, only to be struck by the dagger she hides—just for me—in the heart of every novel.

I'm scared to read this book, scared that it could suck me back into the person I was before.

And, honestly, I'm scared to see what my sister knows.

*   *   *

That night Andrew is home early, after Emma's dinner but before her bath. "I'll take it from here," he tells me. "Put up your feet and relax."

Our grown-up dinner is waiting in the Crock-Pot, so I pour myself a glass of wine, listening to the sound of running water from the bathroom, the deep rumble of Andrew's voice, the piping counterpoint of Emma's. I never thought I would have this kind of life, and relaxing into it isn't easy. Compulsively I run a dishrag over the counter top, even though there's not a crumb on it. I always clean the house aggressively, using products that are safe or even homemade, with vinegar and baking soda. I want it fresh, spotless, safe for Emma. When this all falls down, no one will be able to say I didn't do everything right.

In the hour before Andrew walked through the door, I took a slug from a bottle of bourbon stashed under the sink among the cleaning supplies. The fire in my throat helped me push Ava and her book away as I arranged Emma's bits of cooked chicken, leftover steamed broccoli, and goldfish crackers on a melamine plate divided into three sections.

Emma is an easy child, especially considering that she has passed her "terrible twos" and her "even worse threes." Now that she's four, she likes order, so I made a point of choosing three kinds of food, one for each section, in equal amounts. She went around on her own, taking a bite of chicken, then broccoli, then a goldfish to close it out. Once her plate was clean she held out her hands, and I gave her a kiss on each soft palm, followed by a graham cracker.

We are usually on our own for Emma's meal and the rest of her evening routine. Houston traffic is unpredictably terrible, and we live in the suburbs "outside the loop" of the beltway. On any given evening Andrew might get home in half an hour or over two hours, depending on the situation.

If Bethany's in-laws were Andrew's, they might say he'd found marrying a nanny cheaper than keeping one on. I don't mind yet. Children live in the moment, in the little things of life, so Emma keeps me here, in this happy place. And maybe because she isn't my flesh and blood, I never feel competitive or resentful. Sometimes I wish she were a little older, a little less of all the things a four-year-old child often is—hungry, tired, bored, whiny, messy—but for the most part we get on easily together. Being with her makes me a better person.

Andrew is also easy to get along with. I chose him for his open gaze, his straightforward approach, and his undemanding nature. His wife died giving birth to Emma, something I didn't think happened in America anymore, and eighteen months later he was ready to "test the waters," as he put it. That's how we came to meet on the dating site that served as my smoke screen. He doesn't look for lies in me. And if you don't count the big one, the one I told up front, I don't have to lie to him.

But sometimes I get that sinking feeling in the pit of my stomach. Because lies have a way of surfacing, and I want so much for this Lizzie—wife, mother, friend—to be real. Andrew doesn't deserve a fake.

He returns with Emma in his arms, a fine mist of soapy sweetness hovering over them both. "Say good night, sweetheart." He tilts her toward me.

As her warm, damp cheek presses against mine, she whispers, "Good night, sweetheart," and giggles.

"Good night to you, my Emma bean." For a moment, this is the only thing that's real, this family—a mom and a dad and this loved child. Then Andrew turns with Emma, and I feel the chill of the air conditioning on my abandoned cheek.

I take another sip of wine, a sip that's a little too big. As I hear Andrew setting up Emma's room with the nightlight, special blanket, and lullaby bear, I speed to the fridge. The bottle of white is almost empty, so I swig it down, hide the empty bottle at the bottom of the recycling bin, and fill my glass with a serving from a new bottle. Not cold, but that's okay.

I've put in the wine-saving plug and have the refrigerator open when Andrew comes back into the kitchen.

"You want a glass?" I ask, hoping he'll say no. Drinking warm white wine looks bad, and I'm invested in looking right. We're just weeks shy of our first-year anniversary, and Andrew still thinks I'm a good person.

He nods, then hesitates. "What's for dinner?"

"Beef stew. We have red." I think we have red. Unless I drank it all.

"I'll go with a beer instead." He comes up behind me and puts one arm around my tensed waist, reaching with the other to snag a bottle of Saint Arnold Santo. "Let's watch the news before we eat."

Prime-time television in Texas comes on an hour earlier than it does on the East Coast, where I grew up. There's no way we can watch the nightly news together unless we record it, so we always do. We settle together on the sofa, knees touching, drinks in our hands, and push play.

The newscaster is in the middle of a story, but it's the photo behind her that makes me clench my wineglass. Ava. A publicity photo that shows her leaning against a brick wall, her blonde hair barely brushing the shoulders of her tailored leather jacket. It takes a second for me to make sense of the words written across the photo: "Life Imitates Fiction."

That's how I learn my sister is missing.

2

How is the disappearance of one woman national news? When that woman is a *New York Times* best-selling author whose books are made into blockbuster movies, when she writes story after story about women who are missing or kidnapped or killed, and when her husband makes a teary-eyed plea to the cameras for "any news at all"—that's a guaranteed eyes-glued-to-the-screen scenario.

I'm not prepared. Not for any of it. Not for the rush of fear and love I feel for Ava, even after all she's done. I want to unsee the news, dial the evening back to me and Andrew on the sofa, safe and happy. The way he thinks we still are.

One unfortunate side effect of cutting yourself off from your family is that nobody calls to tell you there's been an accident or a tragedy. And when you learn that your sister has gone missing, you can't let your husband know anything is wrong. Not without blowing up the new life you have with him. All he knows about Ava is that she's a writer on our book-club list. That's on me. I've got the schedule stuck to our fridge.

The final notes of the nightly news theme are fading away. Andrew looks at me. "You should definitely go to book club tomorrow night. This whole thing is going to make the discussion unforgettable."

Unforgettable. I clench the stem of my empty wineglass, remembering the way Ava always sucked the life, the attention out of every space. I can't believe she's missing. I *will* not believe it. This has got to be another one of her games.

As Andrew putters around the house after dinner, I step onto the front porch with the disposable phone I keep secretly charged and hidden in a sugar bowl in the china cabinet. All the china was chosen by Andrew's first wife. Although he encouraged me to choose something else, I loved stepping into this ready-made life.

The air is steamy hot, not cool and crisp like the autumns of my childhood. When the sun goes down in Texas, heat continues pulsing off the pavement, so there's no reprieve. On the front steps, the street stretches away from me on either side, lined with rows of houses in brick. In this planned community, every home is a variant on a single plan. It would be a perfect setting for one of Ava's stories, all the houses made of ticky-tacky.

I open the phone and dial the only number I ever call from it, my parents' landline, but it goes straight to voice mail. I hang up without leaving a message. Bitterly I acknowledge that I could leave them this number, ask them to call me when they know something. But if they wanted to find me, they would have already. The reason I've disappeared so successfully isn't this burner phone, it's that nobody is looking for me.

I stand on my front step for another moment, trying to squash my rising anxiety. Ava is probably just building publicity for her next book, or holed up with a new guy, or looking for a quiet place to write. She's never been overly concerned about the feelings of other people. She'll turn up, and nobody will know who I am.

Ava's fine. I will be too.

*   *   *

I believe my own lie enough to fall asleep, but unease runs through every dream. In them I'm chasing Ava through a forest of gnarled, sentient trees. I wake up with my heart pounding and the sheets twisted like a bandage around my ankles. Beside me, Andrew sprawls flat on his back, arms open, palms up, his breathing deep and rhythmic. I wish I felt that free and open, at least in sleep.

Silently I slip my feet out of the coiled bedclothes and pad to the other room, where my laptop is charging on the counter. Andrew gave it to me last Christmas, and I'm still a little suspicious of it. I don't shop online, and my social-media presence is nonexistent. Our joint family email address is the only one I share with book club and the preschool. Even so, I clear my browser history and power the whole thing off every time I'm done.

Now I think back to the time before, back when my name was still Zoe, before I had a suburban life and disappeared into a cadre of other moms. My hands hover over the keyboard as I remember the crappy student apartment, the babysitting gigs and bookstore job I worked to supplement my graduate student stipend. I type in that old email address—my birth name and the server. To conjure up the password, I close my eyes against the pale glow of the screen and remember the release date of Ava's previous book.

I was working the evening shift at the bookstore, and a huge flat of Ava's books was waiting in the receiving area for the next morning's official release date. Straightening the shelves and pulling special orders, I tried not to think about what Ava might have written. I was tired of being disappointed in my callous parents, tired of being angry, tired of living under a spotlight. Or not a spotlight—more like the focused beam from a giant magnifying glass, and I, the hapless ant, always scurrying away to avoid being burned alive.

The difference with this book was that Ava now had a reason to be angry with me. Before, I hadn't done anything. I was just trying to live my life. But this time I had broken a taboo. Not only had I coveted my sister's man, I had taken him.

And when I sliced open the first box of books and lifted one out to put on the display tower, I couldn't help flipping it open. The story of a husband, seduced by his sister-in-law and then framed for a murder she'd committed. The dedication didn't mention me. It read: "To Glenn, my own true love. May you reap in the future all the joy you have given me."

That was the moment I decided to burn my own life to the ground and start all over again as someone else. There was no way to be free of Ava as long as I was Zoe.

Now, looking at the computer screen, I type in my old password, the one I changed right before I left. ZOE IS DEAD.

I've always been careful about not signing up to email lists or passing out my information. Now I realize

I've been so guarded that no friends from my old life emailed me either. My Texas friends contact me about playgroups and book clubs and wine tastings through the joint account Andrew and I share. Once I killed off the Zoe I used to be, that email account died with her. The most recent email is over two years old, and it's from my parents. That must have been around the time I started calling them from the burner phone, just two or three times a year. I told them I'd be traveling for work but was vague about the nature of the job and where I would be. They aren't the kind of parents who really care.

I compose an email to them now, keeping it short like a virtual telegram.

Just saw the news. Worried. When can I call you?

Then I stop. Can IP addresses be traced? Will I be giving away everything I've worked so hard to create? No, more than that. I might be giving away everything I'm trying to earn. Andrew is a wonderful guy, easygoing and honest, but not even a saint would let a liar stay in the house with his young daughter. An echo of her warmth seems to press against my cheek. I've never had someone I wasn't willing to lose.

I delete the email, and then, paranoid that it might have gone out regardless, click on the Sent Mail folder to double-check. Unlike my inbox, this outgoing mailbox is full. The most recent message dates only a few days ago and was sent to Ava's private email.

Horrified, I read the subject lines: "You Bitch," "You Can't Hide," and "I See You." I click on the most recent one and read:

Ava, the time has come for you to pay. You stole my life, my soul, and now I will steal everything from you. Are you ready to star in your own horror thriller? Better start sleeping with one eye open . . . unless you're afraid I'll put it out. Together we'll see if blood really is thicker than water. Your devoted sister, Zoe.

Frantically, I click on one message and then another, each full of threats. There's one about her first husband, Beckett—how Ava wasn't good enough for him, how she destroyed his life and humiliated the most talented writer she'd ever know. Most of the others talk about her current husband, Glenn. *Do you know what he does when you're out?* the writer taunts. *He has seen the venom in your soul. Do you think he loves you? That he's forgiven you? He's playing a long game. I only hope he doesn't get you before I do. Get in line, Glenn.*

My mind is a staticky blank. I slam the laptop shut and put it away. Some of those thoughts are as angry as anything I might have written, but I didn't. But they sound like me, they sound like someone who hated Ava. Someone who wanted her missing.

The back of my neck prickles, and I can't help glancing at the kitchen windows, discreetly shaded by lace-trimmed curtains. I stand up, my heart racing. I should check the locks, double-check the security system. Someone is after me too. Someone wants to frame me for Ava's disappearance.

Who hated Ava as much as I did? Her former agent, her ex-husband, Glenn, anyone who's ever been in a writing class with her. Anyone could have done it, but I'm the one who will look guilty. Shaking, I open the laptop and it glows back to life. Does the writer of those message know where I am, *who* I am now?

No. I wrap my arms around myself, trying to think. Just because someone hacked my email doesn't mean they know where I am. Probably they thought I'd be an easy target. They don't realize I'm a good person now, a person with a clean house and a loving husband and a beautiful child.

But I don't know much about how the internet works or how IP addresses can be traced. One at a time, I shut every open window and every app, then push a button to disconnect the internet. I clear the browser history. Is that enough?

If only I could completely erase the messages from my outbox and Ava's inbox and the whole internet. The empty wineglasses, rinsed and waiting in the drying rack, give me an idea. I race to the fridge and grab the nearly empty bottle of Pinot Grigio. As I pull out the cork, there's a moment when I long to down the cold dregs, go back to bed, and trust this has all been an alcohol-fueled nightmare. But I'm not drunk, and I'm certainly not sleepy. This shit is real.

Deliberately I pour the wine over the keyboard, taking the time to saturate each and every key. There is still some wine left. Resisting temptation, I tip the laptop to the side and pour the remainder into every hole and port. The screen flickers and goes dark. I shut the lid and tip the whole thing, heavy and dripping, into the trash.

The clock says three AM. The worst hour of the night, when everything becomes bleak and real. It's closer to dawn on the East Coast and my parents get up early. In just another hour, I can call them again.

I sit on the sofa. Perhaps I can find more news now. I keep the volume off, turn on closed captioning, and flip to one of those twenty-four-hour news channels. Nothing about Ava comes on, and after watching the news scroll across the bottom of the screen and the subtitles blur on top of it, in spite of everything I know and all I learned, I fall asleep with the remote in my hand.

* * *

As I struggle back to the waking world, first my neck protests, bent at an awkward angle and jounced by an unseen force. Then I hear the high-pitched noise, closer than the television, and it resolves into words. "Lizzie! Lizzie!"

I'm not really a morning person, so it takes a few more minutes to realize that the jolting and noise are coming from Emma bouncing me on the sofa.

"Hello, sleepyhead." Andrew is in the kitchen. He must have been silent as a housebreaker, because he's already made coffee.

He smiles at me as he fills a mug and adds a splash of milk, the way I like it. "You were really out. Bad dreams?"

I mean to say *Something like that*, but it comes out as an unintelligible garble and he laughs, but not unkindly. I love it when Andrew laughs and the tension in his shoulders releases. That's one of the scars from the loss of his wife, the constant vigilance. He's never forgotten the burden of being a single parent.

Pushing myself upright, I reach out for the mug Andrew brings me, and at the roasted-earth aroma, my eyes fill with tears. Stupid sentimental things like puppies and warm coffee can make me cry, but huge things— distant parents, a missing sister, or the dawning realization that I will have to tell Andrew everything—leave my eyes dry. Anything I say will cost me this home, this safety, this sweet child snuggling next to me on the sofa. I curl my hands around the mug and wish I could stay here forever.

Emma must feel the same way. "I want to sleep out here too. Tonight, Daddy, can I have a sleepover with Lizzie?"

Andrew meets my eyes with a wink. "I think it's easier for everyone if you sleep in your own special big-girl bed."

I can still see CNN playing on mute behind Andrew, and in that moment everything outside the television screen seems to freeze. There is a podium on the screen, and police officers and my parents. With them is a man I haven't seen for three years. Glenn. He and Ava are married now. I hate myself, but I wish they weren't. His shoulders look broader, his face more chiseled than I remember.

I have to hear what he is saying.

I grab for the remote control, but Emma tips over, giggling, and my coffee sloshes over my arm. Jerking away, I send the remote skittering across the floor, before I realize the coffee is warm, not scalding. *I'm okay, I'm okay*, I tell myself, but I feel as wired as if I'd had three pots.

"You really aren't yourself this morning," Andrew says. "Why don't you go back to bed, try to grab a few more hours? I'll get this monkey dressed and off to school." He leans over and scoops Emma up effortlessly, dropping a soft kiss on the top of my head.

Wrapping my arms around myself, I sit in the spilled coffee, letting my pajama bottoms soak it up. I don't deserve Andrew's love, and Glenn is back to make sure I can't keep it. I turn the sound on and rewind to the beginning of the news story.

"We're asking anyone with information about Ava to come forward. In addition, there is some indication that her sister"—Glenn stumbles over the word—"my sister-in-law may be involved."

My skin puckers with goose bumps that have nothing to do with the rapidly cooling coffee. I thought that even if Glenn didn't love me, he knew me, understood me. But there my former lover stands in front of a microphone, throwing me to the wolves. I wish I could feel hate for this judgmental stranger, but there's only pain and rising fear. Someone is setting me up. Is it him?

My parents are just standing there behind him. Walter and Nancy Hallett. The Doctors Hallett. How can they believe I'm involved? All those years they didn't defend me against Ava, all those times they said I was overreacting. They never really saw me. Whatever parents are supposed to be, my mother and father can't manage it.

I pause the television and squint hard at Glenn, standing there in his dress shirt with the rolled-up sleeves. He has changed. I used to think he looked dangerous, sexy, but time has made his good looks softer, more conventional. He's the kind of guy anyone would call handsome and some might call trouble. Not like Andrew. My husband looks like a nice guy, a guy you can trust. He has creases in the corners of his eyes from smiling and a deepening line between his brows from worrying.

Glenn is standing there between my sleek mother and my distinguished father, like part of our family. There wasn't a press conference when I disappeared. Not even in the months before I made my first phone call. No sign of fear or worry, no missing persons report. That must be why I'm such an easy scapegoat. No one cares where I am. Not like precious Ava.

I push play again, and it catches me by surprise how quickly the screen changes to the news anchor. Behind her, much bigger than her head, is a picture of a girl in her early twenties. Her eyes are wide and startled, what Andrew calls crazy eyes. She is looking up from a cutting board with a knife in her hand. Then the picture zooms in—the eyes even bigger, thin lips parted in surprise, the kitchen counter cropped out. I know the girl is finely dicing onion for a mirepoix.

I know, because the girl is me.

From the hallway there's a commotion, loud footsteps, and then Emma's excited voice cries, "Lizzie, you're on TV!"

Behind her Andrew says, "We talked about this, Emma. I'm not Tom Hanks, and Lizzie—" He stops, and I know he is looking at the screen, where the anchor is completing her story about the strange coincidence wherein I have not been seen for over three years.

"But this isn't the first time an author's life has become a real mystery. Over ninety years ago, the 'Queen of Crime,' Dame Agatha Christie, staged her own disappearance and inspired an eleven-day manhunt. Now crime aficionados are wondering if Hallett's disappearance is another elaborate hoax or a case of foul play. Officials ask anyone with information about either of the Hallett sisters to come forward. More news, after this."

I keep my eyes on Andrew, watching him see the screen split with the old picture of me even more wan and pathetic next to a vibrant publicity shot of Ava. Then he looks at me, and my expression must confirm it. I am guilty.

"Lizzie," Andrew's voice is extremely calm. Too calm. "Let's speak in private."

"Me too, meee too," Emma cries, unwilling to be left out.

I put a hand on the top of her head, where the feathery curls are impossibly soft between my fingers. When she was being born, when her mother was dying, I was killing off the person I had been and birthing the lie I am living now.

Andrew picks up the remote. "You can watch *Dora* for one episode. Just one."

Emma lights up at the unexpected treat, usually reserved for getting her nails clipped, taking medication, and other painful occasions. She squirms out from under my hand, flops on the sofa, and sits motionless, barely breathing as the petite explorer appears on screen.

Back in the bedroom, I expect threats or recriminations. The bed where only eight hours ago we both slept back to back is now neatly made. For a moment, with piercing ferocity, I hope Ava is dead. If this is a stupid publicity stunt and it costs me everything, I will kill her.

Then I remember the vicious emails, and I am afraid again.

CHAPTER

3

ANDREW SITS DOWN heavily on the edge of the bed, rumpling the cover he's pulled up neatly, the way he always does. His bedside table has only a lamp and a copy of *New Scientist*. Mine is littered with lip balm and hand cream, crumpled tissues and paperback novels.

"What the hell, Lizzie. Or . . . what did they say your real name is?" His gaze skates away, as if looking at me will distract him from figuring out what to do next.

Can I lie, pretend that picture wasn't me? I want to scramble farther away from the truth until I am the woman I pretend to be. But Andrew is smart, really smart, and I do love him. I can't run away from this without losing him and Emma both. "Zoe," I say softly. "My name was Zoe."

"Zoe," he repeats, twisting his wedding band around his finger. "And your parents aren't dead."

I shake my head, but he isn't looking at me. "No."

"Did they think you were—?" He doesn't say *dead,* but I know he is thinking about Emma. What he would do if she disappeared. He is compartmentalizing his emotions and analyzing the situation, just like my parents would do, if they ever had emotions.

"No!" The word is stronger than I expected, but I need him to *feel*. "No, I wouldn't just . . . I call them." And now he knows the lie has been ongoing, that I've been sneaking off to make phone calls. How can I fix this? "We've never been close, but I didn't want them to worry. I just needed to leave."

"Why? Lots of people aren't close to their parents. They don't change their names and scam themselves into someone else's life."

Scam. Fraud. Liar. My heart is pounding. "I didn't. It's a real name. I changed it legally; my driver's license is real. I just needed to be someone else. Someone not related to her. I didn't plan to meet you."

He looks up, his brown eyes boring into mine. "You were on a dating site. You were looking for someone. And you found me."

My heart feels cold and leaden, like I'm turning to marble. Now that he is looking at me, I feel like he sees all my weaknesses. *Look closer*, I want to say. *See me. See that I love you.*

But he's frowning as if I'm an insect he's trying to identify. "You found me and used me, used Emma to . . . what? Hide? I thought I knew you."

I sink to my knees so we are face-to-face. "You did! You do. I'm the same person."

"I don't know anything about you. Except you're Ava Hallett's sister."

I have to make him understand. "You haven't read her books. They're all about me. She took my life, anything I did, anyone I loved. She took them and twisted them and ruined them."

"What are you talking about?" He has a vertical line between his brows, and I long to press my thumb onto it, to smooth it away.

Instead, I reach out for his hands, clinging to them. "Anywhere I went, she set a novel. Anything I tried to do, she wrote about. Anyone I knew, she used against me. She's not just a writer, Andrew, she's a best-selling author. Haven't you seen her books in the airport or her movies on a plane?"

"You're not making any sense." He shakes me off and stands up, but I rise and follow him around the edge of the bed.

Maybe if I talk fast enough, he will hear what I'm really feeling. "I wanted to disappear. I didn't want her to know anything else about me, ever. When we met, I really was working in a coffee shop. I really did fall in love with you. I really do love Emma, so, so much." My voice wavers, but my stupid, treacherous eyes refuse to well with tears. "You are my family and this is my life. I never lied about anything that really matters."

Andrew holds his hands up to ward me off. "Nothing that really matters? You lied about everything. We're married, and I don't know you at all. And what about your parents? Do they know about me and Emma?"

I can't help it; a bitter laugh breaks free. "My parents? I waited thirty weeks before I called them, and they hadn't filed a missing persons report. They never understood how much it hurt when Ava scooped out my personal life like the inside of a jack-o'-lantern. They told me to be happy for her, to quit being so sensitive." Andrew and Emma are the only people who have ever truly loved me.

Oh, why can't I cry now, when my heart is breaking?

I wrap my arms around my stomach, and I see pity in Andrew's eyes. "Lizzie," he says softly.

He's come to a decision. I can see it in the steadiness of his gaze. Maybe if I grovel, I can change his mind. I have to change his mind. "I know. You don't trust me around Emma. I've lied to you, you don't know who I am, you can't trust me, but—"

"But we've got time to think about all of that later." Andrew's voice is calm. "Right now, you have to go to the police before this thing snowballs. I may not know everything about your life, but I do know where you were last week. I know you weren't making your sister disappear. You've been right here in Texas with me and Emma. The sooner you get that cleared up, the sooner we deal with everything else."

"I'm afraid," I tell him. "Anything I say is going to pull you and Emma into the spotlight."

"All you have to do is tell the truth," he says. "We'll take Emma to day care and then drive over to the sheriff's office. It's not like you'll be talking to the FBI. Emma was in playgroup with Bob's daughter. Just make a statement here at the local office."

"Will you stay with me?"

He doesn't answer, and I can feel the unsheddable tears building inside. My voice rises. "Andrew, please. I *need* you. I can't do this by myself."

"That's not my problem." He sounds like he's speaking to a telemarketer, an annoying stranger . . .

"We're *married*. You can't just—"

"Don't tell me what I can't do. You're a liar!"

And the bedroom door opens. Emma's eyes are huge and accusatory. "You're too loud," she says.

Andrew holds out his arms. "I'm sorry, baby. Let's get you to school."

"I want Lizzie." She runs forward, darting around him, and holds her arms up to me. My knees give way and I am on the floor, embracing Emma, my face pressed against her sweet head. If I keep my eyes screwed shut, maybe I can stay here forever.

Andrew sighs, and I think maybe at least one of my prayers was answered. "Okay," he says. "Okay. I'll come with you."

I raise my head and look at him. Does he love me? I can't tell from his face. But even if this is just pity, it's better than nothing.

Knowing he will be with me to talk to the police, maybe even to see my parents, softens the blow. I can do this. I can tell the truth if he's with me.

For once, the truth really is that I'm innocent.

"I love you," I tell him, but he looks away.

*   *   *

A happy soundtrack of Laurie Berkner, Dan Zanes, and other folksy kid-rock tunes fills the car on the way to preschool. In the back seat, Emma hums tunelessly and kicks her feet in time.

My phone is completely silent. Ominously silent. A number of the playgroup moms are inveterate texters. Usually there's a continuous buzzing coming from my phone. Everything from a slowdown on Highway 90A to a plea to borrow a juice box for a school lunch to an FYI about the PTO (and I don't even have a child in elementary school) to an invitation to meet up at the park.

I know without a doubt that texts are flying around. I'm just not included in them. Someone must have recognized me on the news. Who will be the first to report I am living under an alias? I hope it won't be Felicia or Bethany, but they are the most likely to recognize my picture. The ones who would realize how vague I've been about my past. They were my friends, but I've been lying to them too.

I don't give a shit about a "mean mom" thinking less of me. Playgroup is full of them, the kind of women who specialize in plastic smiles and sweet little burns. They wrap their venom in southernisms like "Bless your heart" or "I'll pray for you" or "Just so you know, sweetie . . ." which is never followed by anything nice. No one says, "Just so you know, sweetie, your child is a genius and you're an amazing mom." It's always something like "Just so you know, sweetie, your child ate the only yellow crayon and I barely stopped her from running into the street." The subtext is clear: "Your child needs help and you're a disgrace."

I don't understand the rules of this kind of girl-game, so I mostly keep a bland, unoffended smile on my face and back away, storing up the most cutting remarks to mock with Felicia later. Felicia was the second person to make me laugh and forget I was pretending to be someone else.

Andrew was the first. I glance at him, but he's looking straight ahead. I'm afraid to say anything, afraid he might not answer me. Maybe I don't exist for him anymore.

We stop at the intersection where the train runs parallel to Highway 90A. From the back seat, Emma starts singing "Little Red Caboose" in time to the crossing bell. Somehow, whenever you're late, you're always on the wrong side of the tracks. I can't tell how long this freight train is, but it seems interminable.

With a jolt I remember I agreed to watch Felicia's son, Sam, this afternoon while she gets her hair cut. Will I be back? I steal another look at Andrew. The longer we go without speaking to each other, the harder it is to be the first one to say anything.

I pull out my phone and text *Can't watch Sam. Family emergency. So so sorry.* She'll have to scramble to find someone else, or bring a squirmy child with her to the salon, or wait five weeks for another appointment while the mean moms give her side eye. One more way I'm letting down someone I care about.

Usually she would text back right away: *OMG Hope all OK?* But my phone is silent. The last car of the train— not a caboose, just a basic boxcar—slides away. The crossing bell stops and the gate swings up.

Andrew doesn't ask who I'm texting, doesn't even look at me. Either he doesn't give a shit or he's trying not to act like he doesn't trust me. Which makes me feel worse. My heart is as heavy as my silent cell phone.

We bump over the tracks and back onto the smooth pavement. I can't go back to who I was. This is my life, my husband and my child. This is where I have friends. *This is where Lizzie has friends. And you're not Lizzie.*

As we pull into the school parking lot, cars are moving in every direction with kids darting between them. It's an obstacle course, but Andrew pulls the car slowly into a free parking place and sits for a minute with the engine off.

Outside, moms and dads trudge into the school with their kids and practically skip out unencumbered. Some are clearly on their way to work in crisp trousers and skirts, holding their children at arm's length to fend off sticky hands. Others are ready for a day at home in casual jeans or even sweat pants and tees. And a few of the übermoms are decked out in coordinated track suits or supertight spandex, ready to star in a workout video. I'm glad none of these stay-at-home parents has a name tag declaring "I used to be a lawyer" or doctor or accountant or whatever. Being a mom let me hide my past as a dilettante. Student of all, master of none. PhD in advanced lying.

Finally, Andrew says, "I'll take Emma in. Be right back."

"Okay," I whisper, not sure whether I'm sad not to have what might be my final hug from Emma or relieved that I'm being spared a moment that might break my stone-cold heart. "Have a good day, bunny."

"See you later, 'gator," she shouts, squirming to get out of the car seat's chest clip. "I can do it my own self, Daddy. You take care of you." With a last grunt, she hits the ground, holds up her hand for his, and trudges toward the school.

Across the parking lot I can see Felicia helping Sam cross safely among the Expeditions, CR-Vs, and Odysseys. I want her to look up at me and smile, to text me that it's all going to be okay. But if she knows I'm a liar, I can't count on her friendship anymore. And then she's gone, disappeared into the school.

Andrew took the keys in with him. Did he think I'd go peeling out of the preschool parking lot in his Escalade and make a run for it? Honestly, if I were going to, I'd have taken my own damn car, a little Ford Fiesta. Half the size of Felicia's SUV, it's the best car I've ever owned. Just big enough.

"Is this really what you want?" Andrew asked when I picked it out. "You can have something bigger. What if you want to carpool?"

"We can fit one other car seat in the back. They'll just have to be cozy."

I'm smiling at the memory when my phone buzzes. Felicia. She did see me. I snatch it up, but the text reads *Get out of the car and run.*

What? I do get out of the car, a rushing sound in my ears, and turn around, looking for Felicia. There's an older woman sitting in the driver's seat of the car parked next to us. Her head is bent over a screen, but when I slam my car door, she looks up and I see the GPS app on the screen.

Another text buzzes. *What are you waiting for? Didn't you see the news?*

Is Felicia trying to warn me? I don't understand. Then I see her coming out of the school without Sam. I tap her number, but as it rings I see her waving open-handed at the crossing guard. She's not holding anything.

I stumble back, my hand with the phone falling down by my side. The emails sent from my account. This must be the same person, stalking me, framing me. Frantic, I look around, but there are phones everywhere. One of the dads is on the phone; so is a teacher standing outside the school; even a little boy is playing a game on one while being dragged through the parking lot.

Another text buzzes. *You're wasting time looking for me.*

Fear skitters down the back of my neck, cascading in ice-cold droplets across every nerve ending in my body. Someone can see me right now. Where are they? I spin around again, but get nothing more than a curious look from the crossing guard at the drop-off lane.

And then my phone rings and I answer it.

A harsh voice whispers, "Don't be stupid, *Zoe*. Run!"

4

I SPIN AROUND AGAIN, scanning the parking lot.

"What are you doing?" Andrew has come up behind me, and I realize that not only do I look like a crazy person, turning in a circle, I've apparently developed tunnel vision. The more freaked out I am, the less observant I become.

"Someone sent me awful texts." I hand him the phone and wait while he reads.

"It's from Felicia's number," he says with the literalness that makes me call him Captain Obvious. He's used to easily definable problems, where you identify each part, make a plan, and find a solution. Usually I find that deeply comforting. Now I'm worried that this problem is too confusing, too scary, and the obvious solution will be to write me—our marriage—off as a loss.

"It isn't her. I saw Felicia taking Sam into school and I called her phone . . . it wasn't her. She came out and got into her car and drove away, the whole time someone else was talking." My voice is growing more shrill with every word. "Someone can see me. Someone knows who I am."

Andrew keeps the phone in his hand and scans the parking lot.

My raised voice has attracted attention. Parents walking their kids are giving me a wide berth. I can see a mean mom standing by the driver's side of a shiny new Lexus minivan, whispering to the driver. As soon as she sees me looking, she makes a little *caught me* face and pulls out her own car keys. *Bitch.* Why don't bad things ever happen to people like that?

"Okay." Andrew puts a hand on my shoulder. "The faster we get to the sheriff's office, the faster we can clear this all up. You'll be safe there, and I'll be with you."

Safe. Hasn't my husband seen any scary movies? That word is the kiss of death. Nevertheless, I swing into my side of the car, shut and lock the door, and then, when Andrew climbs in and gives me my phone, I shut it down completely. I can't remember the last time I did that. There's always the fear that Emma could get hurt or the school might call or something could happen to Andrew. Every crash reported on Highway 59, every twenty minutes he's late getting home, essentially every day he makes the treacherous journey across the looped deathways of Houston, I am worried and my phone is on—in my pocket or my hand.

Now I drop it like a brick into my purse.

As we pull out of the parking lot, Emma's music is still playing. They Might Be Giants wails about the "Alphabet Lost and Found," and I catch a line about slang words that don't belong. There have been times I've felt that way even in my new life—out of place, like a curse word in a church.

I feel that way right now in this car, beside my silent husband. I wish I could make a joke to break the tension, but I'm so afraid it would sound careless, heartless. And if I say something serious, will he answer with something devastating?

I clutch the purse on my lap and wish Felicia really had called me. She felt like a real friend, even though she knew only the lie. Maybe she would like me just as much, or even more, if she knew who I really was. Her subversive edge has always made her seem like she'd want a double life of her own as a spy or a crime fighter or a superhero. We usually talk every day about kids, television, our husbands, and neighborhood gossip, an ongoing conversation that fills the gaps between the face suburbia shows and the truth that runs beneath it all.

Sometimes I drive entire days with Emma's music blasting from my speakers, but Andrew must find the cheery voices grating. With a little too much force, he punches the button for the radio, and NPR comes on. He doesn't want to talk to me either. That could mean he hasn't decided what to do about our marriage. Or it could mean he knows, and this isn't the right time to discuss it.

I squeeze my eyes shut, as if I could wish myself back just twenty-four hours to a happy, safe life. Instead I hear the *Morning Edition* host say:

"In breaking news, we have just learned that Zoe Hallett—the sister of missing *New York Times* best-selling author Ava Hallett—and Glenn Melcher, the author's husband, have been named as persons of interest in her disappearance. In an additional twist worthy of the novelist herself, Zoe's exact whereabouts have been unknown for at least three years, although her parents report phone contact as recently as last month."

My heart rate skyrockets, and I taste sour acid in my mouth. Andrew veers a little too close to a parked car and pulls back into our lane with a jolt. "Don't panic." I can't tell if he is talking to himself or to me. "There was no way you could be involved. You were here with Emma."

He is definitely trying to reassure himself. He was out of town until Tuesday. Ava's been missing since Monday. And that was the day Emma and I stayed home. She had one of those inexplicable high fevers small children sometimes get, and she spent the day cuddled next to me, drooping and damp with sweat, while I coaxed her to sip iced apple juice and we watched *Dora the Explorer* together.

Could anyone verify that I was in Texas that day? Felicia called to see if we were all right, but she didn't see us in person. Surely if we traveled, there would be some kind of record. Or they could check the cell phone towers or something. And no one would stage a major crime with a four-year-old in tow.

"It has to be a mistake," I offer.

"Why would they think you were involved with this Glenn person?" Andrew frowns at the road, and I wish he would pull over and look at me, really see me. I know he means involved with Glenn in Ava's disappearance, but I already feel a flush rising to my face.

No more lies. Lies are what landed me in this mess in the first place. I take a deep breath, or try to, but all I can think about is how I'm about to add another nail to the coffin of my marriage.

Maybe I can shrug this off as a misunderstanding? But that's crazy. Andrew's going to find out anyway. *I can do this. I have to.* I press a hand against my stomach as if I can force the truth up and out of my mouth. "Before he and Ava were married, when they weren't even together, he and I . . . we dated. For a couple weeks." Ten weeks. Almost a whole summer. I thought it would be a lifetime, but then he went back to her. I watch Andrew's face, wishing Glenn and I had lived our happily-ever-after or that Glenn had never existed and I really could be the true love Andrew deserves. Instead I'm not good enough for either of them.

"Do you think he's sending the texts?" Andrew asks. I twist the strap of my purse around my hand as tight as it will go. Is he really asking if I'm still involved with Glenn, if we're not completely over?

"No!" I'm speaking too loudly. "I haven't seen him for years, and he doesn't know . . . he *couldn't* know how to find me. He and I were over long before I met you. He doesn't know who I am now. I love you, you and Emma. My life is here in Texas."

Andrew slows the car as we approach a stoplight. He darts a glance at me, and there's so much sadness in his eyes. "Lizzie. How long has that even been your name? I just don't know who you really are."

"You do! I've been myself every day with you. I'm your wife. My name doesn't matter; it's not who I am."

"You have a whole family, a whole past I know nothing about." His lips tighten, and I can almost read the notes he's making in his head as the light changes.

"None of that matters. It's not who I am now." I did this to Andrew, made him a single parent twice over. I found a grieving widower and then destroyed his second chance. I want to be Lizzie, loving and loved, and I've been working so hard to make her real. Then Zoe fucking killed her. No, Andrew can't lose Lizzie; he can't believe she's gone. How can I convince him to trust me, to believe I'm a good person? I can make myself into the real Lizzie and be everything he and Emma deserve.

"There's the station," Andrew says. "You'll be safe now."

Immediately I feel the absence of the comforting *we*. I'm alone, even though he's right beside me.

I know this loneliness. It's a cot in a shelter, a tiny room in a houseful of students, a job where the name badge belongs to a stranger. Standing alone in court petitioning for a legal name change, as if that could destroy the person I was. Meals eaten out of a can or over the sink, no kitchen table, no family dinners, no Emma singing in the back seat, no Andrew next to me at night. It's the year before I met him, one of the worst years of my life.

We pull into a parking space in silence, and even after Andrew turns the car off, we sit without speaking for a few minutes longer.

I want to ask him if we have to do this. A part of me wants to fling open my car door and run, vaulting the railing that borders the parking lot and darting through traffic. I could get to our bank, withdraw the max from our account, and disappear all over again. A new location for a few months to establish residency, another name change, and presto—a new life. But the other part just wishes Andrew and Emma would come with me. I could be happy in any city, in any anonymous room, by any name, as long as they were there.

For the first time I will have to stay and tough it out.

Andrew must be feeling uncomfortable, even guilty, for bringing me here. He says, "It's okay. Like I said, this isn't the FBI. Just make a statement, and it'll all be okay."

* * *

The station is cold, which maybe shouldn't be a surprise in October, but in Texas buildings are generally only icy cold in the summer when the AC is blasting. The guy at the front desk doesn't understand when we tell him we'd like to make a statement.

"You want to report something?" He looks about my age, late twenties, but he has reading glasses balanced on top of his head and a middle-age spread I wouldn't have expected on a guy in a police uniform.

Andrew leans over my shoulder, and the warmth of him feels so comforting. "Is Bob around? My wife and I need to talk to him."

"Sheriff's out of the office. Leave a message?" He grabs a pen and rolls it between his fingers.

I can imagine how this deputy's face would change if I started explaining who I am and why I'm really here. I glance at Andrew, longing for him to say, "Oh well, we tried. Let's go home." Stupid longing. The kind that never comes true.

"How about a detective? This is a sensitive matter. I can call Bob and get the okay." Andrew's voice is calm, but he's pulled out his cell phone. Not threatening, just as a contingency. He's not going to broadcast my lie, but we're here to Do the Right Thing and we're not leaving until that objective is accomplished. But that's not really fair. Andrew believes that if you do the right thing, everything works out. He must believe that making this statement is the first step to putting our life back together.

The deputy glances at the screen in front of him like he's wishing for an answer to appear there. I'd like to tell him it won't take long, that it's not a big deal, but neither of those things is true. Plus, I feel like a criminal, and anything I said would sound like a lie. Finally, he picks up the phone and hits a button. "Is there someone who can come up here for a minute?"

We wait, and when a detective finally comes to get us, she isn't at all what I expected. She is the tallest woman I have ever seen up close, almost as tall as Andrew, and he's over six feet. She's lean with flaming red hair, like a comic book superhero. Her long, flowing hair can't be regulation. I glance at Andrew to see if he is paying her too much attention, but he looks the way he always does. Calm. I don't know if I even have the right to wonder who he looks at anymore.

"I'm Detective Valdez." She reaches out to me first, maybe trying to put me at ease. Maybe because I look guilty. Her handshake is cool and firm. "I understand you want to make some kind of statement?"

I am tongue-tied. I don't want to tell this strong, confident woman that I'm a liar and a loser. And like the weakling I am right now, I let Andrew answer for me.

"Can we speak in private?"

Detective Valdez doesn't miss a beat. Her face is as impassive as if this happened every day. "Of course. Follow me."

We follow her through the security door and down an anonymous white hallway. She leads us into a small room with a table and four chairs, an interview room like I've seen on television. Very minimal. She leaves the door open, but my heart is already racing.

Before she can ask me anything, before Andrew can start laying out my case, I blurt out, "I didn't do anything. Someone's trying to frame me."

Despite her unreadable expression, I think I can see skepticism in Detective Valdez's eyes. I keep talking, trying to convince her, before she even knows what's going on. "I've been here in Texas, but my sister is missing. And they think—"

Andrew breaks in. "Ava Hallett. Her sister is Ava Hallett. We were on our way to the station when we heard on the radio that Lizzie . . . Zoe is a suspect."

I flinch, and Detective Valdez's sharp gaze misses nothing. What did it cost my husband to make that admission? I want to take Andrew's hand, but I'm afraid he'll pull away.

Instead we sit down next to each other on one side of the table, and Detective Valdez sits on the other. I tell her who I am, how long I've been living as Lizzie, about Andrew and Emma and my normal life. "When I heard on the news that Ava was missing, I tried to call my parents, but they didn't pick up."

Andrew leans across the table, and he's so sincere, with his open face and clear eyes. He's the believable one, the trustworthy one. I desperately want to think he believes in my innocence. But why would he? It's far more likely he's just trying to keep me out of jail. "There is no way Zoe could have been involved. She was here with Emma."

Detective Valdez doesn't look like a woman who needs a man to give her an alibi. I bet she doesn't have kids at home or a pet. She looks completely sure of who she is. Sitting across the table from her makes me feel small and pale. Impatiently she swats a lock of red hair away from her face. "Is there anything else you want to tell me now?"

Now? That sounds like we'll go over everything again, and she'll poke holes in my story and tear it all apart. If she looks for proof I'm guilty, I know what she'll find. I pull out my phone. "Someone hacked my email, my old email. I haven't used it in years, but someone sent hate mail to Ava from it. And I got texts here." I set my phone on the table, happy now to have it out of my hands. I can't help feeling like it's been infected and just holding it made me vulnerable.

"Can you trace them?" Andrew asks.

"And I got a call from my friend's phone, but it wasn't her. It was a threat. Someone told me to run. They knew my real name. I mean, my old one."

Detective Valdez pulls out a pair of thin plastic gloves and puts them on before examining the phone. "Was the voice a man or a woman?" she asks.

That harsh whisper sounds in my memory. "I couldn't tell."

She nods. "Okay. We can certainly examine this, but I'll need you to fill out some paperwork to give us permission."

Doubt floods me again. I'm being stupid. What if handing over my phone seals my doom? If there are weird text messages on there, what else will they find?

And how soon before they pin Ava's disappearance on me?

5

So, Detective Valdez and the lead investigator decide I need to travel back to Virginia. I never intended to go back to my old life with my new identity, and I worry I'll be carried back in time, away from Andrew and Emma. Law enforcement has coordinated with my parents, and all my worst nightmares—my mom and dad, Glenn, and my past as Zoe—are waiting for me in the Arlington Police Department.

We decided that I would go ahead on Andrew's extra air miles, and that he and Emma might follow on Friday for a long weekend. "We can meet your parents," Andrew said. Maybe that means he does want to stay with me. Maybe that means he's checking my story.

I can't forget the whispered conversation he and I had at the police station. "What is it with your parents? Are they the reason you disappeared? Did they hurt you?"

"No!" Maybe my denial was a little too loud, because the deputy at the reception desk glanced up at us. "No,"

I repeated more softly. "Like I told you, it was Ava. She stole my life. I just didn't want her to know about you and Emma, how happy we are. She'd want to wreck it."

"Let's compromise," he offered. "You go first, we'll follow for a long weekend; then if you don't need us, we'll stop by my dad's place on the way back."

"What about work?"

He gave me a look that said *Are you kidding me?* It was true. He had about a million years of vacation saved up. And about two million air miles.

Now he and Detective Valdez have taken me to the airport, right up to the security checkpoint. She's going to escort me all the way to the gate. I wish Andrew didn't have to leave me alone with her.

Andrew hugs me fiercely, but kisses the top of my head. "We'll sort it all out." I can't tell which of us he's trying to convince. The problem with a good guy who specializes in logistics is that sometimes he pushes his feelings way, way down to deal with a situation in progress, and only later do you find out what was really going on in his heart. Maybe after I've left, he'll realize he can get by without me. That life would be easier, Emma would be safer. What if absence doesn't make the heart grow fonder? What if it makes the heart forget?

Detective Valdez goes around security in the fast track, but I'm stuck in a line of people pulling laptops out of bags and tossing water bottles in the trash. My "overhead approved" wheelie suitcase and everyday shoulder bag are easy to maneuver, but the process is still tedious. We're fed through the massive scanner, and as I stand there in my socked feet with my hands raised over my head, I wish this machine could see all the way through me. See that I am innocent.

Once I have my shoes back on, my suitcase in hand, and my bag on my shoulder, Detective Valdez and I head for the gate. We pass a bookstore, the kind disappearing everywhere except in airports. There, right in the front display, is Ava's newest book, *Bloody Heart, Wild Woods*, the one the book club is discussing without me tonight. Provided they're not just discussing me.

Am I in this novel too?

Someone clearly knows where I have been living, who I have become. Maybe Ava staged her own disappearance; maybe she is trying to draw me into a game. Maybe I need to read this book for myself.

Detective Valdez says, "You want to get a bottle of water or something? Go ahead." She pulls out her phone and waits by the entrance of the store.

Hoping no one will recognize me, I sidle up to the display. The cover features a tangle of glossy dark-green leaves overlaid with deep-red letters in a gothic script. *Bloody Heart, Wild Woods*.

Quickly I pluck one from the middle rack and scurry to the register, sandwiching the book between a *Vanity Fair* with Colin Firth on the cover and a *Better Homes and Gardens* special edition on organization. I wait impatiently behind a man in a tweed sport coat who keeps patting his pockets, looking for change.

Finally, it's my turn.

As the woman behind the register asks, "Anything else, hon?" I add a pack of gum to the pile. She doesn't raise her head as she rings it up. "Need a bag?"

Mutely, I nod. As I make my escape, I feel like everyone in the little store is hyperaware of me, knows who I am. It doesn't help that I'm meeting up with a detective. Even in plain clothes, she's striking, and I feel like her posture and the slight bulge of her gun under her blazer scream *law enforcement guarding dangerous criminal.*

When we reach the gate—ten minutes before boarding—the only empty seats directly face the television tuned to CNN. A reporter describes dangerous avalanches in Nevada, oblivious to the news crawl beneath her announcing "mystery writer still missing" and "authorities report her sister has been located and will be assisting the investigation."

I slump down, my face hot. At least there are no pictures this time. And I've been changed from a "person of interest" to "assisting the investigation." Probably they just want to make sure I don't run away again.

Then I realize my cell phone is still back at the sheriff's office. My first instinct is to text Andrew and ask him to pick it up. *Dumbass.* It's like flipping the light switch over and over when the power goes out. I glance at Detective Valdez, her long legs stretched out in front of her while she watches the news.

I should buy a new one from the electronics kiosk, but an announcement is blaring overhead. My flight is boarding.

On the plane, I slip my suitcase into the overhead bin and settle in the relative privacy of a window seat with the gracious luxury of an empty seat beside me. Once my shoulder bag's under the seat in front of me, I open the book. If I had my cell phone, I would text Felicia to tell her I've caved, I'm reading it after all. Then I realize that creepy stalker either took her phone or spoofed her number when he contacted me in the parking lot. She might not even know I couldn't watch Sam. *Shit. Nooo.* One more person I let down.

I lean my head against the cool window and read the opening quotes and the dedication, the places where Ava always embeds her initial clues:

The two children were bonded so deeply that they never went out into the world without holding hands tightly one with the other, and when Snow-white said: "Never shall we two part," Rose-red answered: "Not heaven nor hell nor death itself will separate me from you," and their mother vowed: "You two are as one. What one has belongs just as fully to the other."

To the man in the forest. Through snares and thorns and beasts, may our story wend its way to happily-ever-after.

Not what I expected. Sure, the quote is about two sisters, but who is the man in the forest? Glenn? I can't see Ava wanting the two of us to share him. And I actually don't know much about their life together now. When I was with Glenn, he wasn't into hiking or camping or the outdoors. He was at the U.S. Naval War College for a few months, doing what he referred to as "specialized training." Once he was back with Ava, any internet search I did on him came up empty. In Northern Virginia, that usually means someone works "for the government."

I'm not a conspiracy theorist—anyone could hack emails and track me down—but if Glenn's working for the government, he's probably the one framing me. That stings in a familiar way. Bet he blamed our entire affair on me too. Either he knows I'm innocent because he's the bad guy and he's setting me up, or he's innocent but he thinks I'm guilty. I'll step off the plane and right into my role as scapegoat.

Ava is a good writer, and I really want to lose myself in a story. Even this one. I turn the page and let the words wash over me.

Ava's book opens with a little girl lost in the woods. She wanders alone, hearing the crackling of branches and the rustling of squirrels. Then she comes upon a little house. Ava has written, "No candy lined the front path, the fence was not made of peppermint sticks. The clouded windows were aged glass, not sugar panes, and the bricks were not mortared with icing. Nonetheless, it might have been a fairy-tale house, because once upon a time, when the little girl entered it, the darkness took and ate her, and she was never heard from again."

Creepy. Much creepier than I remember Ava's books being. And thinking of Ava, maybe really missing, maybe afraid and alone in the dark, makes me shiver. I flip the page quickly, as though I might find the answers to her real-life disappearance in this made-up story.

The next chapter focuses on a woman who has moved into a little house in the woods, and we—the readers— know it is the same house. Is she the darkness who took the little girl? Is she the little girl all grown up? Or is she the one who will unravel the mystery of the past?

I have to keep reading to find out.

CHAPTER

6

AVA

I'M SLEEPING WITH *my cheek on my writing desk, but around me the world's in motion, blowing like the wind through branches. My mind struggles to remember why I'm here, but when I open my eyes, I'm still in the dream. A man in a scarlet jacket and trousers the spring green of new leaves stands in the doorway of my study. "Won't you come and dance?" He holds out a hand in invitation, but a slender black asp coils around his fingers, its scales flashing. His thin lips twist in a smile. "Your sister wasn't afraid to come to the Goblin Fair." In the lenses of his round glasses, I see Zoe's reflection, her eyes wide with accusation. Then he tosses the snake right in my face.*

With a cry, I regain consciousness, but this isn't the reality I expect—my own home or even a hospital—no,

I'm lying on a vibrating metal floor with my arms pulled taut behind me. The muscles of my biceps feel the strain. My feet are bound to each other, and I can feel something thin cutting into my ankles. There's enough light to make out where I am, the back of a moving van. Without my hands to steady myself, I'm being jolted as we rattle and bang along.

The last thing I remember is working in my study, lost in a world of my own making. Writing, telling stories, that's who I am, what I do, and my success hasn't just fallen into my lap. Maybe people like Zoe see the publicity shots and the interviews and the movie premieres, but no one sees all the times I shut the study door, all the times I can't hear what other people are saying because of the story flowing through my mind, all the times the words are a wall between me and my actual life.

I must have been drugged. That's the only explanation. Some potion erased any memory that could fill the gap between sitting at my desk and lying here, bound. Now that it occurs to me, my sluggish thoughts fill in the lacunae to build a convincing narrative. Maybe my mind morphed the memory of the actual man who drugged me into a fairy-tale dream. The bite of the dream-snake seems so real, I could swear there's a sore place on my neck—a place like an injection site.

Panic bubbles up through the fog that fills my brain. I twist my hands, but all I get is a stretched-out pain in my shoulders and a penetrating numbness in my fingers. If this were a story, I'd already be chewing through my skin and sinew, trying to break free, but I'm not as rash as the characters I create. They can afford to be reactionary, but as the author, I have to plan.

Wiggling to a seated position, I lean over as far as I'm able. My feet are bound with a zip tie. *Excellent.* I've only written about this technique, never tried it, but I am able to pull my feet up and scoot back through the loop of my arms, so they are now bound in front of me. And they are also fastened at the wrists with another zip tie.

Even as my mind is coolly ticking off the steps of my plan, deep inside me there's a whimpering animal caught in a trap. I ignore it, forcing myself to rise until I'm standing, but when we hit another pothole, I lose my footing. My shoulder and cheek strike the side of the van. My eyes sting with pain and I end up on the floor, gasping.

Finally, I scoot into a corner and use it to support myself until I'm on my feet. When I saw this done, the person had plenty of room to stand and stretch his arms overhead. I'm short, but I can barely straighten up in this space. I take a minute to focus, believing this will work, picturing the move in my head. There isn't room for anything except this single image. Then I raise my arms and bring them down hard and fast, as if I'm going to drive them straight through my own body.

And the zip tie gives way. My hands are free.

I rub them together, trying to restore feeling, to warm them up, but no part of me is warm right now. Extricating myself from these plastic bonds is only the first step in solving my physical problems, and even while I'm executing that plan, another part of my mind is already searching for the guilty party. Every good story has a villain, and I need to know mine.

If I were mapping out the plot of a thriller, the first, most obvious choice for my baddie would be the husband, but my husband Glenn doesn't have a reckless, vindictive nature. Even if he didn't love me, even if he

wasn't my knight in shining armor, he'd never mastermind a kidnapping plot. And the second choice, my ex-
husband, Beckett, couldn't pull it off. The only person I
know who hates me—truly and deeply hates me—is
Zoe.

Just thinking her name brings the darkness inside
me, until I feel as cold and hard as the metal floorboard.
The truck bumps over the road, shaking me like a sack
of mail. No matter who set this up, I'm all alone back
here—clearly I'll have to stage my own rescue and be my
own hero.

I check the pockets of my slinky black trousers, looking for assets—no phone, no wallet, nothing. Not even a
breath mint to chase away the hideous chemical taste in
my mouth. My slim gold watch, a gift from Glenn, is
also gone, as is my wedding ring.

With another bump, I slide down the wall and sit,
hugging my knees.

The metal of this truck radiates cold, forcing it into
my very bones. Maybe it's a crazed fan wanting me to
play Scheherazade or an opportunist wanting a cash ransom. Glenn will pay it, any amount, a king's ransom for
my return.

But he doesn't have access to my money.

While my mind is racing, I work on the zip tie around
my feet. Fumbling, I find the catch and press it, even as
the plastic cuts into my almost-numb fingers, until the
loop loosens enough for me to drag it over my heels.

Points in my favor: three. First, my hands and feet are
free. Second, the driver of the truck can't see me. Third,
I am smarter than they know.

Every time the truck hits a bump, it's not just bruis-
ing me, it's making me angry. I will not be the

victim—not now, not ever. I am the author. If there is an evil mastermind, a malevolent god, that role is mine. I am the one who files for divorce, I am the one who proposes, I am the one who meets Zoe's weakness with strength over and over again. I am *the* Ava Hallett. This is my story and I will take charge of it.

I open the truck from the inside, holding the doors. Once they fly open, the driver will see it in the side mirrors. When I hit the ground, I need to run.

The truck sways from side to side as a rutted dirt road unrolls behind it. All I see on either side is forest—trees and undergrowth. The sun is low in the sky and the shadow of the truck stretches out on the road like the mouth of hell.

My breath is shallow and my knuckles are white as I cling to the doors. This is the only way out, I know it, but my mind whirls, trying to find the best way, the right way. I imagine the options—kneeling down, jumping or rolling out; then I suppress the image of a woman— me—lying on the road with a broken ankle, arm, or neck, dying of starvation, lost in the wilderness. The driver could back the truck over me, run me down, shoot me, or most likely, recapture me.

I shut my eyes and let go.

The shock of landing knocks the wind out of me. My empty lungs burn. I lie on the ground, my body lit up with pain so intense it shuts down thought. Before my brain reboots, I'm running, first on all fours, then sprinting, vaulting over the edge of the dirt road and into the woods.

I catch a glimpse of the truck stopping and a figure, a man, opening the door, but I keep going, darting between trees and around scrub. The farther I run, the thicker the underbrush gets, the more uneven the ground, until I'm flying down an incline with barely a knife's edge of control. I'm the only thing making noise now, I'm filling the world with the sound of crunching leaves and snapping twigs, too much sound to hear if the man, my kidnapper, is behind me.

I need a place to hide.

Trees are flashing by me, the world is so blurred with my speed that I can't look for a safe place; I can't even slow down. I could be going in circles, I could be running straight back to my captor, I could run right off the edge of a cliff or plummet into a ravine. When a thorn-laden creeper snares my ankle, I fall hard on my outstretched hands, plunging them through the dried surface layer of dead leaves to the colder underlayer.

Gasping, I'm on my feet again, running, before I realize I haven't heard anyone behind me. There's a tall pine ahead of me, its lower half bare of branches. Darting around it, I press my back into the wide trunk, breathing hard. The setting sun doesn't penetrate the forest here. Maybe in my dark clothes I'm camouflaged, just another wild thing crouching in the underbrush, straining to make out the sounds of an approaching predator.

Nothing human breaks the silence, no footsteps or revving engines, only the noises of the indifferent forest surrounding me. Somewhere a branch pops, and my muscles spasm; then a bird sings out.

Cold sweat beads under my hairline as I risk one cautious step, then another. In the gathering dusk, I see something larger, darker ahead, and make my way toward it.

The upper part of the hill overhangs and has made a cave, really just a little notch in the face of the earth. I can see all the way to the back wall, and it looks empty.

Before all the light is gone, I grab at the lowest branches, snatching one. As it snaps, I feel a jolt of fear that I'm making too much noise, but the woods around me are still silent.

I take another branch, then another, snapping off the dry ones and twisting the live ones until I have an armful. My face is itchy and I'm trying not to think about all the things that could be in them. I pile them at the entrance to my little cave. Maybe if I hide now, I'll be able to find my way to safety in the daylight.

By the time I finish, I can make out the thick trunks of trees, but wire-thin vines and twigs are impossible to distinguish from the inky air. I'm shivering, only partly from the growing chill.

If this were a story I had written, my kidnapper—the villain—would have thought of everything. He would be wearing night-vision goggles, there would be cameras throughout the woods, he'd be an expert tracker and there would be no easy escape. But I have to envision a different ending, a happy one, where I survive the night and find salvation in the morning.

I scoop up an armload of leaves, trying to get only the dry ones, and creep into the cave. Dumping the leaves on the earth, I pull at the branches, trying to make sure the inside of the cave is totally and completely dark. If no light can get in, not a scrap, then surely no one will be able to see me. I wedge myself in a nest of leaves against the narrowest corner. Tucking myself into a ball like a hedgehog, I close my eyes against the gathering night.

My body is freezing, but my soul is full of heat. There's a puzzle to solve, my life's on the line, and I just need to know a name, the mastermind, someone who hates me enough to have me kidnapped. I didn't recognize the man who was driving the truck from the brief glimpse I got, but he could be just the muscle and the transport. Anyone who's found success knows that someone else is always watching. Someone who wants what you have. Who thinks you don't deserve it. Who wishes you would disappear.

Of course, I didn't have to hit the best-seller list to find that person. I grew up with her.

Once there were two sisters. The older was a storyteller, and the younger was her favorite story. Zoe is the only person I know who lives in Technicolor, not thinking or reflecting or pondering, only living every moment full force. All the noise and action in our house was Zoe, and she looked at me like I was one of them, our colorless, constrained parents. So when I wrote, I wrote about her. I did it to figure her out, or to nettle her, or to give my stories all the energy and life I could channel into them. She's always been my furious muse.

Maybe Zoe and I would have been closer if we'd had another sibling. Two are always in opposition—good and bad, oldest and youngest, smart and dumb, black and white—and with names like Ava and Zoe, it was obvious we were the alpha and omega, the only two our parents intended to have.

I probably should have been a better older sister. I was impatient, often angry, like she had been put on this earth to plague me. Maybe some older sisters teach their younger sisters to put on lipstick or sneak out after curfew, but I was never interested in that kind of thing. She was my unwanted shadow, forever a step behind me, at the edge of my consciousness, waiting.

We didn't overlap anywhere, not in personality, not in school, not socially. When my friends had to take their little sisters with them to the movies or a football game, they heaved gusty sighs of faux exasperation. Their mothers urged them to "be nice" and remember how much their sisters loved them. My parents never said anything like that. They didn't believe words could change the shape of a relationship. Even if they had, Zoe didn't look at me like she loved me—she looked like she wanted to devour me. I can almost picture her bloody grin.

Someone did this to me. Someone wanted me afraid and alone, maybe even dead. Thinking that, *knowing* it, is like having my bones dissolve from the inside, and all my strength turns to water.

As the damp of the night air seeps into my skin and I extinguish any last quivering hint of tears, I build the case against Zoe. Just because she's run away and found herself a new family doesn't mean she's been magically transformed into some sparkles-and-sunshine housewife. After all, those biting emails reached my inbox just days ago.

So I do what I always do when I need to get to some emotional truth. I "write" it out. I can almost feel the pen in my hand, but this will be a mental list. Neither pen nor paper came with me on this nightmare journey.

First, the simple litany of childhood complaints. Zoe stole innumerable articles of clothing, books, even papers I wrote. I'd find them crumpled under her bed, stained in the back of her closet, shoved to the bottom of her backpack. And always she watched me with fire in her hungry eyes.

Second, ever since my first story won an award, I've heard her hissing comments. That feeling you get when you step into a room and everyone falls silent, that moment like a street rat shouting that the emperor has no clothes—that's the game she's been playing with me for years. Zoe stands for every anonymous internet troll, every bad review, every cutting remark I secretly think might be true.

Third, Glenn. Even after three years, I wince at the flash of pain. In the guidebook of basic human decency, surely it states, "Thou Shalt Never Sleep With Your Sister's Husband."

But he wasn't my husband then, I know that. I had told him to leave, that we were done. My words would bring the end to our story, or so I thought, until I tried to live without him. I couldn't write my way out of my love and loneliness, my longing, all those romantic clichés, no matter how hard I wished those feelings away.

So I took him back, forgave him, married him.

But I can't forgive her.

I bite my lip and hug myself closer, imagining the story unspooling without me. Glenn must be wild with fear. My parents won't be worried, but Glenn will work furiously, tirelessly, hounding the police, shouting to the world that I am gone. I miss his strength, his certainty, the feel of his arms holding me close. Even as I try to conjure up the scent of him—birch and leather—some part of my mind coolly repeats that if I were writing this story, he would be the guilty party.

It's always the husband. Always.

Now my arms are wrapped so tightly that it's hard to breathe.

I don't know how long it will be until morning. There are sounds in the forest around me, pops and rustles. This isn't a fairy tale where a talking frog or friendly gnome holds the key to riches, adventure, and a safe return home. The smartest thing I can do now is stay put.

Once upon a time there was a woman who was strong and smart.

At daybreak, she saved herself.

And then she got revenge.

CHAPTER

7

AVA

CLOSING MY EYES, I hold that bedtime story in my heart like a candle against the dark, a promise to get me through the night. I am distinctly aware of the cold, the roughness of the rock behind me, and painful cramps in my calves and neck, but I will need as much rest as I can get, so I turn all my attention inward, imagining warmth and safety, even if they are illusions.

Finally, the darkness ebbs away.

The branches I pulled in front of the opening don't block all the light, but this makeshift screen makes me feel safer, as though I control whether I am seen or not. My hand trembles as I brush aside a few leaves, their musty scent rising as I scan my surroundings. These could be the woods of North Carolina, Virginia, Maryland,

West Virginia, Pennsylvania, or some fairy-tale forest with a witch's cottage and a big bad wolf.

My stomach is an empty crater, and the ending of a darker story rises within me. *The woman disappeared in the dark woods and was never heard from again.* No one knows where I am, not even me.

Shaking off my creeping despair, I crawl out of my hiding hole and head toward the sunlight filtering through the trees, which must be east. Heading seaward feels comforting. Even if I'm going deeper into the forest, I must be getting closer to home.

I'm lucky, I keep trying to convince myself. My feet crunch through the leaves as I count my blessings—lucky I broke free, lucky the temperature didn't go below freezing last night—but I'm having a hard time forming a complete thought as I try to combat the shaking that's spreading through my body.

And that's when I hear it—a metallic buzzing sound that doesn't belong in the forest. It slices through me, and I freeze with hope and dread. I don't want to be caught again, but I can't pass up a chance at salvation.

Forcing myself to move carefully, quietly, trying to subdue even my ever-quickening pulse, I head toward the distant sound. Sometimes it pauses, as if someone is listening, and I stop cold until it starts again. Some kind of power tool, I think, and my heart pounds in my ears. I am getting closer and closer, I think I see movement through the trees, and then suddenly everything goes completely silent.

If I move now, the person will definitely hear me. Either my attacker will grab me and I will be caught like my escape never happened, or I will have help, something to drink and eat, a safe haven until I'm in Glenn's arms again.

I steel my nerves for another step. Leaves rustle and a branch breaks under my foot. Nothing happens in response. If this is an innocent person who just happens to be in the woods, one of us should call out a greeting to the other, but there is only the watchful silence.

I wish I could take that step back again.

An animal—a wolf?—explodes from the under-growth, crashing into my chest, all gray fur and fangs and hot breath. I cry out as we fall to the ground and turn my head to the side, trying to press myself into the earth.

A woman's voice says, "That's enough, Zeus. *Aus*, drop it."

With a last push, the weight of the dog leaves me and I can see his mistress clearly.

Backlit by the filtered sunlight, she stands above me in muddy hiking boots, brown pants with cargo pockets, and a cotton jacket in army green, her dark hair cropped close to her head. She doesn't look much older than I am, and she stands, one arm akimbo, like a fairy huntsman at rest.

I am about to gasp out a plea for help when my brain registers the slim cattle prod in her right hand. She follows my gaze and raises an eyebrow.

"I'm not going to need to use this on you, am I, Ava? You'll come with me and Zeus without any problems."

Shaking, I stagger to my feet, chilled by her use of my name.

I have no idea who this woman is.

A small part of my brain issues one command after another: *run, shout, demand answers, plead.* But I am chilled and weary and afraid. And the futility of that small rebellious voice would bring tears to my eyes if there were a drop of moisture left in me.

"Poor thing." The woman studies me dispassionately. "You look dead on your feet." There is the strangest disconnect between her tone and the words she is saying. My brain struggles to reconcile them as my body struggles to stay standing. Then she says, "Okay now, let's move."

When I only stand there, swaying, she pokes me with the prod, and I flinch away before I realize she hasn't armed it. Not yet.

"That's it." Again the encouraging words are delivered flatly, and she looks at me as if the prod isn't long enough. "Zeus, *fuss*."

The dog comes to her, a handbreadth from her knee, and the two of them move in unison around me. Then the woman pokes me in the back. "Keep walking. I'll tell you where to go."

A whirligig of fear spirals in my stomach, and I resist walking toward what could very well be my own death. But no. All she had to do to kill me was leave me out here alone, and starvation or dehydration would have done the job. I try to speak, to ask what she wants, but my dry throat fails and I produce only a rough cough.

"Zeus, *brummen*," she says, and the dog starts a low, rumbling growl.

Painfully, I force out the words, "What do you want?"

In answer Zeus growls louder, no longer a rumble but a revving engine, as if he is building to action. Another brisk command—"*Ruhig*"—and the sound stops abruptly. This dog is so big, so well trained, like a hundred-pound extension of the woman's body.

I don't have the strength to do anything except walk.

Without another challenge, I let the woman and her wolf-dog force me through the forest. Perhaps I don't have much of a choice, but I choose to allow this.

Moving takes all my energy, so I couldn't argue or fight with her even if I dared. But my mind is churning, trying to solve this puzzle. She knows my name, and the mere thought makes me stumble against a tree trunk. My hand is already scraped up, and it stings.

She says, "Careful," but I can tell she doesn't mean it. She just wants me to keep moving forward.

I go as slowly as I dare, picking my way across the slippery mix of moss and pine needles and fallen leaves. The pain has cleared my mind like a jolt of caffeine, and I pluck the most likely story from the swirling possibilities. Money. If Glenn pays, or my parents, I can go home. If money can solve this, I'll pay anything, *do* anything, sign any papers, sell any assets, even spin straw into gold.

But panic pinwheels faster and faster in my gut.

My brain isn't interested in false comfort or fantasy. This woman striding through the forest with her gray wolf-dog isn't making any effort to disguise herself, and she hasn't covered her face with a mask. Maybe she hasn't hurt me, maybe she doesn't want me dead, but she's not afraid I'll identify her.

Like a bird in a snare, I'm trapped, and she doesn't intend to let me go.

CHAPTER

8

ZOE

I'M A SLOW reader, and I'm only a fourth of the way into *Bloody Heart, Wild Woods* when we land at Baltimore/ Washington International airport. As I pull my carry-on from the overhead compartment, an idea hits me. *International.* I could walk up to any ticket counter and be gone.

Despite the people streaming off the Jetway and veering around me, I stand still and look up at the arrival and departure boards.

In less than an hour, I could be on a plane to London or Prague or Mexico City. If I had a valid passport. But Los Angeles and Anchorage and Honolulu are still options. I could fly away from all the shame about lying, all the fear about being framed, and all my mixed-up feelings about Ava. That's what I want, so badly. To slough off Zoe and go where I can't be found.

I would leave, if I didn't have Andrew and Emma wrapped around my heart. Wherever I flee, I'll bring my love and longing for them with me. Houston, that's the only place I want to go. Home.

I won't be here long. I'll tell these new detectives the same thing I told Detective Valdez. And if there's any doubt, I'll hang out just long enough for Ava to get tired of this stupid game. If she isn't back in a week, swear to God I'll find her myself.

Some asshole wheels his stacked bags—a bulky carry-on topped with a laptop bag and a rolled coat—right over my foot. I yelp, but he doesn't even turn around. My own suitcase isn't heavy enough to bother pulling the handle out. Maybe I'm tempting fate, but I hope I won't be staying long enough to need a bigger suitcase. I'm traveling light. At least when it comes to luggage.

Then I see an older man in a suit jacket with a gun on his hip watching me, and I recognize him as the detective who's been sent to meet me. Despite how chill and trusting Detective Valdez seemed, she escorted me all the way to my departure gate. Now her counterpart is here at Arrivals to pick me up. Andrew might know Sheriff Bob, I might have a sort-of alibi, but that just meant I got to fly alone. It doesn't mean I have an opportunity to flee.

This policeman has gray patches at his temples and the kind of crow's-feet that come from smiling. He looks like someone's grandfather. As he raises his hand in a wave to me, I see a well-worn wedding ring on his finger.

"Zoe Hallett?" he asks, as I bow to the inevitable and approach him.

I nod, and he holds his hand out to shake mine.

"Detective Davies. Any luggage?"

"Just a carry-on and a personal item." I heft my trim black suitcase to illustrate, like I'm trying to prove that every word I say is true. Ava's book makes my shoulder bag feel heavier than usual.

"I'll be taking you to the station. We'll go over your story again on this end." He motions for me to follow him and we make our way through the airport, his gait somehow a casual stride that moves quickly.

I'm hustling to keep up. I don't want this man to think I'm afraid or to know how angry I am with Ava. At this point, I can almost believe her disappearance is simply some publicity stunt and those emails and calls were just Ava dragging me into her drama. Trying to conceal my breathlessness, I ask, "Has there been any news?"

He doesn't turn his head to look at me. "Nothing new."

I don't know if this is the truth or if that's all he can say to someone who may be a suspect. I asked about my sister, didn't I? That's what an innocent person would do. And I am innocent . . . of Ava's disappearance, anyway.

Detective Davies loosens up a little as we approach the exit. Maybe he's also relieved to be leaving the noise and chaos behind. Maybe he wants me to relax. "I'm not sure you're going to be warm enough in that little jacket. It's gotten cool early here. What's the weather like down there in Texas?"

"Hot," I tell him. "Sometimes it's eighty degrees, even in January." I'm *not* going to relax, but he doesn't need to know that.

He's left his car right in the loading/unloading passenger lane. A perk of law enforcement. It's not a cop car with a cage in the back, and the detective holds the front passenger door open for me. "Well, if you get cold on the ride over, I might have an extra sweat shirt in back. Throw your suitcase there too. After we finish at the station, you can always pick something else up. You'll be going home with your folks?"

"I guess so." Actually, my parents and I haven't discussed it. After I went to college, my parents moved into an elegant townhouse in the historic district. That place is not my home. My mother and father have never known how to make one, and the thought of staying with them makes me feel small and uncertain.

I slide into the front seat and keep my shoulder bag by my feet. Detective Davies shuts the door, and as he walks around the car, I think he must be a very, very good detective. I've known him for ten minutes, and he's managed to make me feel like he's on my side. But I'm not an idiot. I know his "Let me take care of you, little lady" routine could all be a calculated act.

He gets behind the wheel, and we pull away from the airport. We maneuver past the tangle of traffic quickly, too quickly, and approach downtown Arlington. I am afraid to reach the police station, but at the same time I wish we were there and it were all over. Waiting is almost as bad as fear.

I clench the strap of my shoulder bag like a tether to Texas. This is the bag I bring with me when playgroup goes to the zoo or when Andrew, Emma, and I take a family trip to the ice cream factory in Brenham. It holds up to four library books, plenty of snacks, and a change of clothes for Emma. Now it has my wallet, a cardigan, and Ava's novel. And probably some leftover ziplock bags of stale cereal.

But it holds nothing that can slow the inevitable. Detective Davies has put on the turn signal to bring us into the parking lot of a municipal building.

We are at the police station, closer to my parents than I have been in three full years. Driving straight past the crowded rows of parked cars, Detective Davies pulls around the side of the building and parallel-parks the car, quickly and efficiently, between two identical sedans lined up by the concrete wall of the building.

"Have enough room to get out?" he asks.

I really want to run, but Detective Davies has shut the driver's side door and is taking my suitcase out of the trunk. My door is bounded by the municipal building. And I have nowhere to go. There's at least a foot and a half of space, so my door opens. I squeeze out and drag my shoulder bag after me.

Carrying my suitcase instead of rolling it, Detective Davies leads the way to a squat building, boxy and blank. Just like at the Fort Bend County Sheriff's Office, the lobby has echoes of a waiting room, with chairs and magazines and an officer at the front desk behind glass.

This time we walk right past to the security door. Detective Davies offers the woman at the desk a cursory nod and waves his ID badge across the electronic lock. He holds the door open and waves me through. On the other side, he sets the suitcase down. "Remember to pick this up on your way out," he tells me.

I guess he doesn't intend to book and jail me yet, anyway.

Everything is glossy white, a nightmare corridor of doors. Anything could be behind them—a murder board with pictures of Ava's dead body, an interrogation room where I'll be handcuffed and dragged off to jail. And when Detective Davies opens the first door on the right, the nightmare is real. Because the three people getting to their feet are my mother, father, and my brother-in-law, Glenn.

I bump into Detective Davies and realize I've taken a step back. His hand lands on my shoulder, and I am steered through the door and into the room.

This isn't an interrogation room, it's more like a conference room. In addition to the table, big enough to seat eight, there are cushioned office chairs, and the walls are lined with cabinets all shut tight. I don't want to look at the people in here with me.

"Let's have a seat," Detective Davies says. "We have a few things we'd like you all to know, before we ask Zoe some questions separately."

Nobody sits down. My parents are side by side, holding on to the backs of the chairs in front of them. Glenn is coming toward us, his fists balled. He is still handsome, so handsome, like an action figure, all sharp, defined edges. But now his muscles aren't sexy; they're scary. He's a big guy, way more built than Andrew, and he's angry at me with all the force I once mistook for love.

"Ask your questions right now," he insists through clenched teeth. "She's obviously behind this."

My heart hurts like he's punched me in the chest. "Excuse me? I've been living my own life. You're her husband. You probably did it. I haven't even *seen* Ava for three years."

"Whose fault is that?" Glenn's looking at me with real hatred, something I've never seen on his face before, and it feels like I'm being sliced open.

My mouth was snapping out retorts, but my feelings have finally caught up with me, and I turn my back on him. I imagined our reunion so many times—him apologizing, desperately explaining, coming back to me. Never this. I can't let him see how I care.

I turn toward my parents, their faces perfectly composed, ignoring all my drama. There's no help here. I'm drowning all by myself.

Expressionless, my mother says, "You must feel overwhelmed. Do you need to sit down?"

My parents never have to worry that their faces will betray an emotion, as they clinically identify "anger" or "grief." Now that I'm taking care of Emma, I use those techniques when she's having a tantrum. I mirror her distress, affirm it, and distance myself from it. Because it's never about the cookie she can't have or the juice that spilled. The problem is too big for her to articulate. The problem is being a small, powerless thing in a world full of rules you didn't make and don't understand.

I feel like Emma now, like everyone is trying to blame me or pry me open or get me to confess and I don't know what is going on or what the rules are. Like one of those dreams where everyone has been talking about you behind your back, except that in this case, they really have.

At the risk of seeming defeated, I do sit down in the chair Detective Davies has pulled out for me. He sits down right next to me. His techniques are transparent. We're the only two people seated, right next to each other, on the same side of the table. But I'm not stupid. He's not really on my side.

Ignoring everyone else, he looks at me. "Let me bring you up to speed. We're monitoring the phone lines and Ava's email, as well as going through all the correspondence she has received in the last few weeks."

Email. Heat rises inside me. Did Detective Valdez tell him my email was hacked? Do my parents know? Does Glenn? The vicious words—words I didn't write, but ones I could have. I have been that angry at Ava; I have wished her dead and gone.

As if he can see everything inside me, Glenn says, "This is a waste of time. We know Zoe was involved."

"I wasn't!" I protest, but there's no point. Whatever he felt for me once has soured, and I feel that acid pain inside my own gut. Maybe the only way he can justify our affair is to blame it all on me. I have to ignore him. I don't want anyone to see how much his words hurt, and not just because it might make me look even guiltier. Beside me, Detective Davies is watching, taking everything in. He's a little closer to me than I find comfortable, but I don't think I can scoot away without looking defensive.

I ask him, "What really happened? I only know what I heard on the news."

Mom sinks into a chair opposite me. There's a box of tissues on the table near her, but I know she won't need one. "We must have been on the phone with Ava just before it happened," Mom says. "She called and sounded quite distressed that we didn't have time to talk. Your father and I were trying to get out the door to the annual JJJ Gala."

My mother's eyes are a deep, vivid blue, the same color as Ava's, with a darker ring around the iris. Her reading glasses hang from a slim gold chain around her neck. She still wears her hair in a swingy bob, the same silvered gray it's been as long as I can remember.

"What did Ava want to talk about?" I search her face for a sign that three years have passed since we've seen each other, but my mother is ageless. She looks exactly the same.

She reaches across the table and captures my hands, holding them as if she's trying to warm me. From someone else, this gesture would be comforting, but this is my mother. I can't tell whether she believes I'm innocent or is just trying to establish "rapport." Not something you need to do if you really have a relationship.

"I'm afraid I wasn't giving her my full attention. Something about research for her book. I told her we'd talk later."

Dad remains standing, one hand resting on the back of her chair. His glasses and tweed sport coat give him a professorial air. I can see more lines than I remember around his eyes and mouth, and there is a slight added weight to his jowls, as if his thin face is giving in to gravity. I know that by standing silently above us, he's trying to establish dominance. Glenn's hypermasculinity, his shouts and threats, are amateur compared to my father's glacial control.

I risk a glance at Glenn. His face is impassive, he's rigid, and his fists are clenched by his sides. I'm pierced again by the loss of our time together, the softness of the rumpled bedsheets, the smooth bulk of his muscled arms and the tender places behind his ear and on his throat that I loved to kiss. "Where were you?" I ask him, more softly than I mean to.

He leans over the table, slapping his hands down with a sound that shoots right through me. "I was at a conference. My flight got in the next morning, and when I got home, the front door was open, the phone was on the floor, and Ava was gone. But you know that, don't you? You crazy jealous freak!"

I'm out of my chair now, shaking off my mother's hands, trying to get away from the hate in Glenn's eyes.

My father puts a hand on his shoulder in one of those beautiful gestures that's both a comfort and a restraint. "Now Glenn, let's give the detective a chance to talk."

"Yes, well." Detective Davies clears his throat. I can't see his face. Why did he let Glenn shout at me? "We're waiting for confirmation from Houston, but right now it's not clear in what way, if at all, Zoe was involved."

"I wasn't!" He *knows* that. "I was in Texas. I had nothing to do with it."

As I tense up, my mother's hands tighten around each other on the table, and I remember the last time we were together. There is a reason my parents and even Glenn might think I planned my sister's disappearance. In fact, there is a reason they might fear I have even planned her death. A chill spreads through me. Even though I didn't do this, maybe I do deserve the blame.

"Okay, everyone. I think Zoe and I need a few minutes to ourselves," Detective Davies announces. "Please return to the waiting area, and we'll meet you back out there when we're done."

Glenn storms out, clearly angry he isn't allowed to beat the answers out of me. My mom reaches out like she's going to grab my hand again, and I flinch. She shakes her head, and I can almost hear her thinking *typical Zoe* as she stands and smooths the wrinkles from her skirt.

"We'll be right outside, sweetie," my father says, and I wonder if the endearment feels as strange in his mouth as it sounds to my ears. It's almost a relief when they are all finally gone and I am alone with Detective Davies.

He is lean, with cheeks that are nearly hollow and angular cheekbones. One eye is slightly narrower than the other, and his chin juts just a little to the opposite side. My immediate fate rests in the hands of this man, and those strange eyes make it impossible to tell what he thinks about me.

"Before we get started, I need you to know we're recording this session." He doesn't set anything on the table, and I scan the room. *There.* On one of the shelves opposite me, above a double-doored cabinet that clearly holds something with a screen, there's a black box with a light. I had thought it was a wireless router or something, but it must be the camera. It wasn't an accident that we're seated on this side of the table, facing it. I need to remember: just because this isn't an obvious interrogation room doesn't mean this isn't an interrogation.

My heart starts beating double time. "Are you going to read me my rights?"

"I don't think that will be necessary." He smiles, but I see warmth in only one eye. The other still squints in permanent disbelief. "I read the statement you gave Detective Valdez, and we have corroboration from a few other sources."

Who? Felicia and Bethany and I texted and spoke on the phone. Maybe Emma's pediatrician. I call that office every time she has a fever, just to hear them tell me it will be okay. Or maybe the detective has heard back from the airlines. But I could have taken a smaller, private plane from the Sugar Land airport. I didn't, but he doesn't know that. I should be relieved that he seems to believe me, but now I doubt his competence . . . or his sincerity.

"Okay," I tell him. "Record me."

"Thank you," he says gravely, and I know the recording has been going on this whole time, through Glenn's accusations and my denials. But he continues the charade by looking up at the black recorder and saying, "Interview with Zoe Hallett. October thirteenth."

"McPhee," I correct him. "I'm married."

"Right. Elizabeth McPhee." I know he thinks changing my name was just magical thinking. You can't change who you really are. *Screw you for humoring me* I think back at him.

He continues. "The time is five thirty and we are in Conference Room B. Zoe, will you state for the record that you are chatting with me of your own free will and are not under any coercion?"

"That's right." But I am coerced. If I refuse or balk at any point, I'll look guilty. Surely he knows this, which makes everything we are doing feel like playacting. I am acutely aware of his eyes on me, and of the camera, which could be showing this scene in real time to anyone. My face feels as hot as if there were an interrogation lamp overhead.

"Will you tell me, in your own words, where you were and what you were doing on Saturday the eighth and Sunday the ninth?"

I tell him everything I told Detective Valdez, in even greater detail. I don't know if it gives my story added credibility or makes it sound like total fiction.

If I were planning an alibi, I wouldn't have come up with this one. When Emma is sick, she wants to cuddle, heavy and sweaty against me. We watch television, shows in bright primary colors with simple songs. We both suck on hydrating push pops full of electrolytes. We don't leave the house. No receipts, no eyewitnesses, nothing to prove where I was or what I was doing. I wish I were there again, and time could thicken to hold us together.

Detective Davies blurs, and I realize there are tears in my eyes. Maybe, if I am lucky, he will think they are for Ava.

Without comment, he slides the box of tissues closer to me. "That corresponds to the statement you gave in Sugar Land. Now I have some follow-up questions, and it's crucial that you answer me truthfully. Do you understand?"

I reach for a tissue to dab my eyes, but my heart is hammering. "Okay."

"When is the last time you saw Glenn Melcher?"

"Three years ago."

"More specific, please."

"August, three years ago."

"Have you had any contact with him since that time?"

"No."

"Please describe your relationship."

"He's my brother-in-law. I haven't seen him for three years."

"And prior to that period?"

I don't want to say it out loud in this room to this man. It will be documented. A matter of record. My hands clench the edge of the table, but then I remember everyone will see this and I force them down into my lap. "Prior to that period, we . . . dated."

"You were romantically involved?"

"Yes."

"What brought your relationship to an end?"

"He left."

"Do you know why?"

"No." I don't want to say anything else. I know all of this can be used against me.

"Did anything unusual happen in the week preceding the last time you and Glenn saw each other?"

Ava happened. Ava always happened. Under the edge of the table my hands are clenching again, my nails digging into my palms. "My sister published a book dedicated to him."

"What was their relationship at the time?"

"Nothing. They weren't dating. They had broken up." At least that's what I had believed. And then she reached out and took him back.

"That must have been upsetting."

I shrug. He's looking for a reaction, and I can feel it building inside me. The same fury that throws chairs and flips tables. If I had anything in my hand, I would hurl it at the camera. Instead, all this anger is vented on myself. My nails have drawn blood, and I twist my fingers against each other.

"How long after that did they get married?"

I will not move a muscle of my face. I will keep my voice soft and even. "A couple months." Three. Three months.

"Did you read her book?"

"No." My answer must be more forceful that I intended, because he raises an eyebrow and that squinty eye on the other side almost closes. "No," I say more gently. "I don't really care for thrillers." At this I remember the copy of *Bloody Heart, Wild Woods* in my shoulder bag, and my face grows hot again. Do I look guilty or like a bitchy younger sister?

"How would you describe your relationship with Ava?"

"Distant."

"Because of Glenn?"

I've been holding my breath, and a huge sigh finally breaks forth. "God, no. Glenn was just a symptom."

Detective Davies tilts his head to one side, as if his skeptical eye is heavier than the other. "Then why?"

"We don't have much in common."

"Would you say you have an adversarial relationship with her?"

"No, not necessarily." Did my parents tell him that? Did Glenn?

He slides a few sheets of paper across the table to me. At a glance, I see the hateful emails. "Did you write these?"

This is just a test. "No. Like I told the other detective, I haven't used that email address in years. I don't even remember the last time I emailed Ava. Maybe never." And then I can't help myself. I ask, "Did you show these to my parents?" Did he show them to Glenn?

He purses his lips and shakes his head. What does that mean? I can't tell if he believes me or not. He folds the papers in half, and I am suddenly sure he knows more than he is telling me. He taps them with a finger and asks, "Do you know anything about Ava's disappearance? Or about her movements and activities over the last few days?"

"No. My sister and I haven't spoken in over three years."

"Any other contact?"

"No." I put all the sincerity I can muster into the words. "No calls, no emails, no postcards, nothing. I haven't seen, spoken, or heard from her in all that time."

"But you didn't have a bad relationship?"

I push my chair away from the table and cross my arms.

"We didn't have a relationship at all."

CHAPTER

9

AVA

As the strange woman and her dog herd me through
the woods, I keep my head down, enduring rather
than marking time as it passes—an hour or two, maybe
more. Then one by one, gray and white-flecked stones
appear in the thin grass and mossy earth. A few steps
farther and the forest floor gives way to gravel with the
occasional scrubby plant poking through it. I am so tired
I could fall asleep on those sharp-edged stones, but I look
up.

We are approaching a wood cabin, not the kind where
hunters rough it or a cunning little cabin for dwarves,
but instead the luxe contemporary kind Oprah would
use for a weekend away. The rich brown beams of the
walls are glossy and the windows are spotless. I can

almost feel the soft thickness of the beds and the soapy heat of a shower.

I veer toward this sanctuary, but the woman gives me a hard rap on my hip. "Not yet. Stay to the left."

At the side of the house stands a small shed, metal like a shipping container, and I can't help it. My feet stop moving. It's smaller than the back of the van. I will not be confined, helpless, in another box.

Behind me, Zeus growls again, low and steady.

"I can't." My scratchy voice sounds weak.

"You will." The woman gives me another solid poke with the goad, but my muscles are locked and frozen.

This isn't a child's playhouse, a cute plastic cabin with little windows or even a rickety pile of sticks that might let some light in through the cracks. This metal box with a padlock on the door might serve as an innocuous place to dump lawn equipment, but to my eyes it's an oversized coffin, a little too big to bury.

I don't have enough strength to argue with myself, to explain that the poking stick could become an electrified bolt of pain, that the growling dog could bite and rip. I am deeply, viscerally opposed to going in that shed. My body is delivering an unequivocal refusal that my mind cannot override.

The shock of the cattle prod steals all thought and breath. The world is bright, harsh pain. Then it is gone and my muscles spasm. I stagger forward, shaking on limbs I can barely control, until I'm right in front of the shed.

I balk again, turning to scramble away, but Zeus's jaws clamp around my arm. His teeth don't break the skin, but his grip is inexorable, unyielding.

The woman steps over me and unlocks the padlock. She swings the metal door open. "*Fass*," she says, and he gives me a firm shake. "He will release you and you will go through the door." Her voice is calm. "If you do not, I will have him attack. Do you understand?"

She keeps looking at me until I nod; then she says, "*Aus.*"

Zeus does release my arm, slick and bruised. Shaking, I wipe it off. "What do you want?" I ask.

"You're wasting time." She wants me to go into the shed. That is the only thing she wants right now.

So I stumble over the threshold.

The door closes behind me, and there is total darkness. When I close my eyes, I can picture the afterimage of the interior—empty, metal, small—and stretching out my hands, I can touch each of the four walls without moving my feet.

There has to be a way out. Methodically, tamping down my rising hysteria, I turn to one side and then another, patting and pressing each wall, searching for anything, a gap, a weakness, but find none. When I follow the wall down to the seam where it meets the floor, I collapse, wrapping my arms around my knees. My body shakes and I can't control it. I can't control any of this.

No light. No air. No space. I try to force my rapid breathing to slow down. Tiny muscles in my body are still spasming. I *groveled*. I pleaded and cried in front of that woman, that stranger. This is not who I am.

I have never known fear like this, fear that could make me break. *It fell out that the woman was captured by a wicked witch and she thought that all was lost.* But it wasn't; the story never ends this way. Every fairy tale starts with a person who undergoes trials and struggles, before reaching a triumphant conclusion where virtue is rewarded and evil punished. Without her dog and her weapon, that woman won't have any power over me. Right now I may be weak and scared, but I'm remembering how it feels to be angry. That will be the thing that saves me.

I close my eyes and focus. *Breathe in. Breathe out.*

Time passes, and I spend it huddled up, conserving my waning strength. My body is weak, but I feel my mind getting sharper. I am an ascetic, fasting in the desert, waiting for a vision. First I will determine who this woman is and what she wants; then I will figure out my escape.

When the door finally opens, I'm not prepared. It's painfully, blindingly bright. Before I can recover and hurl myself forward, something has been dropped inside and the light is gone again. The lock snaps shut.

I grope along the floor and discover a rectangular shape in a wrapper. Food.

Against the wall I find a smooth plastic bottle. Almost frantically I unscrew the top, a distant part of my mind registering the comforting snap of the plastic seal being broken. I gulp the water down, feeling it slosh in my empty stomach, until the last drop is gone.

There isn't enough—I should have saved some, made it last. I am beyond hungry, but eating whatever is in this packet will make me thirsty again. I have made a mistake. These people have made me so stupid.

I turn the bar over and over in my hands, considering. The water has cleared my head enough for me to start forming a narrative. First, food and water mean this woman isn't going to kill me yet. Second, she knows my name, so this is not a random crime. But finally, she's a stranger, and I have to believe she's working with someone else, someone closer to me.

One of the worst things about being a writer is looking at your life like a story. If this were a story and a rich woman had been kidnapped, I'd think the husband had done it. Everyone would. My cheating first husband Beckett could be taken as proof that I'm not good at reading men. But Glenn knows I would give him a divorce the second he asked for one, because I wouldn't want him if he didn't want me.

Plus, my cold inner voice adds, surely there are easier ways to get rid of me. My heart twists. I love Glenn more than I let myself believe, and I long to curl back into a ball of self-pity, but I refuse and stamp those feelings of weakness down hard. There's productive thinking and then there's obsessive thought, and I choose the former.

Now I'm composing a plan for survival. There's nowhere to hide my bar of food, but I am going to save it. If there is more water, I'll eat the bar before I drink anything. And I promise myself I will save some water too. The empty bottle and the bar go beside me, so I can grab them.

The next time that door opens, I am going through it.

Time passes. Minutes or hours. The darkness makes it all the same. Asleep is the same as awake. My mind throws out images like a projector on a screen: Glenn backlit by the sun. The window over my own desk. Even the cover of my last book with its glossy green leaves. And Zoe facing me in a frame of jagged glass shards.

The last time I saw Zoe, she hated me, and I have a scar on my forehead as proof. Maybe I deserved it. Maybe I even deserve this.

The darkness is everything. I blink to make sure my eyes are still open. Now my stomach twists with hunger.

I grope for the bar and pull back the paper. The first bite overwhelms me. The darkness is full of sounds, gulping and tearing. Clutching the torn wrapper, I bow my head. I have nothing. No reserves. An empty water bottle and an empty food wrapper. I am failing.

Zoe probably still hates me. I can imagine a scenario where she wanted me afraid and weak, but not one where she methodically planned all the details of a kidnapping. This plan isn't like her; any plan is not like her. Zoe is all impulse and attack. And it's been three years since we've seen each other, three years she's been living in Texas. Of course I found her; I'm the queen of research. If she were the one who'd gone missing, I could have found her. After all, she wasn't in any trouble at all and I tracked her down. I could have rescued her, even if she didn't deserve it, but now I'm the one who's been taken, and even if she wanted to find me, she isn't equipped. It's just not who she is.

I drift in and out, my dreams and thoughts all mixed up. I am conserving my strength. I have no strength.

When there's a noise, the door banging open, I'm not prepared and I don't run. Instead someone stands, silhouetted in the door; then it is slammed shut. Now we are together in this too-small space.

A blow to my cheek. Pain lighting up the dark. An elbow in my side. My nails against skin. We are battling against nothing. Against each other.

Panic makes me flail and punch. He is fighting too. He is bigger than me. I slam against a wall.

"Stop!" My throat hurts. "Stop!"

And he does. We are still too close. I can smell sweat and something else, something I remember on a visceral level. "Who are you?"

"Who are you?" he asks. "What do you want?"

Maybe this is a crazy trick—someone put in my cell to gain my trust, someone to use as leverage, someone to tell all my secrets to—but nobody's even asked me any questions.

I press myself into a corner. "Sit down."

But he is still standing. "I'll sit down if you sit down."

"Who are you?"

"Who are *you*?" he asks again, more desperately.

We are both here, two of us, locked in this tiny space, and there's something about him, something so familiar. I have nothing to lose by telling the truth. "Ava."

Then he reaches out and finds my shoulder. "Ava?"

And I recognize this man.

My first husband. Beckett.

10

AVA

THE RELIEF OF being with another human being overcomes any awkwardness I might feel about it being *this* human being. My ex isn't some dashing prince who'll slay a dragon or defeat a giant with grace and aplomb; he's more a languid, ethereal Romantic poet, although right now he's absurdly solid, bumping into me with every breath. His hands seem to be bound in front of him, and he's using them like a billy club.

As a bonus, we're jammed together in this far-too small space, and Beckett won't stop talking, firing off questions and working himself into a frenzy.

"Are they going to keep us here?" he pants.

"I don't know."

"Did you see them?"

Before I can answer, he asks, "Do you know who they are?"

"No. But they know my name."

"Mine too." His breath smells rank.

I press myself farther away from him and ask, "What happened to you?"

No one has to prod Beckett to talk about himself. It's one of the ways he deals with tension. The month before his midtenure review, he almost lost his voice, and after a week of his nonstop monologue, I wished he had. Now I want to know how his story compares to mine.

"I was at the university, working late on a new piece—a deep exploration of the psyche through reverse point of view, experimental and very exciting—and I completely lost track of time."

He's tripping over his words, an excessive amount of them, as if he's trying to smother the fear and uncertainty of our situation under the weight of his own narrative. A ball of irritation gathers in my gut, but I just let him talk.

"When I left, I was still completely immersed in that mental state—you know? And they took advantage of that. They must have been waiting for me to come out. I felt a sting and I got dizzy, and I woke up in the back of a van with my hands tied together. I don't know how long I was out. I couldn't see anything, but I think we were going uphill. Then the road got really rough, like gravel, and we pulled up here. But that woman wasn't driving. She opened the back of the van, and somebody else drove it away. A man."

All the pieces of his story—the van, the male driver, the drugs—match what happened to me. "Let me see your hands." I feel the familiar zip ties around his wrists. "These are what they used on me too."

"They untied *you*?"

"I broke out of them." I can tell by his sudden silence that he doesn't want to believe me. "It's easy if you know how."

If you know how, and if you have more space than we do, and any practical knowledge or coordination or an infinitesimal amount of competency.

"Show me." Beckett must be terrified if he's asking me for help, and I feel a pang of pity.

Blindly I'm trying to scoot him into a corner to give him enough room to raise his arms and bring them down hard enough to break the tie, and he's explaining to me that this will work because the zip tie is weakest at the junction, when the door opens again.

The woman and her dog are silhouetted in a painful rectangle of light. Behind them the windows of the house shine in the early morning. Before I can move, Beckett shoves his way outside, stumbling out of the shed, and runs. The woman's eyes never leave mine as she says, "Zeus, *fass*!"

Beckett is not athletic on a good day, and with his hands tied in front of him he runs like a character in a sketch comedy. I didn't marry him because of his physical ability. Beckett seemed smart, interesting, and had a pallid, dreamy intensity. Now terror rises in my throat and I shout, "Beckett, stop!"

But Zeus gets there first and brings him down. It's frighteningly efficient, and the analytical portion of my brain marvels at the dog's beauty, pure muscle avoiding the flailing legs to seize the upper arm, completely immobilizing Beckett.

My own body is shaking. I'm crying and gasping. The woman's mouth purses in disgust. *That's right, I'm weak. Just a girl.* She doesn't know my mind, my will. My cheeks are wet with tears, but there's steel in my heart. *I will survive.* I step out of the shed.

Beckett is curled into a ball on the ground, and the dog's jaws are still around his bicep. Zeus's tail swishes back and forth with pleasure. That dog could kill Beckett. I am helpless, as helpless as I felt when Zeus brought me down yesterday. Underneath my fear lies anger. If that dog attacks me again, he'll lose an eye.

Despite my apparent hysterics, the woman keeps her gaze on me and her cattle prod at the ready. "Mr. Coughlin, are you quite finished?"

Beckett moans.

"Enough. Zeus will let you go, and I expect you to stand up and walk over to me. If you don't do exactly as I say, he'll rip your throat out on my command. Are we clear?"

Somehow she interprets the noise Beckett makes as assent. "*Aus! Pass auf!*"

Zeus releases and takes a step back, keeping watch. Beckett pushes himself to his knees and stumbles upright. His face is blotchy and he ducks his head, avoiding my eyes, his humiliation tearing at my heart.

The woman isn't cutting him any slack. "Come here."

Slowly, Beckett walks over, stopping right next to me. Reflexively I reach for his hand, but he twitches it away, a stinging reminder that he's still my petty ex-husband.

Zeus returns to his mistress and stands at attention by her side, and I imagine using German to command his obedience, but the way he glances up at our captor makes me think he wouldn't obey just anyone. She's his handler, his alpha, his everything.

She motions us forward with the cattle prod. "Go on."

None of our drama has deterred the inevitable—we are going to the house. It looks like an upscale cabin in the woods with exposed logs, a wood-shingled roof, and a wraparound porch with Adirondack chairs. Those empty chairs face the yard like seats in a coliseum, watching the spectacle of our pain and degradation.

The woman follows behind us. "Go on," she urges. "Up the steps and through the front door."

My heart is fluttering, my fists are clenched. I glance back and see on her lips the flicker of a smile. I don't know this woman well enough to judge whether she enjoys our distress or revels in her own power, but I do know she's hyperorganized, with a headquarters in the wilderness, isolated from the world for a reason I don't yet know but dread.

Zeus presses against my knee and Beckett hurries ahead. I will not shrink or run away as Beckett is doing. This dog is a tool, this woman's tool, and I will not betray my fear to either of them, even as I try to remember how to walk, how to move my body with the animal so close, approaching a house that must hold terrible secrets.

At the front door, Beckett stops, his hands still zip-tied in front of him.

"You, Ava. Open the door." She does not have a German accent, but she certainly has the attitude.

The polished door is unmarked by time or weather, shining dark. If I could open it quickly enough, I could get inside and slam it shut, leaving the woman and her cattle prod outside. Maybe I could find a phone, maybe . . .

I can't keep myself from looking back, and our captor has a gleam in her eye, like she knows exactly what I'm thinking. She's not even a little bit worried I'll escape, and sending us through the door first could be a kind of test, or a trick, or one more excuse to cause pain. I remember the dark figure who drove me here—this woman has an accomplice, so even if I slammed the door in time, I bet I wouldn't be alone in the house.

And Beckett is in the way.

I reach around him to turn the knob, and he stumbles through the door before it's fully open. No matter how quickly I move, the woman's right behind me, already shutting the door and shooting the dead bolt.

Inside, everything—the concrete floors polished to a high gloss, the stainless-steel kitchen counters, the minimalist black leather sofas—is high-end, contemporary, and cold. This does not look like a cozy retreat. Oddly, it's the kind of decor my parents would love.

Beckett moves to one of the unwelcoming sofas, raising his bound hands to maintain his balance.

"No!" the woman snaps at him. "Don't sit."

Startled, he staggers to regain his footing, needing his arms but unable to use them. Lurching sideways, he sends a lamp crashing to the floor, and the sound of metal against concrete rings like a gong.

I look past the woman, past Beckett, to the door. Now could be my moment. Zeus growls, and I freeze with my foot barely raised, calculating—the dog's right behind me, the woman's between me and the way out.

Not yet.

The woman looks at Beckett and the fallen lamp with equal amounts of disgust. "Goddamn idiot. Don't touch anything, either of you. Zeus, *pass auf.*"

Don't touch anything. My pulse is racing, but so are my thoughts. One of my sources, a cop, told me that every time he pulls a car over, even for a routine traffic stop, he touches the trunk as he approaches the driver, just to mark it with his own fingerprints in case he doesn't walk away. *Once there was a woman who disappeared, leaving no trace, not even a fingerprint, behind.*

The constructive part of my brain keeps spinning, making notes, planning. First, our captor's not holding a gun, not even a Taser. Second, the cattle prod has only as much range as it has length, no more. Finally, Beckett is standing against the wall, chewing his lip, not looking at me. If we both ran for the door, Zeus could take only one of us down. I could get away, run for help. Beckett might not get out, but I could do it . . .

The woman pulls out a phone and starts fiercely texting, but her gaze never completely leaves us. I turn a little so she can't see my face.

Look at me. I will Beckett to wake up, to engage. I need to get his attention, but in a normal, not-planning-to-escape way. "Beckett, are you okay?"

He is lost in his own world, completely shut down. If I'm the only one who runs, Zeus will kill me. It has to be both of us to work.

While I'm looking at him, I can't see if the woman is paying any more attention to us, but I can hear her hiss in frustration. If I glance over at her, I'll look guilty, and my skin is crawling with the effort of keeping calm.

"Beckett!"

Finally he raises his head, tears in his eyes. He whispers, "Why is this happening?"

I jerk my head toward the door, roll my eyes, do everything I can to convey *run*.

But Beckett just stares at me blankly. Maybe he's afraid of the dog. Maybe he's in shock. I am buzzing, electric with adrenaline.

The woman looks up from her phone, and her dark gaze seems to lay my intentions bare. She doesn't take her eyes from mine as she raises the phone to her ear.

It's too late. Disappointment lies bitter on my tongue. I could spit at Beckett.

Her voice is low, but so intense that I can hear every word. "No phone, no computer, no excuse." With her free hand, she taps the inert cattle prod against her leg. "Track her down and smoke her out. It's your job to keep the pressure on." Another forceful exhale, and she hisses, "Figure it out or you won't get paid. I'll be out of range for a while."

She jams the phone back into her pocket, and I note which one—the left hip. Some analytical part of my brain, a gift from my mother, keeps whirring, trying to find a way out. Solve X for Escape.

But this isn't the time. Our captor comes closer, her heavy hiking boots thumping on the floor. "Move."

She motions us over to the opposite wall and waits, holding the cattle prod at the ready, between us and the front door. Almost without realizing it, I'm backing away from her, bumping into Beckett. Zeus growls.

"Now don't start that again." She sounds almost amused. Her eyes steady on mine, she reaches out to a keypad embedded in the wall and types in a code.

A code is a security precaution, another kind of cage. I don't want to be locked up again. Zeus is pressing hard against my leg right now, and I kick out in panic. He snaps and I choke on my own gasp, air and fear and a muffled scream all catching in my throat.

A panel in the wall slides open, some kind of high-tech door. Zeus has a firm grip on my forearm and is tugging me toward it, and I can't help resisting, even though I know it's futile. "Go on down the stairs," the woman says, gesturing with the cattle prod.

"I don't want . . ." I don't know what I'm saying. I don't want to go down there? I don't want to cause trouble?

Behind me I hear Beckett finally moving, obeying her orders, and my anger flares again. If he'd only run when *I* told him to, but now he steps in front of me, like he's trying to earn extra credit by following directions.

Then we hear a voice, a man's voice, from the bottom of the stairs.

"What's taking so long?"

I freeze. It could be the kidnapper, the one from the truck. I should have kept running through the woods; I should run now. There must be a reason they've kept us alive so long. Even if they've caught me and plan to hurt me, they won't kill me, not yet. Any true-crime aficionado knows not to let your captor take you to a secondary location, especially a secret room nobody else could ever find.

I try to twist away from Zeus, but his grip tightens until pain pierces my wrist.

"Help us!" Beckett calls down the stairs.

"*Idiot.*" The word escapes my clenched teeth. The front door is locked, the alarm is on, we're in the middle of the godforsaken woods, and now the woman gives her cattle prod a burst of electricity, just enough to remind us who's in charge.

No one knows we're here, no one except our captors, and once we go down those stairs, we'll be lost in whatever pits of anguish they have planned.

Zeus tugs at me again, then releases my arm. Swallowing my fear, I push past Beckett. It's not hard to pretend I'm stumbling with panic as I lurch against the doorframe and slap my sweaty palm hard against the wall. My body is shaking for real, but I hope my fingers are leaving clear prints.

I may not be coming back, but by God I will not disappear without a trace.

The woman gives me a shove and I'm on the first step, flanked on either side by concrete walls. The air is colder, and there's a moment before I can take a real breath.

Instead of a monster at the bottom of the stairs, I see a gangly man in an ill-fitting lab coat, his thin wrists extending beyond the cuffs. He's standing beside a heavy metal door like the door to a bank vault. I wish I didn't recognize it, but I do.

Any delusions of escape I'd been harboring vanish like so many soap bubbles. I know exactly where we are, and when that door seals shut behind us, there will be no way out.

CHAPTER

11

ZOE

WHEN WE ARE finished at the police station, my father asks, "What's the next step?"

"Go home and rest," the detective tells us. "We'll follow up tomorrow morning."

I wish I could go home. My real home in Texas. But Ava hasn't reappeared yet, and Andrew and I arranged things so he and Emma could meet my parents. There is no way I can leave without looking like a complete monster. Failing that, I'd take a sterile hotel room without the memories. But I have a role to play here, dutiful daughter and supportive sister, and I need to act normal. That means staying with my parents.

If I think of a childhood home, it's the house in the suburbs where my parents were expanding their psychiatry practices. The lot next to ours was empty, so Ava and I used to gather blackberries there in summer and build elaborate snow forts in winter. We had tiny bedrooms that faced each other on opposite sides of the upstairs hallway. Mine looked out over the cul-de-sac and hers had a view of the forest.

As I walk through the front door of my parents' new townhouse, the familiar smell hits me: lemon furniture polish and new magazines. I've never lived here, but it smells like that long-ago house. A home that smelled absolutely nothing like children. No fruity bubble baths, no play dough or markers, nothing baking in the oven.

From the entrance I catch a glimpse of the "family room." More like a psychiatrist's office, a home version of what my parents have at work. Modern and impersonal with nothing that invites you to kick off your shoes and relax. This is a house for adults, with sleek leather furniture and abstract paintings depicting harsh angles in neutral colors.

My mom stops in the front hallway and turns to look at me, as if searching for the right thing to say. Her hands flutter up to the reading glasses hanging by a chain from her neck, then back down again. "Do you want something to eat? Soup?"

"No," I tell her, although I am a little hungry. "I'm okay." My parents never had much interest in food, even when we were little. She must be making a real effort.

"Okay." She looks at my father for help.

"Towels," he says decisively. "You'll need clean towels."

"And sheets?" my mom asks him.

"No, I washed them after the last guest and put them back on."

My father takes Mom's arm and helps her up the stairs. She looks frail in a way that surprises me. I always thought my mother was made of steel, but she moves slowly, as if she needs my father's support. Time didn't stand still while I was in Texas, but I can see its effects only in the way my parents look. They still feel as distant as ever.

As they talk to each other, they lead the way up the stairs. I trail behind them like the little kid I used to be, one who could never get their attention. The only other person in the world who would understand how normal this weirdness feels is Ava. Before we hated each other, we were allies in this family. Her gaze was proof I existed, even when my parents didn't notice anyone except each other. I almost miss her now.

We reach the top of the stairs, and Mom pushes open a door. I enter a small bedroom with a four-poster canopied bed flanked by small bedside tables with china-shaded lamps. If the rest of the house is cool and modern, this one room is almost a throwback, a little girl's Victorian dream.

This is it, the closest thing to a childhood home I have. My old bedroom with the furniture I pitched a screaming fit for one Christmas. Just like in the showroom: the bed, the tables, the lamps, and the marble-topped dresser with its matching mirror. Of course, now my parents have removed the plush carpet, so the mahogany bed and tables are adrift on a polished oak floor. They've even removed the gauzy canopy so the posts of the bed reach futilely upward, supporting nothing.

This room should be like something from a storybook, except my parents have spoiled it. The bare floor has a judgmental gleam, and on the wall I see two more of those abstract paintings I hate. When Emma does something like that, at least she uses lots of color. Her art is active and messy and alive. These paintings are dead.

"You still have my old furniture?" I ask. Surely that means they care a little.

My dad looks at me blankly. "Did you want it?"

"If you can use it, just ship it home. Texas, you said?" My mom looks almost eager. *Stupid.* They didn't keep my furniture because it reminded them of me; they kept it because they needed to furnish a guest room. They've done everything they could to force it to fit their modern aesthetic, and they'd be only too happy to replace it. That's my parents. Pragmatic, thrifty, never sentimental.

"Maybe." I wheel my suitcase into the middle of the room and drop my bag beside it. I want to ask if they're worried about Ava, if they think she's okay, if they think (like I still do) she's just pulling a stunt. But I don't think I can take another reminder of how little they care. It's Ava's fault I'm here at all, and for just a second I miss her more than I'm angry at her. She's the only person in the world who had the same childhood as me, no explanation necessary.

"If you have anything to hang up, there should be coat hangers there." Mom gestures as if I am incapable of recognizing a closet.

"I put a clean towel and washcloth by the sink in the bathroom," Dad announces.

"Okay then." Mom steps out into the hall, and I can see a flicker of relief pass over her face. She's almost done having to act like a mother. "Call us if you need anything."

"Good night." Dad pulls the door shut behind him.

It is eight o'clock at night.

There are no chairs in this room, so I sit on the edge of the bed. This could be any one of the quiet nights from my childhood when Mom and Dad were clearly being whoever they were once they were finished pretending to be parents. I remember the way they whispered, even when Ava and I should have been asleep, the way they stopped talking when one or the other of us walked into the room. When it was "our time" at dinner or over homework, they hovered and asked us about our day, but it was hard to shake the feeling that they were playacting. Even now, it's as if they had to ask themselves, *What would real parents do for a daughter who came home to spend the night?* And the only answer they could muster was to supply clean towels.

I wouldn't mind being treated like a child, as long as that child was loved.

If I ever get back to my home in Texas, I will make sure Emma knows how much I love her, no matter how old she gets. I will make a big deal about her every time she comes home—having her favorite dinner (currently chicken nuggets), playing her favorite games (Chutes and Ladders), and never ever leaving her alone for a minute. I'll probably drive her crazy.

I feel like I'm going crazy now. The silence is creeping under my skin, building up. No wonder I screamed and raged so much as a kid. There's nothing else to do. I grab my bag and get back on the bed, messing up the white counterpane. That's better. I scoot back and gather the bedspread around me like a nest, as if it could give me the warmth I need.

I'm not going to have to stay here long. Ava will get tired of this game. I just have to wait her out. And in a few days, Andrew and Emma will come up. Then I

realize that Andrew doesn't have any way to contact me.
My parents have an unlisted home number. My phone is
in Texas with Detective Valdez.

I wrap my arms around my knees. Everything will be
okay. I'll call Andrew tomorrow from the landline, probably one of the last landlines in America. I'll tell him
everything that's happened. He still loves me. He has to.
Emma doesn't know I'm a liar. God, how I wish she were
in my arms. But I don't want her in this house. The last
thing I want is to see her joy and confidence replaced by
insecurity and loneliness. Maybe when I call Andrew, I'll
tell him not to come, for Emma's sake.

The two windows in my room are bare, no blinds or
curtains. The sun has set, but the darkness outside is
punctuated by lights from the townhouses on either side
and across the street. Maybe I should change my clothes
in the bathroom or the closet, but I don't give a shit. I
strip and pull on an oversized T-shirt. This oppressive
house is making me reckless, just like it always did. I'm
tired, bone-tired, but not even a little bit sleepy. Tonight,
I won't go prowling in search of alcohol, but that's something to look for tomorrow.

Inside my bag I find allergy pills, a forgotten baggie
of cereal I put together for Emma, and Ava's book. I tri-
ple the dose of the pills, hoping a good hit of antihista-
mine will knock me out for the night. Once I've turned
off the overhead light, the lamps on either side of the bed
glow like stage lights, waiting for the curtain to rise.

I take *Bloody Heart, Wild Woods* and crawl back into
bed, pulling the covers up around me. Glenn is fresh in
my mind, the way he looked at me with hatred. The last
book Ava wrote is the one that killed our relationship. I
haven't found myself in this one yet, and I don't know

which would be more painful: not to appear in it at all, or to find that she still knows everything about me, all the worst bits.

I hold the book in my hands for a moment. Maybe the opening quote about two sisters is the only part that's for me. That fragment of a fairy tale reminds me of a different Ava. Not the one who eviscerated me in prose, laying out my every secret fear on the page, but the one from years ago, who crawled into bed with me during thunderstorms. The big sister who told me stories.

"We are in a boat," she would whisper. "A boat that looks like a bed. All around us are waves, and underneath the waves is another world."

As she spoke, the room around us seemed to melt away and the darkness became black water underneath a starry sky. Beneath the billows, I believed there was a city of coral and pearl, where mermaids swam and strange music rose in bubbles. Ava made it all seem real.

In my memory, I hear her say, "Hold on to the covers and take a deep breath. We're going down."

CHAPTER

12

ZOE

I DREAM THE POSTS of the bed elongate, stretching up and out, becoming trees. Between their spreading branches is a spider web where the canopy should be. Caught in the middle of it is a girl, Ava, the way she looked at eight when I was only five. Her hair is tangled with the filaments of the web and her eyes are huge, dark holes of panic. The bed shakes, and I know with certain dread that the massive spider is coming for me. I can hear its razor-fanged jaws clicking together.

I wake with a start and the sense that I really did hear something. My heart is racing, but my limbs are weighed down with the medication I took. I reach out for Andrew, but then I remember, and the pain of it snaps my eyes open.

I'm alone in this bed.

My parents' house is quiet, and there's no clock in the room. Without my phone, I have no idea what time it is. Then I hear it again, something pattering against my window, like a sudden gust of rain. Pebbles. The sound of pebbles on glass.

Silence.

I slide my legs out from under the covers. My head is full of cotton wool and my thoughts come slowly. There aren't any trees near my window, and nobody knows I'm here.

No one except Andrew, my parents, and Glenn.

Somewhere deep inside me a smarter Zoe is telling me to get back in bed, go back to sleep. I don't know what fresh hell tomorrow will bring, but I need to be rested and ready to fight. But what if it is Glenn?

All I can think about at this moment is how much Glenn hurt me today and how happy I used to be in his arms. Even if he doesn't love me, he can't hate me. If Glenn hates me, then Andrew could hate me. If Andrew hates me, there's no happiness for me anywhere. I have to fix this.

If Glenn is throwing something against my window, if he wants to talk to me, I have to find him.

The bare floor is icy on the soles of my feet, and the cold seems to travel up my legs. The silver moonlight is tempered by the golden glow of a few errant porch lights. I cross the luminous grid on the floor and look out the window.

No moisture on the glass, nothing to indicate it was rain or freak hail. No one standing in the street, holding a boom box over his head, ready to declare his love. Not a single smoker on a porch or a stray dog or anything suspicious. Nothing.

I should go back to bed.

Instead I open the door of my room and hesitate, listening.

The world is so quiet, I could believe I imagined the sound. I take one cautious step into the hallway, but everything is still. There's no light from under my parents' closed door, and I know they wouldn't have heard anything anyway. Not if they sleep the way they used to, with eye masks and ear plugs and a white-noise machine. In our house, if you had a bad dream, you were on your own.

Peering down the stairs into the front hallway, I see nothing, hear nothing.

The absence of sound echoes in my head like the roar in a seashell. Maybe this is still my dream and earth has been emptied of people. I am alone in the house, alone in the night, alone in the world.

Tap. Tap. Tap.

Not pebbles this time, but something singular, rapping on the front door.

Ava would wake our parents, or call the police. She would make a smart choice and never get carried away by her curiosity.

I can't stand playing it safe.

My bare feet are silent against the stairs, but the tapping stops, as though someone is listening for me. I speed up, unable to stand the suspense of creeping forward with painfully cold feet. On the mat inside the front door, I stop again. There's no window, no security peephole, no way to know what's on the other side.

It could be Glenn, come to apologize or accuse. It could be Andrew, to wrap me in his arms and make everything better.

It could be Ava, messing with my head. Showing up only after she's blown my life apart.

Angry now, I wrench the door open. No one is there. The street is still empty, the row of townhouses on either side as devoid of life as empty sets on a sound stage. A breeze rises, warmer than the inside of my parents' house, but nothing else moves. All I hear is a faint chirping from my parents' security system.

Then, "Lizzie?" The familiar voice, a child's voice, pierces me with longing. "Lizzie?"

I step out into the night, my heart pounding. "Emma?"

She can't be here; I know she can't. But I scan the darkness, squinting at the shadows between the houses, terrified that she is out there.

"Emma!" I shout, but I don't know where she is, where the voice came from. I take the front steps too quickly, something crunches beneath my foot, I lose my purchase on the path and go sprawling.

My knee is skinned and the heels of my hands sting. Wincing, I push myself onto my butt and look around frantically. I can't see anyone, and the voice doesn't return. Am I going crazy?

No. I know I heard something.

This must have been a trick. Just like the text messages and the phone call. Emma is in Texas. Her school would never release her to anyone except me or Andrew. She isn't here. She isn't.

I keep telling myself that, but I am shaking. I press my hands against the pavement to stand, and something cuts into my palm. The stupid thing I tripped on in the first place. My fingers close around it and I glance down at a slim gold wristwatch. Someone's lost treasure. The face is cracked, probably because I stepped on it and skidded, grinding it into the path as I fell.

Then the night fills with sound, the shrieking of the security alarm.

I leap to my feet as if the police are on their way. The sound cuts through me, and I would do anything to stop it.

Maybe I can figure out how to turn it off. I charge up the front steps, desperate to silence the alarm before God and the neighbors come to strike me down.

And there are my parents, awake after all, in the doorway. My father squints at me as if he doesn't recognize me; then he ducks back inside and the alarm cuts off.

My mother steps out of the way so I can come in, and I notice she is wearing slippers in the same muted gray as her tailored pajamas. Her sleep mask is pushed up like a headband and she looks completely unrumpled and calm. Pajamas, pantsuit, she's ready to therapize me. "What were you doing, Zoe? It's two in the morning."

"I heard a noise." I feel as stupid as I know I sound, but I can't stop. "Someone was knocking on the door."

She leans close to me, and I freeze, not sure if she intends to embrace me or offer comfort. Instead she grasps my chin and examines my eyes, checking my pupils. "What did you take?"

I jerk away. "Nothing!" *Allergy pills don't cause hallucinations. What I heard was real.*

The phone rings, and I can hear my father telling the alarm company it was a mistake. A guest opened the wrong door. A *guest*. I want to shout *I'm your daughter!* I want them to believe me, or comfort me, or worry about me.

Instead my father is already hanging up and shuffling past us toward bed. On the way he says, "I reset the alarm. Stay put until morning."

My mother is still examining my face speculatively. "You had a dream?" she offers.

Oh, she'd love that, wouldn't she? An easy explanation and another way to analyze me, neatly fitting all my thoughts and worries into labeled cubbyholes. There's no point in trying to persuade her. No matter what I say, she'll think it was all in my imagination.

I open my hand, displaying the broken wristwatch I've been clutching. "I stepped on this out front. Is it yours?"

She picks it up from my palm and holds it at arm's length, trying to focus without her reading glasses. Finally she shakes her head and drops the watch back into my hand.

Before turning to follow my father up the stairs, she says dismissively, "It's broken."

13

ZOE

THE NEXT MORNING I'm slow to wake. I stumble downstairs, and my father tells me we're going back to the police station.

My heart gives a hard thump. Maybe it's over. Maybe I can go home.

"Is there news?" And just like that, my hope is chased by guilt. There could be bad news, but I still believe Ava is behind her own disappearance.

My mother sets down her coffee—black, no sugar or cream. "I don't know. Glenn said we should meet there again this morning."

"But why?"

She looks at my father, who shrugs. Apparently they are letting Glenn dictate "normal behavior" in this situation. Anyone could see my mother and father would rather just head off to work. I can imagine Mom thinking, *After all, it's not like we can* do *anything for Ava, so why waste time?* At least they are pretending to pretend to care.

I care, but not about Ava. I care about Emma and Andrew. Does that make me a monster too?

My parents wait with unveiled impatience while I dial Andrew's cell number from their home phone, but the call goes straight to voice mail. Is he ignoring me? My voice sounds high and strange as I leave a message with my parents' phone number and address.

I've written his cell number dozens of times on forms at Emma's preschool and doctor's office, on the waivers for trampoline parks and playgroup outings. But I always called it from my cell phone, where he's listed as my "in case of emergency" contact. This feels like an emergency, but my parents are no comfort at all.

Once I'm settled in the back seat of their car like a kid, all I can think about is hearing Andrew's voice and talking to Emma. My life in the Lone Star State seems so far away, a fading echo, like the child's voice I thought I heard last night. I need my own cell phone. I need a way to reach my family in Texas.

I need to know if Andrew still loves me.

Before I am fully awake, we are back at the station. Neither Glenn nor Detective Davies is waiting for us, but the officer at reception buzzes us through.

The watch is in my pocket, and as I follow my parents into the same conference room, I finger the metal. Yesterday Glenn was so angry, blaming me. Last night some part of me hoped he had come to make peace. This morning I know that was just another dream. I can't expect him to be sorry for the way he treated me. But maybe I can convince him of my innocence.

Bringing up what happened—the tapping, the voices—will make me sound crazy. It's not like anyone was hurt or the house was invaded. There's no upside to saying anything.

Experience tells me that keeping my mouth shut is the best way to stay out of trouble.

Before we even sit down, Glenn comes through the door in front of Detective Davies and he's scowling, his eyebrows drawn down at an angle as sharp as his cheekbones. I can feel the pit open up inside me, sucking down my last vestige of hope.

But he's staring back at the detective, practically spitting out the words, "You spent an hour, an *hour*, grilling me and you have nothing. No new information, no plan, nothing. You're not even *looking* for her."

With the kind of patience earned by years of dealing with people on their worst day, Detective Davies speaks mildly. "We're gathering information, talking to everyone who—"

"You need to talk to *her*." Glenn whips back around, and his gaze on me is like a blow to the sternum. "You read her fucking emails."

My face grows hot. "I didn't write those."

"Bullshit. You hated Ava."

"She hated *me*," I say fiercely. "I just wanted to be left alone."

"You wanted anything she had. What did you do to her?"

"Nothing. What did *you* do? Everyone knows it's always the husband."

Glenn pushes a chair out of the way, and I grab the one nearest me, either to attack him or defend myself, but Detective Davies puts a hand on Glenn's shoulder and says, "That's enough." And whether it's the authority in his voice or the realization that we are, in fact, in a police station, Glenn shakes free and throws himself into a seat, scowling down at the tabletop.

My father pulls out a chair for my mother, and she sits gracefully. They aren't afraid, I realize with a jolt. They think Ava is fine, wherever she is. They don't seem concerned that she might be missing. They sit at this conference table like there will be an agenda with a PowerPoint presentation and a coffee break. As though this weren't a case of us all being here because Glenn is trying to control a situation Ava obviously created.

But when Detective Davies sits down, that seat becomes the head of the table. And I think he was letting Glenn and me shout at each other just to get a feel for our relationship. Glenn fills me with hot anger, but the detective's self-control, his calm watchfulness, tempers that rage. In the real world, it doesn't matter what Glenn thinks of me. Detective Davies is the one who needs to believe I'm innocent.

I look right at him, relaxing my face and widening my eyes. "They're checking my phone, right? Trying to see who sent me the texts?"

He nods without expression. "And they've got your laptop and are working with the email provider. We'll get to the bottom of this."

So Andrew gave them my laptop. Even though he and I agreed we'd cooperate, I can't help feeling disappointed. And not just in my husband. I should have known a glass or two of wine wouldn't permanently erase a hard drive.

My father asks, "What do you need?" I can hear the unspoken ending to his question: *from us?* He and my mother don't want to be here. They don't think it's necessary. And that makes me feel so lonely, because I know they'd act the same way if I were the one missing. Ava and I were only ever duties to be fulfilled.

"Actually," Detective Davies says, "we'll need to talk to you all again, together and separately. Just to cover our bases. But at this point we don't have any evidence of foul play."

Glenn's head snaps up. "She's been missing for four days! She left her phone and her laptop, she missed a meeting with her agent, she didn't leave a message or—"

Detective Davies raises a hand as if to hold back Glenn's torrent of words. "I know. And we are investigating. But her wallet is missing. And there have been no demands for ransom or indications of violence. Our team is committed to finding your wife. But we're just getting started, and we'll be looking at a number of scenarios and talking with everyone who knew her. We need a solid understanding of her movements and her state of mind."

Her state of mind. I blurt out, "You think she went missing on purpose?"

"It's something we have to rule out." Detective Davies won't give anything away, but I feel a rush of triumph. "Only a small percentage of disappearances are the result of criminal action."

Glenn's mouth twists. "You think she's just taking a break? Or that this is some kind of stunt? Ava would never do that."

My instinctive snort is covered when my mother speaks, her voice as clear as if she were addressing a lecture hall. "No history of mental health issues, no tendency toward overwhelm, risk-averse . . . I don't see it."

Dad adds, "She's always been very confident, but stable. Not prone to reckless or impulsive behavior."

And there it is. Ava's not crazy. Not like *me*. That stings. My parents know, Glenn knows, what Ava did to me. They just don't think it matters.

I have to say something. "What about her books?"

They all look at me. I can't meet Glenn's eyes while I say this. The light glints off my father's glasses, so I can't tell what he is thinking. If I look at Detective Davies and see pity or amusement in his face, I will die.

"She always put something about me in them, made me the murderer or the paranoid detective. Or straight-up killed me. It's why I took off. It's been three years since she saw me."

My mother's tone is professionally neutral as she says, "You think Ava is doing this to you?"

Okay, I know it sounds crazy, but I believe it. And if I back down now, Ava will win all over again. I pull the broken wristwatch out of my pocket, clenching it in my hand. The solid metal is real, proof that something happened last night. "The police know about the text messages and the phone call, they're checking out those emails, and last night someone tapped on the window and used my daughter's voice to lure me outside. All I found was this."

I toss the watch, and it slides clear to the end of the table, right in front of Glenn and Detective Davies.

Glenn picks up the watch, stares at it, and the color drains from his face. "Where did you get this?"

"I told you, I—"

"This is Ava's watch."

My breath catches in my throat. I should have kept my mouth shut. But then I think of Ava laughing her ass off, and I'm furious again. "Of *course* it's Ava's watch. That bitch is behind this whole thing. She hates me."

"You. It's always about you. Jealous, spiteful—"

My mother interrupts. "You heard voices? That's why you went outside?" I know what she's thinking. *My daughter is delusional.*

Detective Davies pulls a pen from his pocket and lifts the watch out of Glenn's hand. "You recognize this watch as your wife's?"

Glenn nods. "There's a dent on one side. It was always hitting the side of the desk when she typed. She'd take it off, then put it on again. That's why the clasp is so loose."

"When was the last time you saw your wife wearing this watch?"

"She puts it on every morning." Glenn shoots me another suspicious glare. "And you just happened to find it in the middle of the night."

I grip the edge of the table. "I didn't just *happen* to find it. Ava tricked me into coming outside. Ava wanted—"

Glenn slams his hands on the table. "Enough about Ava. She didn't do this. She's *missing*. And if I find out you had anything to do with it, I'll fucking strangle you myself."

He shoves past Detective Davies, slamming the door to the conference room on his way out.

As though taking this as a sign that the meeting is adjourned, my mother stands. Looking at Detective Davies, she says, "You'll contact us with any additional information?"

Without waiting for an answer, she holds out a hand for my father and extends the other to me. "Time to go, Zoe."

* * *

On the ride home, I stare at the back of my parents' heads. It's so strange being an adult under your parents' care, staying in their house, following their rules. My car, phone, and laptop are all back home in Texas, and my parents don't even own a television. I know the news is out there, that the world might be hearing something about Ava, about Glenn, about me.

From the back seat, just like the child my parents still think I am, I say loudly, "I need to stop at a drugstore." Then to forestall any questions, I add, "It's that time of the month."

"Ahhh," my mother says, and I can tell she is ascribing some aspect of the way I've behaved over the last twenty-four hours to my hormones rather than my missing sister.

They wait in the car while I sprint inside. I do pick up feminine products to flank my real purchases. Moving on instinct, I grab a top-up card for a cell phone and an extra pair of socks. At the front register I ask the clerk for a disposable cell phone.

When I am settled again in the back seat, I ask casually, "So you'll both be going in to work this afternoon?"

Silence. I can picture the thought balloons rising over the backs of their heads. *Staying at home makes no sense. There is work to be done, and no reason not to do it.* I have to believe, on some level, that my parents realize their own analytical reactions aren't normal. They just don't care.

"We were discussing it," my father admits.

My mother half turns in her seat. "You don't need us at home. The police don't need us. And we'll have our phones turned on."

Dad adds, "Unless . . ."

She nods. "Or at least we'll check them for messages. We can get work done and be home this evening."

Excellent. I nod as if this makes total sense. "I don't guess you know what Glenn will be doing?"

My mother almost raises an eyebrow. Despite the silver in her hair, her skin is as smooth as if she's never frowned or worried or been afraid. "Zoe, I expect you to refrain from fixating on Glenn's animosity toward you. These stressful circumstances have affected him, but neither his scapegoating of you nor your self-victimization are productive."

Reflexively I slouch down in the seat, feeling completely shitty. Even though I want my parents to go to work—it's part of my plan—I feel so alone right now. I clutch the plastic drugstore bag to my chest. "Yeah, all right."

She turns around to face the windshield, and I can feel the pressure building inside me. I want to kick the back of her seat, throw myself from the moving car, anything to let out the pain and rage. But I'm not an angry teenager anymore.

I lean my head against the window and watch the world flash by. Once my parents are gone, I'll prove to everyone that Ava's perfectly fine. Glenn and my parents and Detective Davies will understand she's the bad girl.

And I'll go back to Texas and never see any of these assholes again.

CHAPTER

14

AVA

Poised for a second on that staircase, I inhale as if it might be my last breath. Then the woman gives me another push, and I have to move my feet to keep from plummeting to my death. Taking the stairs too quickly, almost tripping, I'm starting to realize where I am.

When I'm not actually writing or promoting my books, I do research for them—digging through archives, interviewing professionals, and scouting locations. Locations like this abandoned missile silo in West Virginia.

Even though I only saw it online, in person I recognize the inspiration for my most recently planned novel. I can picture the stairway that continues behind that vault door. I know it leads to a room built around a central concrete column. Beyond that is a tube-shaped metal hallway and the missile chamber, a drop of over one hundred fifty feet encircled by rusted-out metal walkways and scaffolding.

I'm light-headed with exhaustion and fear, unable to process the reality of stepping into the very nightmare I'd intended to use as a fictional backdrop. The man in the lab coat struggles to type in a code on a security pad, then wrenches the wheel to crank the door open. The sound cuts through the fog in my head. Even if this is a dream, I'm not going to stand here waiting to be forced to my death.

I lurch at the man wrestling with the door. Inside my slow, sluggish body, my heart is beating like a panicked bird in a cage. With all my strength, I slam my head into his.

The world explodes in colored lights as we stagger apart. Something slams into my side, and I fall under a heavy weight. My stomach churns with the pain in my head, and someone's elbow is in my ribs. Beckett.

The woman's hiking boots are in my peripheral vision as I struggle to untangle myself. She says, "That was stupid, Ava. I expected better."

Beckett rolls away and lies gasping next to me.

She sets one foot gently upon my throat. I can feel my pulse trembling against the thick rubber of her sole. She speaks again. "Phil, pull it together and open the damn door."

I hear Phil scrambling and the grating of metal and realize my eyes are closed tightly. My whole body is rigid, attuned to the single point where her full weight could crush my windpipe, but I'm not going to give this petty tyrant the satisfaction of seeing my fear. I open my eyes. *Do it*, I think, *I dare you.*

She's staring right at me. Her lips twitch as though she's amused or even proud that I'm looking her in the eye. Softly she whispers, "Just relax. This isn't about you."

But I'm the one on the ground, her foot on me filling my nostrils with the scent of mud and leather, unable to speak, barely able to blink.

There's a rush of air and a scraping sound, and Phil says, "Cristina? It's open."

Cristina, that's the name of this militant woodwitch, and as I look up the length of Cristina's khaki-clad leg, all the way to her cold brown eyes, I stop breathing for a moment. No zip ties. No drugs. Not even a cattle prod. But I am still helpless.

"Cristina?" Phil asks again.

I could swear I see in her assessing gaze the same contempt Beckett inspires in me. But all she says is "Get the other one in first."

I don't move at all. I don't look away, even as there are more sounds of scuffling and moaning. Beckett says, "My ankle. When she pushed me, my ankle got fucked."

That's what happened—I slammed into Phil, then Cristina pushed Beckett into me, and now Phil's taking Beckett back into the bowels of the missile silo while I lie here helplessly, my body vibrating with my need to escape.

Cristina raises her foot a millimeter. She lets the hiking boot hover, and I can't help it. I flinch.

"Remember this." Her voice is soft. "Get up. Slowly. We have work to do."

She steps back and watches as I awkwardly push myself to my feet, unsure if I can even stand anymore.

It's not only the dryness in my mouth that makes it hard to swallow. Defeat is bitter as a poisoned apple.

Through the door, there is another staircase, a narrow metal one, leading into the depths of a concrete shaft. At the bottom I can see another blast door, this one standing open, offering the only light. These steps are so steep that slipping now might kill me, but maybe that would be better than what we're walking toward. The concrete walls swallow the sound of our feet on the metal. Somewhere I can hear small noises like pebbles or drops of water echoing, but I can't tell if I'm just hallucinating them. Surely no sound could penetrate this far under the earth.

There is no going back. But when my feet reach the concrete floor, I balk again.

Cristina's hand clamps down on my shoulder. "Keep going. You're almost there."

"Where?" Anything could be behind that door—a torture device, a slaughterhouse, Bluebeard's bloody chamber—but my mouth is too dry and my spirits too low to form those words.

Footsteps approach from the room ahead of us, the sound dying almost as soon as it's heard. Phil stands in the doorway. "Need any help?"

He has a bottle of water in his hand. I can't stop looking at it. My brain is shutting down. That water is the only thing I can see. More than escape, more than life, I want it. It's been a day since I had anything to drink, and I'd gone another day without water before that. I didn't realize how much my exhaustion, my fear, was actually my body dying of thirst. In the distance, Cristina and Phil are talking, but all my attention is on that bottle.

"He's already in place?"

"All set."

Cristina gives me another little shove and I'm closer to the water, my hand reaching out for it. Phil pulls it back, then looks past me.

Cristina's voice, almost amused, comes from behind my shoulder. "Go ahead and take her through. I don't think you'll have any more trouble. I'll deal with the doors."

I can tell Phil's looking at me, but I can't tear my gaze from the water. Now I know how cheaply I will sell myself—I will grovel, beg, whore myself for a few drops. Anything I might say or think is nothing next to this. I am just an animal after all.

With a step backward, Phil tells me, "You can have it if you follow me. Come on, now."

So I do follow him through the door, even though I don't want to, and into a room that opens around me in smooth curves around a central concrete column flared at the top like a giant funnel. But I can't really look at it, can't really see anything except that bottle of water, catching the light.

When Phil stops walking, I reach my hand out again, but he shakes his head and motions me forward. "Over there."

I don't want to move even a single step away from the water, but then I smell something amazing. Fried, meaty, and rich, making even my dehydrated mouth salivate. My head snaps around, and I see Beckett sitting on the floor against one curved wall. Not just sitting. Eating. His zip ties are gone and he's cramming fried chicken into his mouth with grunts.

Two steps and my own hands are in the bucket, my mouth full of greasy meat. Even if it were poisoned or rotten, I'd still be eating it. I could weep with relief. The entire world is this—crunching and snuffling and almost choking in my haste to get the food into my system.

Too soon the chicken is nothing but bones, bones we suck until they are smooth and clean as marble, until my stomach hurts, but there's water, an entire flat of bottles. I fall on my knees, fumbling with my slick fingers to twist off the plastic caps. I drink one and then another, even though my stomach clenches with pain. I've been dimly aware of Beckett, his hands groping for chicken alongside mine, the sound of him gulping water, but now I raise my head and look at him. He's standing, sweaty and pale. He must have eaten even more than I did, and just as quickly.

"Sit down," I tell him. "Let it settle." Because we can't get sick. Our bodies need this food. We need to stay strong.

I press my back against the wall, breathing slowly, willing the food and water to stay down. I force myself to catalog every detail of our surroundings, even though my heart is pounding. The room is circular, with track lights running around the joint between wall and ceiling. The door we came through is now shut and sealed. Against one wall is a broad table with two laptop computers, an external hard drive, file cabinets, and empty shelving.

Beckett and I have scant assets—the remains of the flat of water, a single folding chair, and a paper bucket full of bones.

Phil is struggling with something affixed to one wall, and Cristina goes to help him. Together they pull a metal scissor gate free and drag it, screeching, across the room. Another cage.

I scramble to my feet, my stomach flipping over and over. "No. No. You don't need to lock us in."

Phil pauses, but Cristina ignores me. "Get the other side," she tells him.

I run forward, but not fast enough. The two halves of the fence meet just as my hands slam against the harsh metal. Cristina snaps three padlocks into place.

Ignoring me, she stands up and looks at Phil. "Did you get all the paperwork set up?"

"I did." But the expression on his face implies he's not so sure he did it right. I know that look and I assign him a role—henchman, the weak link, the one I have the best shot at defeating.

Cristina gives a short sigh. "I'll look it over now. Everything has to be in order for tomorrow."

She crosses the room in two steps, flips open one of the laptops, and motions to Phil. "Show me."

I want to see, *have* to see what he has. If I knew what they wanted, why they captured us—but I can't see enough, not with the implacable cage holding me back.

Phil pulls a sheaf of papers out of one of the file cabinets. Even from across the room I can tell they're crumpled and not precisely lined up. Cristina stares at him a moment, then reaches into a desk drawer and pulls out a clipboard. She takes the papers, squares them up, and clips them into place.

My face presses up against the cold metal of the fence as I try to fathom exactly what kind of scenario is playing out. This doesn't look like the setup for cannibalistic serial murders or satanic blood rituals; instead it looks almost . . . scientific.

Phil seems stung at Cristina's implied criticism. "Everything's online anyway. The paper records aren't necessary for publication."

If they plan to publish the results of an experiment, Beckett and I must be the lab rats. I slip my fingers between the bars of the metal grate fencing us in, clenching it with ice-cold, trembling hands, willing myself to be the strong hero I need. God knows Beckett won't be. Our first, more important weapon will be information.

"Screw publication. We're going to sell it." Cristina still sounds impatient.

"How can we sell something we have to keep secret?"

"Classified crap gets sold all the time. To governments, mega-businesses, the military. Where do you think the tech for smart bombs or computer viruses comes from? They just need a better plan for the human problem."

I can't breathe. This is the answer to why we're here, Beckett and I—somehow we are the answer to the "human problem," and Cristina doesn't care that we know.

She sets the clipboard down carefully, then leans over the computer to check something on the screen. "Reverse-engineering SERE was stupid. And then the APA got involved and it was all human rights this and ethics violations that. This is the right way to go. Nancy knew that. She was on the edge of a breakthrough, but the idea of publishing, of getting peer reviews and public approval, held her back." She sounds like she's making an argument she's made in her own head a dozen times.

"Nancy *and* Walter," Phil adds.

Hearing Phil name my mother and father is like being given a jolt of anesthesia that blows my consciousness up and out of my body. I know the word SERE—the Survival, Evasion, Resistance, and Escape techniques used by CIA operatives. This isn't the first time my parents' names have been associated with this kind of research, but I can't even feel the inevitable fear and grief though the dizzying storm of disbelief.

Reverse-engineering SERE, the phrase Cristina mentioned so dismissively, was the kind of program that yielded the enhanced-interrogation atrocities of Abu Ghraib and Guantanamo Bay. My parents aren't warm or loving, but they couldn't have anything to do with torture.

I glance back at Beckett for confirmation, but he's sitting against the wall with his head in his hands, not even listening, and the flash of anger I feel snaps me back to reality. I want to shake him awake. This isn't the time for his feckless beautiful-dreamer routine. We both need to pay attention.

Cristina scowls at Phil. "Screw Walter. It was her idea, her vision. And then she just . . . lost her nerve."

Cristina's words wake all the worst fears I had about my parents—that they don't care about people, that they don't care about me, that they only care about research. If you substitute writing for research, they're the same charges Zoe has leveled against me.

I fight the bile back down. No, there's absolutely no way my parents have anything to do with this, and I'm nothing like them.

Phil doesn't let it go. "Like you said, it was illegal. And the funding dried up."

When I was doing research about torture techniques for a novel, a familiar name came up—James Spiegler, someone I knew my parents had worked with in the past. But they worked with so many people over the years, it wasn't as though these old "enhanced interrogation" studies were based on their current research.

Nancy and Walter. Mom and Dad.

My body goes heavy, sagging against the metal fence. The metal protests with a creak and Cristina's gaze flicks in my direction, then away again dismissively. The separate pieces of the puzzle—the kidnapping, this strange location, my parents, psychological testing—are all swirling in my mind.

Cristina slaps the clipboard on the desk. "We won't worry about the funding. We'll crack the problem and collect on the back end."

"Fine." The two of them bend over the laptop as Cristina's fingers race over the keyboard.

Beckett raises his head and catches my eye. He has been listening. Thank God. I wish we could talk it out right now, but I don't want Cristina and Phil to hear us.

Back when I was researching my next book, the one that will come after *Bloody Heart, Wild Woods*, I pulled on that thread, searching for more information on Spiegler, and instead of leading me to my parents, it sent me down a rabbit hole. Tracing James Spiegler took me from one website to another, from government labs to prison studies to university faculty.

Chilled, I realize another place those digital bread crumbs led—this location. This abandoned missile silo that had been converted into a house by James Spiegler. Clearly it's been updated since then. Now the connections—my parents, war crimes, enhanced interrogation—narrow down to a single question.

My body goes as rigid as the metal slats I'm gripping. What's going to happen to me and Beckett?

It doesn't matter if we talk to each other or scream or cry. Cristina and Phil don't care if we overhear them, and they haven't bothered to cover their faces. I've known what that means since I first saw Cristina—they won't be letting us go.

Desperate, I look back at Beckett. For a moment I feel for him the way I used to, back when we could communicate with a glance. Silently I tell him *I need you.*

He reaches up for my hand, but it feels like he's pulling me down, sucking my strength.

My mind is spinning with images of prisoners hooded, electrocuted, abandoned. I slide to the floor, sitting beside Beckett with my back against the wall. His hand is the only warmth, the only comfort. It's not enough, but it's all I have.

We're no longer lost in the woods; we're in the maw of the beast.

15

AVA

CRISTINA AND PHIL leave, and when the door seals shut behind them, Beckett and I are alone in the darkness of their scientific lair with the faintest hum of electronics and just enough ambient light to discern the metal gate. The cold seeps into my bones, and my mind won't stop turning over everything I've heard, trying to follow these crumbs of information to a real conclusion.

I let go of Beckett's hand and stand up. Now we're finally able to talk together, and this time we won't fire off questions or flail around struggling to figure out the basics.

There's a pale-blue light from the security panel and another from a power strip by the computers. As the minutes crawl by, our eyes adjust and it's easier to see.

Scanning the room, I notice a small red light in one corner near the ceiling, and I think it must be a camera. I turn my back on it.

Beckett hoists himself to his feet, just a shadow beside me. "Did you hear them talking about Nancy and Walter? Is this about a ransom?"

"I don't know. I think it's more than that." I've been unfair to Beckett. He was paying attention, not just zoning out. But he processes everything verbally, and I wish he'd be quiet so I could think.

No such luck. "Because you're a big-deal writer? Just pay them. You must have plenty of money. I'm not worth a ransom, not on my salary. Nobody pays to read literature."

Familiar irritation flares inside me. He means I've got money only because I'm a sellout, pandering to the masses—that's his favorite excuse for failure, believing he's unappreciated and artistically better than me. It still stings a little, as though my pursuit of my dreams cost us our marriage. That's exactly why I wrote my first novel in secret, when I was supposed to be marking student compositions or working on the collection of interlocking short stories that would have been my thesis. A garland of unhappy relationships, generation after generation of ennui.

"They don't want my money." *You idiot.* Even if they do, paying it won't set us free. They've already shown us too much to let us go. I can't believe he hasn't picked up on that, but then, he's historically terrible at noticing anything outside his own head. Beckett is solipsism on two legs.

Whatever their end game, it's not as simple as bind, torture, kill—no, this is something less personal, more scientific. Or at least, Cristina thinks it is.

But as a writer, I know something she doesn't—it's always personal. We all tell ourselves stories to justify our actions, but believing your own story is a foolish mistake. The more personal Cristina's motivation, the less she might even realize it, and that could give me an edge.

Beckett's still talking. "I bet you've got money to pay them. Or Walter. Your folks must have a ton saved up."

He's putting the information together, but it's taking too long. Hearing him make every mental step out loud might kill me. And I know I'm being unfair, but my teeth are gritted as I say, "They were talking about research, about SERE—"

"Your parents won't pay for me, of course." Beckett runs both hands roughly through his hair, like he can wipe the slate clean. "What am I even doing here?"

I try again. "They were talking about military torture techniques—"

"So they might make torture videos and send them to get your folks to pay up? I think your publisher would pay more."

"Just listen for a minute. They were talking—"

"I *have* been listening." His gaze darts past me in constant motion. "They're coming back tomorrow to get started, they're not covering their faces, so they're not going to let us go even if your parents pay them—or your husband, your new one."

The pieces are falling into place, but I'm irritated instead of relieved that he's caught up. Not only is he ignoring everything I've been saying; now he's taking a swipe at Glenn? "Not that new. I've been married to Glenn twice as long as I was married to you." Oh, it feels good to say this. After all, it's his fault our marriage failed.

"So where is he now? Why didn't they take him?" Beckett asks, like he's trying to imply something.

"Because you were easier. Glenn's a fighter." That feels even better. In a horrible way, quarreling with Beckett feels so right, not least because I'm *so* good at it.

He flushes, and I know I've hit him where it hurts. "Then the two of you are a great match. That's probably what happened. You were a total bitch and he set this up to get to your money. Let me guess, you have a prenup, right? He gets nothing if you dump him."

I will not flinch, but my nails are cutting into the palms of my hands. "He's got nothing to worry about."

"You think he's not cheating on you?"

"Because he's not jealous of me. How long did it take after my book deal for you to start sleeping with students? A couple weeks?" I pitch my voice high. "Congratulations, honey, on your success; now I'm going to start screwing around."

His eyes narrow, and one corner of his lip twists into a sneer. "Maybe if you hadn't been such a stone-cold bitch—"

"I didn't brag about it, I didn't get to celebrate or enjoy it, I was so careful of your feelings—" Even though my new success was blooming, the possibilities expanding, I'd get home and tamp it all down. I felt like I was playacting—*this is how an ordinary woman loads the dishwasher, reads the mail, pretends to listen to her husband talking about his day*—like Snow White singing while she kept house. Except I couldn't seem too happy, or Beckett might feel too bad.

"You looked at me like I was nothing."

"So you found some random adoring eighteen-year-old and killed our marriage. Forget writing; you couldn't even cheat creatively."

Beckett fires back, "Our marriage was already dead. Your contempt killed it."

"You mean, my success."

"Whatever." He turns his back on me.

If we don't get out of here, if Cristina and Phil don't kill us, I am totally going to kill him.

I clench my hands. Hitting Beckett would be like hitting my pillow, soft and unyielding. If he were gone, I could just focus on saving myself, and when I got out there'd be no nagging sense of his petty jealousy brooding out there in the world, no ex who found me undesirable, no one to remind Glenn I might be doomed at marriage. Right after the divorce, well-meaning people were always asking about Beckett, how he was doing, and I wished fiercely he was dead.

I steal a glance at him, and his hunched shoulders look so vulnerable. I could kill him, anyone could, but the way he looks with his head bent reminds me of our first days together. He wasn't just my lover, he was my writing companion. We wrote in the same room, together but in our own heads, Percy Bysshe and Mary Shelley. When I needed a break from the long solitary work, I would look up, and if his head and shoulders were curved over his pages, I didn't speak but turned back to my own writing and left him to his. But sometimes his head was raised and I could offer to make us tea or ask for a synonym or invite him to take a walk.

Since Beckett, I've never had anyone to write with.

In silence, I examine the barrier trapping us together. The padlocks closing the two halves look solid, but the fence itself has some movement. I shake it hard, violently. I'm thinking about Beckett, and I rattle the fence longer than necessary.

Yes, it's an accordion style, designed to be dragged and moved, but it is set into a grooved track in the floor and ceiling and there's no gap. We could push on it until it bowed, but I don't think Beckett and I could create enough space for either of us to fit through. We need someone with paramilitary training, or at least someone stronger.

We need Glenn. And I can't help an unfair flash of fury that it's Beckett, Beckett who is so much like me, so cerebral and uncoordinated, that I'm stuck with, Beckett who's rubbish at listening and following directions—even when we haven't been fighting—almost as dreadful as he was at being a husband.

I should tell him about all my speculations, about Spiegler and my research and where we are, but that will lead to more talking, more arguing, and first we need to focus on escape. Plus I don't feel like wasting time spelling it out for him.

"Do you see anything we can use to get out of here?" I ask, trying to make my words sound neutral.

"We could do something to the gate." At least he's making suggestions, even if he sounds sulky.

Beckett shakes the fence ineffectually. Noise fills the empty space around us, and I hold my breath, but no one comes. And it doesn't create a gap.

"Maybe we can break it?" he suggests. "I'll get a chair."

At first he hits the gate with the folding chair, and the noise reverberates again. I can't imagine this insubstantial weight shattering the massive barrier. If Glenn were here, he would have one of those magic tools that looks like a pocketknife, but he wouldn't be running at the gate. He'd try to break it at one of the joints. Fiercely, I swallow against the lump in my throat. Some part of me longs for Glenn to save me and hates Beckett for needing me to save him.

"Wait." I put my hand on Beckett's arm, thin, more like mine than Glenn's. "Maybe we could put it through a gap? Like a lever."

He angles the chair, slipping one of its feet through a diamond-shaped opening in the gate. "Yeah," he tells me. "This could work. Help me push."

There's just enough room at the top of the metal folding chair for both of us to grip, our arms interlaced and our faces very close together. He stinks, but I probably do too. Beckett is not as brawny as Glenn, and that makes me feel more valuable, more useful.

We put all our weight on the chair as it slips and skids around, and finally it catches just right on the place where a bolt holds two pieces of the fence together. I push so hard my feet almost leave the floor, until I am supporting myself by my arms on the chair. And then it moves, something gives way, and I lose my balance. I fall heavily on the hard floor, and the chair comes after me.

Becket doesn't run to my aid. He kneels in front of the gate, running his hands over it to see what damage we've done.

I take a few more moments to let the pain settle, but it is just a banged knee, after all. I reach out for the chair, and as I grasp it by the leg, I realize what has happened. My fingers find a fold in the metal where our pressure has crimped it.

"We bent the chair, not the fence," I say.

"Fuck."

He sits heavily, resting his arms on his knees. I know how he feels—frustrated and helpless. I do too. Beckett may be a delicate flower of a human being, but he's the only one on my side right now.

I try again. "About Cristina and Phil . . ."

"And your parents."

Exactly. That's the part that matters, why Cristina and Phil were talking about my parents and their research. Maybe Beckett and I can figure it out together. "Yeah. Can I just tell you what I know? Then you can tell me what you make of it."

He doesn't answer, so I start talking, laying one brick on top of another, watching to see if he's following.

First, the ways the entrance to the missile silo seemed familiar. Second, the location—only hours away from home. I don't know how long I was unconscious in that van, but it wasn't more than half a day. Then my parents' names, and the phrase *reverse-engineering SERE*. How I had been researching military interrogation techniques for a book and came across a name I recognized: James Spiegler, a colleague of my parents'. He'd been involved in developing a new version of SERE, one that relied more on psychological torture than physical torture.

I realized how little I knew about what my parents actually do, and instead of researching the novel, I turned my attention to researching them. I found a picture of them with Spiegler in front of a cabin in the woods, one that could be this one. One I discovered had been built over an abandoned missile site. I found my father's name with Spiegler's and other authors' on an article about psychological manipulation and reverse-engineering SERE.

Now I feel like someone has spilled a box of puzzle pieces on the table and I'm holding only five in my hand.

Beckett is unnaturally quiet, his eyes wide, but I can tell his brain is sifting through the information. "What you're saying—it fits with the lab coats and clipboard, the talk of getting results, but it's crazy."

He trails off, and I wonder if he's doing the same thing I'm doing, assessing my parents' possible involvement. Then he shakes his head. "Whatever's going on, it's got nothing to do with me."

I thought he might be my ally, but we can't break the damn barrier, we can't escape, and he can't even stand to work with me to find answers. Angry fear floods me and I snap, "Because this is all my fault? Just like everything else? I'm the reason you're a failure?"

And for once he's silent. I stalk over to the wall and lie down facing it, overwhelmed by fatigue. I can hear Beckett moving, but I'm not going to look.

I'm no longer hungry or thirsty, but my mind is spinning. I think there's no way I'll fall asleep, but my eyes won't stay open. Somewhere in the distance water is dripping.

I struggle to stay awake, but I'm drowning.

And there are monsters in the dark.

16

ZOE

M Y MOM AND dad finally leave me alone in the house. And I've never been so grateful to have the kind of parents who think more about their work than their daughters. I can imagine their own relief at dropping the pretense of being worried and caring, almost smiling as they drive back to the professional lives that define them, even at the risk of appearing callous.

Even with Ava missing.

Alone, I take a few minutes to explore this strange house full of familiar objects. The old house was bigger, suburban, but even then my parents chose modern, uncomfortable furniture and abstract art that was different from anything our neighbors had. I see the canvas covered with black, gray, and red slashes that hung above our fireplace instead of a family portrait. This town-house doesn't have a fireplace, but that hostile picture still has a place of pride, centered above a black leather chaise lounge that looks like a refugee from a therapist's office.

Fitting.

Next to an end table where I used to set my drink without a coaster, there's an unfamiliar floor lamp, stainless steel, with a menacing arc, looming over a matched set of club chairs, so tight and sleek it's impossible to imagine sitting on one. In another corner, placed almost like an afterthought, is an abstract sculpture with angular metal spikes shooting out like an explosion, but without any symmetric beauty.

Everywhere I look, my eyes find something unwelcoming and discordant. No cozy chairs for snuggling up and reading to a child. No personal photos of family time or charming mementos from trips abroad.

That's the thing that makes this feel like my childhood home. The overwhelming sense that I'm not welcome.

I have to find Ava and get the hell out of here.

In the kitchen, I find a paring knife and tear into the packaging of my newly purchased cell phone, tossing the instructions aside in my haste to plug it in. But I can't wait for it to charge up or power on. This house is creeping me out.

I call Andrew again from the landline, and again it goes straight to voice mail. The little flutter of anxiety I felt this morning is pounding against my rib cage now, the steady beat of panic.

He doesn't love you. He doesn't love you. He doesn't love you.

I run upstairs to my bedroom, dump out all the detritus from my shoulder bag, and pack it lightly with the pair of socks and my wallet. I race back downstairs to check the phone. The battery's at seventy percent, and that's good enough. Hello, internet.

I'll start by finding out where Ava lives now. The last time I saw her, she was in Delaware, but I know she moved. During one of our awkward phone check-ins, my mother let that slip. Something "closer to Glenn's work." Translation? The greater DC area.

I type in her full name, then cross-check with Glenn's, and bingo. There's an address right here in Arlington. Closer to our parents than I would have guessed. Close enough for me to drop by. And there's a home number, so hopefully I can make sure the house is empty when I get there.

I am sick of all this drama. The sooner I prove Ava's alive and well and behind her own "disappearance," the sooner I can go home.

Of course, I'll need transportation. After the agony of waiting for an app to install, I find a freelance driver just ten minutes away. While I wait for him to arrive, I call Ava's home number, but thankfully no one picks up. Either Glenn is not at home or he doesn't answer calls from numbers he doesn't know. Either way, I'm going to risk it.

The ride is uneventful, the driver hip and chatty. He doesn't mind my monosyllabic responses. I'm buzzing with anticipation, the same kind of pre-adrenaline rush I used to get when I snuck out at night. We leave the tidy townhomes that line the streets where my parents live and enter a straight-up suburb. Large homes, but different from the sprawling ones in Texas. These are definitely

East Coast homes, Colonials and Victorians and Geor-
gians. And I know that even the deceptively small ones
command a high price. This is a neighborhood for politicians and power brokers, bankers and best-selling authors.

I get out on the sidewalk and the car speeds away.
Now I am free to stare. Looking at Ava and Glenn's
home, I feel like she's cheated my expectations again. Ava
bought this house after I disappeared, a new house for a
new marriage. It should have been a fairy-tale mansion
for a modern-day Snow Queen, something imposing and
imaginative, entirely unique.

This is just a generically pretty, Victorian-style home
with gabled windows and curlicues around the porch.
Not old. Not special. It could belong to anyone. In fact,
it's got the same sort of look as all the other houses on the
street. Same builder using a master plan, changing it just
enough to make each house slightly different from its
neighbors.

Like most modern neighborhoods built for a certain
income bracket, there's no sign of life during business
hours. Adults are at work, children are at school or day
care, it's very quiet. I'm the only thing that doesn't belong.

Time to quit stalling. I square my shoulders. Obviously, I can't just march up the front steps and beat down
the door, but I can see if anyone's home. And if it's Glenn?
That thought doesn't stop me. I'm not finished trying to
persuade him of my innocence, and if that doesn't work,
I'm not finished fighting with him either.

I walk with faux confidence up the front walk, up the
three little steps, and rap briskly on the door, my heart
booming. Nothing. I press the doorbell, a few seconds
longer than usual. I can hear the distant chime, but no
other sound. The house is empty.

My first feeling is rising triumph. If the police thought Ava was kidnapped, they'd be monitoring the house or staking it out or something. They must really believe she's doing this herself. A publicity stunt. Typical Ava Hallett.

Then I get the neck-crawling sensation that someone is watching me, but not from inside the house. I step away from the door and shrug, conscious that I may have an audience, but when I turn around, the streets and yards are still deserted. Each house has windows shaded by white curtains, giving them blank, unassuming gazes.

I don't waste any more time at the front. I need to shake this feeling. Out here in the open, I'm a mouse in a grassy field with a hawk circling overhead. Walking briskly, like someone with a job to do, I skirt around the corner and down the side of the house, grateful for the size of the yard and the privacy afforded by the lush evergreens planted between Ava's property and her neighbor's. In Texas, our yards are divided by pine fences mandated by our HOAs. The trees are prettier, and with a pang I imagine Emma playing like Ava and I used to, using a fallen pine branch as a make-believe broom or filling the lower branches of the trees with our dolls.

If I were still at home, Emma would be at school. I might be pushing a loaded shopping cart through the produce aisles at H-E-B or accepting a sample of chicken salad. Maybe I'd be at home with the washing machine and the dishwasher both running while I wiped down the counters and swept the kitchen floor. Or I could be playing hooky with Felicia over a cup of coffee and a kolache, the soft yeasted roll giving way around sharp sausage-and-jalapeño filling almost as spicy as our gossip. If I want another morning like that, I will have to be strong now.

There's a sun-room jutting from the back of the house, a kind of glassed-in porch. That door is also locked. I take a step back to scan the windows, a little surprised to be standing here, battling a growing sense of despair. All the ground-floor windows are shut tight. Then I notice it. A dormer window set in a corner, facing east. Open. And somehow I know that has to be Ava's study.

Ava always used to open a window in her room. Our parents hated it. They complained that she was wasting money and electricity, making the AC and heat inefficient. That even with screens, insects were getting inside. That it was an unnecessary security risk. What if it rained while we were out, and her floor and curtains got wet and rotted? Once my father even unearthed a hammer and nails from somewhere and nailed the window shut. Ava's fingers were red and raw the next morning, and I knew she'd gotten that window open again.

Now that she has her own house, I bet her window is never shut.

Even if there is an alarm system, it can't be armed without every window closed. All I have to do is get up there. But I don't see a ladder or step stool around, and the pine trees are too far away from the house. Even if they weren't, they don't look easy to climb. I walk across the yard, considering. There's no way to spider-crawl up the wall, and when I step closer and give the drainpipe a shake, I can see it's too flimsy to be any use either.

I have almost given up when I turn the corner to the side yard. There, someone—surely not Ava—has planted a little herb garden with brick paths in a simplified, miniature labyrinth. In addition to the plants, all dulled by the end of summer, there's a sundial, an opalescent gazing globe on a stone pedestal, and a wrought-iron bench big enough for two people to sit.

Tall enough, I think, for my purposes, if I stand it on end.

This is reckless, crazy, the kind of thing I thought I'd never do again. I'm a nice suburban mom now, not some loony who uses garden furniture to break into a house. I almost give up. Then I remember. If I don't do this, if I don't find Ava, I'm going to lose Emma and Andrew. If I can't clear my name, that life is lost to me.

It's hell to drag the bench over to the sun-room, and I leave deep gouges in the lawn. There's not going to be any way to cover that up. My lungs and legs are desperate for oxygen, and my fingers are on fire with the weighted edge of the iron as it cuts into my hands. I have to be careful at the end. I want to prop the bench against the house, but if I slip, if it veers too close to one of the huge glass windows, this could be a very literal break-in.

When I think it's mostly stable, I take a deep breath and brace my hands against the wood of the house, trying to make myself as light as possible. My stomach feels hollow with fear. If I slip, I could kill myself. Worse, I could knock myself unconscious and wake when Glenn pokes me with his foot or when the police show up. My insides cringe at their imagined contempt.

As I stretch upward and start to lever myself off the second armrest, I feel the bench shift, and I leap. For a moment I'm not on the bench or the house, but then the roof of the sun-room catches me under my arms, and I lean into it.

I refuse to fall.

Pushing and scrabbling through sheer force of will, I am on the broad roof of the sun-room. Below me the bench has fallen on its back, thankfully not through a pane of glass. As I lie on my belly, I am close enough to touch the open window just in front of me. My whole body is shaking.

The gray shingles are rough and warm under my hands and cheek. I push up a little, aware of how high this is. Anyone could see me. Is someone calling the cops right now? I reach out for the windowsill and scramble through.

As my feet scrape across a table set right beneath the window, I knock books to the floor. I land heavily, loudly, and hold my breath for a beat, waiting for someone to come storming up the steps and find me. But the house is silent. My heart is pounding so heavily it's hard to believe it makes no sound.

I was right—this is Ava's study. There's a straight-backed chair in front of the table, so she must use it as her desk. No drawers to search, but bookcases line three of the four walls. The fourth has a door and Ava's mood board. At least, that's what I guess it is. From floor to ceiling the wall beside the door is covered with bits of paper—newsprint clippings, postcards, photos, notes written in Ava's bold, spiky script—and a few are even affixed above the door itself.

I haven't seen her handwriting in years, but it's burned into my memory. The open window, the familiar shapes of each letter—it's strange to consider that some of the things I knew about her are still true. People think sisters know each other better than anyone else. Ava and I don't have that kind of relationship, but we aren't strangers either. Seeing her handwriting now gives me a jolt of recognition, followed by a gut-tingling sense of foreboding.

Looking around the study, I know I shouldn't touch anything. If by some remote chance Ava really is missing and they dust for prints in here, I don't need them finding mine.

A quick dig through my shoulder bag yields those new socks I bought at the drugstore. I didn't let myself admit it earlier, but I was preparing for this moment. I will do whatever it takes to get my life back. Feeling ridiculous, I pull them over my hands and wipe down every incriminating surface. Just to be safe, I'll leave these makeshift "gloves" on while I snoop around.

Straining my ears, all I hear is the eerie silence of an empty house.

I pick up the books I knocked onto the floor, but they are nothing special. Two oversized paperbacks marked as "Advance Readers," neither of them by Ava, and an Audubon field guide to the birds of North America. I drop them back onto the desk. There's no computer here, and I wonder if the police have taken it.

I approach the wall covered with notes. Ava was always collecting bits of paper, even as a child. Some she tore from magazines or envelopes, some she covered with words or phrases in her own scrawled handwriting, or little sketches, unintelligible to anyone but her.

Seeing this fills me with resentment. I don't know why I come across as the crazy one. From a distance, this wall has a freaky *Beautiful Mind* vibe. In addition to the torn paper and Ava's black writing, there's the impression of the colors she chose: forest greens, Valentine reds, and rich gold tones. Once I get closer, I see things grouped together that don't make sense.

It's almost like two sections. The lower part is blanketed with a swirl of words and pictures that seem to go with *Bloody Heart, Wild Woods*. I see snippets of fairy tales, pictures by Arthur Rackham and Trina Schart Hyman, and bits of sheet music for old folk songs. The top half is less colorful, mostly black-and-white printed text and handwritten notes. I step closer and read "a psychiatrist, a lie-detector expert, and a hypnotist," "Mindszenty," "Survival, Evasion, Resistance and Escape," and "MK-ULTRA."

There's even a folded piece of paper that looks like a blueprint, accompanied by a word—"Spiegler"—in Ava's handwriting. I put that one into my bag. It's the only thing that remotely resembles a location. Maybe that's where she's holed up.

As for the rest, I wonder if it's research for her next novel—or has my sister become a tinfoil-hat conspiracy theorist? I pull my cell phone out of my bag and fumble to find the camera on it. The screen flickers, and then my cheap phone starts rebooting. Fuck. I turn back to Ava's desk, and there is a pen on top. Instead of trying to figure out where the hell she puts all the paper and things a normal person would keep in a desk drawer, since this table doesn't have any, I open up one of the advance reading copies and tear out the back page. The violent ripping echoes through the house and makes my pulse race.

I copy the strange words and tuck the scrap of paper into my bag.

Being here has a weirdly familiar feel. I used to babysit as a teen, and it was impossible to resist the temptation to see how people arranged their books, what clothes they had in the closet, what was hidden in their drawers. Now that I have a chance to dig into Ava's life, I can't stop, even though I'm running on adrenaline and nerves.

I have to check out the rest of the house.

Stepping out into the hallway, I'm hyper-aware of every sound.

Next to Ava's study is a storage space with dusty boxes, trunks, and old furniture. On the other side of the staircase leading down to the first floor is a guest bedroom, anonymous and boring. I ignore it and the little closet next to it. Downstairs, there is a room that's slightly raised, just two steps above the ground floor.

Glenn's study.

My heart is pounding the way it used to before we met for a date, thrumming a beat of danger and desire. If I am discovered here, I really will look crazy obsessed. The smallness of the room, barely larger than a closet, makes the size of the furniture even more dramatic. Glenn's desk is easily twice as heavy as Ava's. While hers is a simple wooden table that wouldn't be out of place in a farmhouse kitchen or a workshop, his is made of a highly polished mahogany look-alike; it's the kind of desk that demands attention. A show horse, not a workhorse. He gets to sit in a leather-padded ergonomic dream chair. The surface is dominated by a desktop computer and its keyboard. Why haven't the police taken it too?

His desk doesn't face the window like Ava's does. He keeps his back to the view and his gaze on the door. The same alpha-male quality that I used to find sexy now seems controlling.

One wall is lined with dark bookcases, but each shelf holds only a few books. These shelves are for display. There's an assortment of manly knickknacks: an abstract glass sculpture, a bronze eagle, a pyramid-shaped award of some kind. And there are so many framed photos of Glenn—holding up a giant fish, in outdoor gear on a ski slope, with his arm around Ava as if she is just another trophy. The ocean is behind them, and with a pang I wonder if it is their honeymoon picture.

The silence of the empty house is beginning to creep me out. I slip behind Glenn's desk, glad I can keep an eye on my escape route as I rummage. For all the fancy wood and brass-handled drawers, nothing is locked. It's tricky to handle the papers with my hands in socks, so I slip them off. It's not like anyone will fingerprint the entire house.

In a movie, I would find incriminating evidence right away. Instead, all I learn is that they pay extra for the premium sports channel, they support Doctors Without Borders, and Ava makes more money in a year than I could make in a lifetime, which makes me feel like even more of a failure.

Not as much of a failure as if I will be if I'm caught. Time's slipping away like the dripping of a faucet. I can't stop until I find something, but I can't stay too long.

I tentatively touch the keyboard of the computer, and it hums to life, but the screen is locked. Although feeling invasive and creepy with my hands on the keys, I remind myself I'm doing this to find Ava, whether or not she wants to be found. The password isn't any variant or combination of Ava's name, or Glenn's, or "password." I'm not some tech genius, so I just leave it and hope the computer will put itself back to sleep before Glenn gets home. Then I scrub the keyboard with my socks.

Next to the computer is a business card holder in the same rich wood as the desk. I pick up a card and study the sparse details. Glenn's name, his email with its dot-gov domain, and his cell phone number. No address, no job title, not even a decorative picture of some kind.

Seems strange to have this in a holder. Ava probably gave it to him. She always sucked at gift giving.

I pocket the card, not that I can imagine wanting to contact Glenn, but I need any information I can gather right now.

Before leaving, I pick up the picture of Ava and Glenn. He looks like he's really smiling with his mouth and eyes, and I can feel my insides dissolving a little.

I only saw Ava with her "new boyfriend" Glenn over one Christmas break. I didn't talk to him or make eye contact. I didn't look at the two of them, and I always left the room as quickly as possible. The next summer I ran into Glenn in Providence. When he said, "Zoe?" I was startled, not recognizing him for a second. Then he stepped forward to give me a hug, our first, and asked warmly, "How have you been?" and I was lost.

We were together only ten weeks, because of Ava. She was done with him, and then she wasn't. All she had to do was stretch out her hand and take him, and I was alone in the cold again, always second best.

I study the Ava in this picture. Her hair is blowing across her face, and she looks like she is about to laugh. There is motion and joy in the sunlight on the ocean waves and in the way Glenn and Ava hold on to each other. If I'd never known either of them, I would want to meet the woman in the photo. This couple looks perfect for each other. I would wish them both well.

I put the picture facedown on the shelf and leave the room, feeling again like I'm on the wrong side of the glass, looking in.

For a moment, I am opposite the front door. Light shines through the beveled window, and the back of my neck prickles again. Every second I stay here is tempting fate. I should walk right out that door and be done with it.

But I'm rash and sometimes stupid. And if I can prove where Ava is, there's no way I'll stop now.

I whip around the corner and down the hall. The soles of my shoes catch and squeak against the hardwood floors.

There's a formal dining room and a little room with a piano in it, but I'm hurrying now, knowing my time is running out. I open doors and find a coat closet, a half bath, then finally the master bedroom.

The first thing I notice is the darkness. There are windows along two sides of the room, but heavy floor-to-ceiling drapes block any light except that from the hall-way behind me. There is a scent to Ava's master bedroom, feminine and masculine mixed, light citrus and some-thing woodsy. If the staircase made me feel exposed, this room is like a safe cave, hidden from the world. I avoid looking at the bed.

This is the most intimate space of Glenn and Ava's life together. Waves of emotion surge through me—jealousy, resentment, fury, and even a wisp of yearning.

I yank open the drawers of one bedside table, then the other. Tissues, coins, an old copy of *The Economist*. Must be Glenn's side. Ava's side has a bedside table with only a lamp. No books, not even an e-reader. I'm kneel-ing down to peer under the bed when a phone rings in another room and I startle, banging my head hard enough to bring tears to my eyes.

Crap. I explore the bump with my hand. I'll just check the closet, then get the hell out.

Inside Ava's walk-in closet, I systematically search through expensive suits, flannel pajamas, and oversized sweaters—even inside soft leather boots. When I pull out a scrap of paper, I hang on to it. The loose change, lint, and candy wrappers go back where I found them. There's a rhythm to the work, and I'm completely engrossed when suddenly I hear the front door open.

Fear surges in my stomach, sending chilled tendrils throughout my body. A housekeeper? I can bluff my way past a housekeeper. But that's a wild hope. Odds are it's Glenn. I can already see the contempt in his eyes, hear the words he won't need to say—*psycho, criminal, loser.* My breath catches in my throat.

There's no way I can leave the master bedroom without being seen. I'm not even sure I shut the door between the bedroom and the hallway.

Only bad choices remain: stay hidden in the closet, hope I have enough privacy to climb out a bedroom window, or take a deep breath and charge straight out the front door.

Every muscle is tensed with the desire to go, *go, go.* I know the smart play is to stay put. Sooner or later whoever has come into the house, even if it's Glenn, will leave, or go upstairs, or fall asleep. But I suck at waiting. The tension and suspense are so much worse than anything else that could happen. I know this is my biggest weakness. I always lose my temper, or cut and run, or make the drastic choice instead of playing it cool. And this closet is full of Ava, reminding me, smothering me.

The person has gone into the kitchen. I can hear sounds, too faint to identify. If I come out of the bedroom, I'll be in the hallway, not really visible from the kitchen. *Just wait. Be smart.* But even as I think the words, I am ignoring my own good advice. On one side of the closet is a hooded sweat shirt. If I make a break for it, maybe they won't be able to tell it's me. I pull it on over my shoulder bag and everything else. As it goes over my head, I feel safely invisible. I really, really want to run. I stand up, tensed and ready.

I won't run. Not yet.

I sit back down and shove my hands into the sweat shirt's pouch pocket. Then I feel something crumple under my fingers and pull it out.

A torn piece of notebook paper. And on it, my address. My own address in Texas where I live with Andrew and Emma. My address, right there as though I had brought it with me. Those familiar words, the house number I've practiced with Emma, but written in Ava's distinctive handwriting.

My neck tingles like she's standing right behind me.

This scrap of paper is proof that someone looked for me. Proof that someone found me.

Ava.

And then the bedroom door opens.

I freeze.

My nerves are screaming with every sound from the other room. A drawer opening, the swish of a curtain. Carefully I scoot deeper into the closet, and the sound stops. I stare blindly at the closet door.

Then, a miracle. A creak from the bedroom, footsteps in the hallway. I crawl cautiously toward the closet door, but my heart won't stop pounding. With the tips of my fingers, I push, and the door swings open enough for me to see through the bedroom door and into the hallway.

For once, I should be smart.

Instead, I run for the front door.

17

ZOE

Six feet. That's how far I make it down the hallway before someone swings over the banister and grabs me by the shoulders hard.

I am so focused on the front door that my feet try to keep running. Then I see who's holding me.

Glenn.

Trapped. My mind freezes on that thought, and my animal instincts take over. I'm flailing, hitting and kicking, trying to break free. My elbow knocks something out of Glenn's hand that clatters on the floor. Swearing, he seizes my wrists, holding me at arm's length.

"Just stop," he shouts. "What the fuck are you doing?"

"Nothing. I was looking for Ava." I try to twist away, but my wrists are pinioned. I hate him right now. I'm panting and I hate him.

"What are you doing in my house?"

"Looking for Ava." I spit the words out this time.

He shakes me. "You know she's not here!"

"Bullshit. You probably killed her."

A strange look crosses his face, and he studies me. "You really don't know where she is?"

"Of course not. I just want to find her and go back to my family." I can't tell what he's thinking, but at least he's not shouting.

"Don't freak out again. Just stand there." He looks at the floor, and I see that the thing I knocked out of his hand was a cell phone.

Panic floods me. *The police. Breaking and entering. Person of interest.* I try to yank myself free. "Let go!"

"Shit. Zoe! Zoe!" He shouts my name like he's trying to get me to grab a lifeline, and I stop struggling, shocked at how much I want to trust him.

"I'm not going to call the police. Calm the fuck down." He keeps hold of one of my wrists and leans down to grab his phone. "How'd you get in here, anyway? The front door was still locked when I got home."

Is this a trick? "Study window."

"Which study?"

"Ava's."

"That's the second story."

"I used a bench to get to the porch."

"Christ." He sounds exasperated, but not angry. "Look, you can't stay here. I'll drive you home."

So, we walk out together. In the driveway there's a black Lexus sedan, elegantly practical. Glenn opens the passenger door.

"Get in the car."

Some instinct makes me freeze.

His jaw tenses. "Get in the damn car, Zoe."

I don't have to go with him. But I have a phone, so I can call for help if I need to. And he seems to believe I didn't hurt Ava. I don't believe he did either. Mostly.

So I get in and pull the door shut.

He slides into the driver's seat, hits the accelerator, and we pull away.

Sitting next to Glenn, I study his profile. He used to wear his hair longer, but the bridge of his nose, the angle of his jaw are still the same. Physically he's more similar to Andrew than I realized. And Glenn's take-charge attitude is a more volatile version of Andrew's cool focus on logistics.

A warning chimes deep within me as the memories unfurl. Glenn and me in the sheets of his futon bed while sun streamed through the curtainless window. I remember sitting on the dock of the boathouse with a book, waiting while Glenn sculled. Then the deepest memory, Glenn's closed door, his empty apartment.

I can tell he's driving me straight back to my parents' house and I shouldn't waste any more time, but I can't help myself. "Why didn't you even tell me you were leaving?"

He knows what I'm talking about. Three years ago I read the dedication in Ava's latest book, I told Glenn about it, and the next day he took off. Now he's staring straight ahead, like he can leave this confrontation in the dust. "I'm sorry."

He doesn't say it like he means it. He says it to shut the conversation down. There's a sour taste in my mouth, but I'm not the kind of angry that picks a fight, not right now. My heart isn't broken, it's just bruised. And I don't care what he thinks of me, so I ask, "You know I didn't do anything to Ava. What do you think happened?"

He sighs, and the edges of his eyes and mouth droop.

"You think someone *kidnapped* her?" It feels like he is taking her side, like I am the horrible person everyone else believes I am.

"Zoe, I don't know what to tell you." The car turns into my parents' neighborhood. "You say you're married, you've got a life. I think the best thing you can do is get on a plane and go home."

"She's my sister. If she's in trouble, really in trouble—"

"You'll do what?" He brings the car to a hard stop right in front of my parents' house and cuts his eyes at me. "If Ava's in trouble, you *should* fucking run. I told you before. Go home."

CHAPTER

18

AVA

I AM FLEEING THROUGH the woods, and a full moon gives the scene the flickering light of an old filmstrip. I need to find a refuge, but I can't catch my breath. I stop, clinging to a tree for support, my fingers clutching the rippled bark. Then the tree gives way under my hand, a small door opening, and inside the tree is a tiny room with a fireplace. A man bends over it, feeding twigs into the flames. He straightens and I see it is Beckett, but a younger version, the man I fell in love with.

He smiles and holds out a hand in invitation. "'Come live with me and be my love.'"

I put my hand in his. Relief floods through me, but then the sky darkens and a cage falls down around us. We are caught.

My mother stands on the other side, a clipboard in her hand. She frowns at it, then at us. "You're not nearly fat enough. Stick your finger through the bars and let me see how plump you are."

There's a chicken bone in my hand, gnawed clean, and I poke it out of the cage.

Now she looks at me with Cristina's piercing dark eyes, and her face begins to sag like an oversized rubber mask. "Don't try that trick on me. You're the damn witch in this story. Just ask Zoe."

I wake with a gasp. The room is still dark, and now Beckett is sleeping behind me, almost touching. I don't inch away. The dream felt so real, not like sleep, not like a fairy tale. Zoe probably does think I'm a witch, but I don't think she's behind all this, I'm crossing off one option after another—not Zoe, not a crazy fan, not a random psychopath.

The signs point to my parents.

But that's insane. I can't believe it, but I can't refute it either. Setting aside the secret research and the connections to all the terms Cristina rattled off, the most damning evidence is the way my parents always take a minute to decide on an emotional reaction. When I first brought Beckett home and told them we were engaged, they just looked at us. The silence grew more and more uncomfortable. Then my mother took a breath and said, "Congratulations, sweetie." The endearment sounded like a word in a foreign language, one that she'd read mothers should say.

Behind me, Beckett whispers, "Ava?"

"What?"

He pauses. "Did you ever think it was Zoe?"

"Maybe." Of course I did. Now I almost wish it were.

"But it sounds . . ." He draws a deep breath. "Do you think . . . maybe your parents are involved? Somehow?"

I squeeze my eyes shut. My *parents*.

Nothing can dispel the loneliness and fear of that thought. This is exactly how I felt as a child, when my parents' presence in the house was no comfort at all, and Zoe always fell asleep straightaway. Some evenings I couldn't stand lying awake by myself and I would slip into bed next to her, the solid fact of her breathing the only comfort I could find. This chill, this isolation, brings it all back.

But I still can't believe it. Their research was a mystery to me and their attitude toward me and Zoe was clinical, sure, but I can't wrap my head around the idea of my parents actually doing this.

I lean back just a little, so I'm closer to Beckett. We are frightened, cold, disoriented, and exhausted, and even though it's been five years, my body remembers the shape of his.

"It's going to be okay," he whispers into my hair, and the sweetness of the lie makes me tear up. Maddening, infuriating Beckett. If only I could hate him all the time.

I was never sure what my parents did for a living, and I never felt love or emotional connection from them, only a sense that Zoe and I were some kind of family experiment.

I don't doubt that my parents would prioritize their research over my health and well-being. I know the grim truth—they are absolutely capable of this. I just can't believe they would go to all the trouble, or that my mother would delegate a massive research project to anyone else, much less somebody like Cristina. I tell myself that if my parents were really involved, I would have seen them by now.

I close my eyes against the dark. My dream still eddies around me, and I wish this were only a story, the kind I used to tell Zoe.

When a nightmare woke her in the wee hours of the morning and our parents were bundled up with sleep masks and sound machines, I'd hear a whisper from the doorway of my bedroom. "Ava? Are you awake?" She'd slip under the covers, we'd press our foreheads together, and I'd whisper stories to her. Some were "real" fairy tales like Hansel and Gretel or Rumpelstiltskin, and others I made up—two sisters exploring a magic forest, dragons tamed and princes rescued and witches plunging off cliffs. Now I'm the one in the cage and no one's coming to defeat the witch. If I disappeared forever, that would probably be Zoe's happily-ever-after.

But I try to find comfort in the warmth of that long-ago memory, when I wasn't alone and stories could hold back the shadows.

Minutes or hours pass, before the sound of the blast door unsealing shakes me awake.

My head still aches from slamming into Phil, but it's one ache among many. Every muscle and joint hurts. Beckett is already up, seated against one wall, his legs crisscrossed, as if he's meditating.

Cristina comes into the room, leaving the door open, and I'm fully alert, my body tensed, cataloging her every move. Nothing she does will escape my notice, because no matter how clever she thinks she is, she won't outwit me.

Her army-green coat is gone, replaced by a trim white lab coat that she wears without a trace of self-conscious pretension. The container of coffee in her hand trails a familiar scent redolent of morning comfort, and there's something in her other hand, but I can't quite see it. Glancing at us as if she's confirming we're still here but not as though she's particularly interested, she stops at the computer and hits a few keys. Shaking her head at the screen, she takes a sip.

Slowly I approach the gate.

She turns around and slips two energy bars through a gap in the fence, then quickly steps back. The diamond-shaped gaps are not wide enough for a hand, but the food slides through easily and falls onto the floor. We still have bottles of water, and a bucket in the corner. A slight smell lets me know that Beckett has used it during the night.

I pick up the energy bar, but I'm not ravenous, I'm furious that this witch thinks she can kidnap me, cage me, and then ignore me. All the leftover edginess from my argument with Beckett is redirected right at Cristina. I've been trying to be strong, holding back, not letting her know how scared I am.

Now I want to get a reaction—that's the only way I'll learn anything new. If Cristina were someone like Beckett or Zoe, it would be easy to needle her, just enough to make her crazy.

I start small. "You've been working with my mother."

She doesn't even look at me.

"How does she feel about your little plan?"

Of course, Cristina's nothing like my sister or ex-husband. She's paying attention to the laptop, absorbed in her thoughts like my mother always is, impervious to my usual methods—a cutting remark, a refusal to rise to the bait, attack and withdraw, withhold. I need to become someone else, someone loud and impossible to ignore. Zoe.

I know how my sister operates—Zoe slammed doors, hurled objects, and single-throatedly generated epic bouts of screaming. My parents dislike emotion, but even they couldn't withstand the ferocity of her onslaughts. If they didn't leave the room—or sometimes the house— quickly enough, they were forced to deal with her, as if Zoe had suddenly snapped into focus in front of them and they really saw her, while their eyes skated over me. I don't know if I can work that kind of magic with my words, not in real life.

I need to be as bold, as fierce as Zoe.

"Hey, Cristina!" I shout, and I shake the fence with all my strength.

Phil comes through the blast door with an armload of folded sheets. "Where do you want these?"

I speak at the same time she does, trying to drown out her answer. "Let us *out, out, out!*"

His eyes widen, but Cristina just jerks her head, indicating where he should set down his burden.

Grabbing the battered chair, I beat the fence with it, trying to fill the world with noise, but nothing happens. Cristina leans over and whispers something in Phil's ear, and he leaves. I'm slowing down, getting tired, when he returns with a cardboard box, Zeus at his heels.

Phil sets the box down on the desk, then touches Cristina's arm and nods toward a door on the other side of the room, a normal door like a broom closet or a bathroom, not a blast-shielded bomb shelter entrance like the way we got down here. She hands him what looks like some kind of wireless router and he heads out. Zeus flops down at her feet.

I let the chair fall. Whatever alchemy Zoe uses to turn noise and anger into attention doesn't work for me.

Without even looking over, Cristina says, "Are you finished?" She bends down to unlock a cabinet.

I glance at Beckett, and his eyes are wide. *Come sit down*, he mouths at me, but I'm not giving up until I get a reaction. I have to say something.

"Look," I say. "It's not that I'm not impressed with your cut-rate Dr. Evil routine, but it's a little B-movie, don't you think? Half-baked, ill-conceived, derivative . . ."

"What the fuck," Beckett whispers. "Are you trying . . . ?"

I see from his face that he understands I *am* trying to make her mad. I may be inept at physical feats of strength, but I can play psychological games with the best of them. Just ask Zoe.

Cristina carefully sets a blood pressure cuff on the desktop. Her movements are precise, maybe too precise, as she adds a thermometer and a few other items I can't make out.

"Heard you talk about Nancy and Walter. So you're one of Mom's groupies?"

There's no reaction at all from Cristina, although the very act of mentioning my parents out loud makes me feel shaky, like I'm making it real. I cling to the barrier, forcing myself to watch, to think, not to let the swirl of grief and fear swamp me.

Think. She must be preparing to take our vitals, and she'd only do that to subjects of an experiment. My hands tremble and the gate shakes, but I let go before Cristina notices. We really are lab rats and the games are about to begin.

But first she'll have to take one of us out of the cage, and that's an opportunity. My pulse leaps in anticipation.

"Hey Dr. Evil, what's Mom think of your pathetic post-apocalyptic lab?"

She shuts the cabinet with a little more force than necessary. So my mother is her trigger point. Then I know exactly where to push, because Cristina's fears are mine—stupidity, weakness, failure.

"When my mother was your age, she'd already published her first book," I go on. "She had a faculty position and a place on an international research committee. What's on your CV, Cristina?"

Cristina focuses on her desk, smoothing out a coil of the blood pressure cuff with much more concentration that the task warrants.

"Maybe I remember you. You were her assistant, but she fired your ass, right? Too bad you couldn't bully her with your little dog and electric stick. Too bad you couldn't measure up. Mom doesn't suffer fools."

Her head lifts, her face a frozen mask. "Do you think this routine is going to get a reaction? You think you're pretty sharp, don't you, Ava? Sharp enough to cut yourself. Your mother's a genius about everything, except you. She deserves better."

She takes a step closer, the gate bisecting the inches between our faces. "You look just like her, do you know that? Especially the eyes. Go ahead, say whatever you want. It won't make any difference."

We stand eye to eye for a long moment, Cristina and I, until the ordinary door opens again and she turns away.

Phil comes in without the router and gives a decisive nod. Whatever he was setting up, it's ready to go now. Cristina picks up the cattle prod.

They are preparing to take at least one of us out of the cage. Cristina is giving instructions to Phil in a low voice, and I can't make them out.

I turn to Beckett and urgently whisper, "If they take you, get to the door."

But I want to be the natural choice, the first one they'll pick, because I want to take Cristina out. It's time to slay the dragon.

Almost as if she can hear my thoughts, she raises her head and looks at me. Then she smiles, a smile that's unnerving precisely because it is filled with anticipation.

"*Pass auf,* Zeus." With her dog at her heels, she and Phil approach the fence.

Phil tells me, "Go stand against the wall."

"Go fuck yourself." But my voice sounds watered-down and insubstantial.

Cristina activates the cattle prod. At the staticky buzz, my body flinches, remembering what happened in the yard, but now there is a fence between us. I will make her rue that petty threat.

Phil tries again. "I'm going to open the gate, and Beckett will come out. You move back."

Beckett's right behind me, but my eyes never leave Cristina's face. This is my moment.

Slowly, deliberately, she turns the key in the top lock, then the bottom one, leaving the middle one, the one that will really open the fence, for last. I'm coiled, ready for that moment.

She says matter-of-factly, "Ava, if you don't move away, you will regret it."

I know this game. I've played it with Zoe for years. And I don't back down.

19

AVA

Now I AM burning from the inside—my mouth making noises, my muscles convulsing, my thoughts a wordless scream. Time stops. Language fails. My mind shatters. Electricity has stolen everything human and left me nothing but pain. When I come back to myself, I am lying on my side, hugging my knees. *Once there was a woman, a stupid, stupid woman . . .*

Cristina's face is placid as she slides the gate closed again, the cattle prod now inert in her hand. I struggle to get up, but my body refuses. Shaking, I collapse while she snaps the locks shut again—one, two, three. She doesn't bother to say anything to me. She's not bothered at all.

Through the film of tears, I see Phil and Beckett at the table with the medical supplies. Beckett is sitting in a chair, and Phil leans over him. A surge of fear turns my stomach and I roll onto my knees.

Over my body's revolt, I can hear voices, Cristina and Phil speaking softly. I have to be stronger than this. I need to know what's going on. I wipe my face harshly with the edge of my shirt and crawl closer to the fence.

"Just take his vitals and move on," Cristina snaps.

"Shouldn't I do a CBC too? Just in case?" Phil moves something on the desk, but I can't see around him.

"Fine. But hurry."

"Hold still," Phil says to Beckett.

Beckett cries out and I flinch, my hands reaching out to clutch the fence. Then I see the syringe in Phil's hand. Of course, a CBC—a blood draw—the first step. I don't know what they are planning, but this is minor pain, nothing compared to what will probably happen next.

"Don't forget the hood." Cristina nods at the table impatiently.

Phil looks at it blankly for a moment. Then hastily he gathers up what looks like a handful of black cloth. "Is this part necessary?" he says.

Beckett looks from one to the other, then to the door. I know what he's thinking—can practically see his inner dialogue writ large on his desperate face—but I'm helpless. I can't tell what Cristina and Phil are fighting about, and I can't stop Beckett from making a huge mistake. I was wrong to suggest it—our captors are literally standing right next to him, and Zeus is lying against the wall. This is not the right time.

"We didn't go to all this trouble not to use it." Cristina's voice is calm now, but there's steel in it.

"*You* aren't going to be using it!" Now Phil is clenching the black cloth.

"Oh, is that the problem?" Cristina leans forward, her hands on her hips. "Are you afraid of—"

Before I can warn him or beg him not to, Beckett lurches out of his chair, knocking Phil to the floor. Cristina's hand moves to the cattle prod, but before she can activate it, Zeus uncoils and springs. Beckett turns to the side, taking the brunt of Zeus's charge on his shoulder.

I have risen to my feet without realizing it, using the fence to pull myself upright. "Beckett!" I scream.

Incredibly, he still tries to stagger toward the closed blast door, even with Zeus's jaws locked around his arm.

Phil stands up, looking more aggrieved than hurt. He takes a step forward, but Cristina stops him. "Wait."

Zeus keeps tugging and shaking Beckett's arm, but I see he isn't breaking the skin. He's simply holding Beckett, not wounding him, and Beckett is getting tired— not enough food, water, or rest. His body doesn't have the fuel to keep fighting.

Cristina is right. Phil doesn't need to expend any energy subduing us. Beckett and I, we are already defeated.

The second Beckett surrenders, Zeus releases his arm. Without a command, he returns to Cristina's side, sits, and resumes his guard.

Cristina looks at Phil. "See, they're ready. Go ahead."

He picks something up from the table and walks over to Beckett. "That was stupid. Give me your hands right now."

When Beckett sticks his arms out in front of him, they are as stiff and awkward as the arms of a puppet. Phil wraps a zip tie around Beckett's wrists and pulls it tight. Beckett drops his arms, and his head droops too.

He doesn't look at Phil or Cristina or me. *That could have been me*, I want to tell him. *I would have tried too.*

But I don't have a chance to tell him anything. Phil pushes Beckett in front of him. "Come on. No more drama."

Then he picks up a sagging tote bag from beside the table and follows, shoving Beckett whenever he slows. *Petty little bully.* I will gouge Phil's eyes from his head and swallow them whole.

"Wait." Cristina bends down and scoops up the black cloth hood from the floor. She slips it into the top of the bag.

"Thanks," Phil says, reaching out and opening the completely ordinary door.

"I've got the screen pulled up," she tells him. "If you've got the list of questions, everything's in place."

All I can see in the open doorway is darkness, a creeping penumbra bleeding into the thin light of the lab.

Then Phil pushes Beckett into that void and it swallows them both.

20

ZOE

GLENN HAS DROPPED me back off at my parents' house and driven away, but as I stand on the front steps, I can't stop arguing with him in my head. He thinks Ava might really be in trouble and I should run. Why? Because I was so much safer in Texas? That's where I was in the first place when my email was hacked. Good thinking, Glenn.

I unlock the front door. If Ava was taken, kidnapped, they could come after me. There's no way I can go back to the home I share with Andrew and Emma. Not while Ava is missing. I have brought enough darkness into their lives.

Stepping into the front hall, I pull the door shut and flip the dead bolt. Alone again.

If I were in Texas, it would be time to pick Emma up from preschool. We might head to the playground, where Felicia and Bethany could tell me all the latest gossip, or we might swing by the library. When we got home, I would fix Emma a little snack and we might read together, snuggled up on the sofa. I'd have a load of laundry to do, or some prep work for dinner. There'd be a purpose for me in every room, something I could do to make life easier and more pleasant for my family.

In this house, I'm in the way and nothing is restful to the eye. Even the decorative touches, like the spiky sculpture in the corner, are hostile.

It is so frustrating to be home by myself, trapped. No car, nowhere to go if I had one.

This is not the house where I grew up, but it has the same suffocating feel, as if it is saying, *Be quiet. Don't touch. Sit down.* As a teenager, I reacted by shouting, slamming doors, breaking things. I painted my bedroom walls black, ruining the beige carpet. I borrowed the car without asking, failed science classes, and never cleaned up after myself. Anything to get a reaction. Anything to prove I existed.

Spending this morning investigating Ava's house has made me feel invisible again. She's not an impostor like I am. Everything inside her house is hers, not someone else's. She doesn't have to prove her usefulness or defend her position. She defines her position, and everything in her house has to prove its usefulness to her.

I am tired of sneaking around, tired of pretending to be good. I suck at it anyway.

It's afternoon and I don't have a car, so I go to the kitchen, pull a bottle of white wine out of the fridge, and uncork it. A quick rummage through the cabinets and I have a wineglass and an unopened can of fancy Virginia peanuts. The kind given as a gift by people who don't know you. Makes sense. Not even Ava and I really know our parents.

I have no interest in sitting in their leather chairs, but I try to get comfortable on a modern chaise lounge. It could use more stuffing, arms, and throw pillows, but I put my feet up, pull out my phone, and start Googling the words I found in Ava's study—"Mindszenty," "Survival, Evasion, Resistance and Escape," and "MK-ULTRA." A slug of wine, a handful of nuts, and another page of information I'm struggling to understand. There's a lot of medical jargon and abbreviations. Ava is so freaking smart; she probably figured this out in seconds. She never failed her science class or needed a tutor for French.

The bottle of wine is empty and the peanuts are half gone when my data plan finally runs out and I take a break. I have read through so much information, but all I have are more and more pieces of a puzzle I don't understand.

MK-Ultra is a declassified CIA mind-control program; Survival, Evasion, Resistance, and Escape is military training to evade capture and resist torture; and Cardinal Mindszenty was Polish, an opponent of Communism, tortured during Stalin's regime. This must be research for Ava's next dark thriller. It's not a clue, just a dead end.

With the data plan used up, my phone is good only for calls and texts, so I drop it into my bag and lean my head back, closing my eyes.

Why is my sister so obsessed with darkness? What drives her to write about serial killers and stalkers, hatred and obsession and loss? And the biggest question, the one I've never understood: why does she keep writing about me?

The sister who was my storyteller and my refuge began to rebuff me once she started school. Little by little, books and daydreams gave her the same distant expression I saw on my mother's face. And the more Ava retreated inside herself, the more I battled for her attention. Sometimes it worked, like the time she slapped me for tearing pages out of a library book. I had a hundred percent of my sister for about five minutes then. Other times she just walked away, like I was behind a thick pane of glass, my mouth moving with no sound crossing over.

I was a senior in high school the first time I recognized myself in Ava's words. Her debut novel had come out in galleys and my parents had a copy. I picked it up, hoping to learn something about the stranger my sister had become.

Instead, as the story unfolded, I began to notice details about one of the main characters, a criminal profiler.

This character was named Chloe—a name so close to Zoe as to be laughable. Ava was never quite that obvious again. Chloe had the same hair color as me, the same habit of saying "liberry" and "ax" instead of ask, things I did just to annoy Ava, and she shared my then-obsession with combat boots and long skirts. In one scene after Chloe leaves the room, the protagonist, a police detective named Natalie Wilson, says, "Someone that angry, she's a ticking time bomb. I bet she can't make it five years before she snaps and does something horrific, something violent." And she did. The character became obsessed with the killer, joined forces with him, and then he killed her. Stupid, angry Chloe deserved to die. Was that what my sister really thought about me?

The wine has made my body warm, almost enough to blunt the memory of that first moment of betrayal. The things Ava was researching before she went missing, information on manipulation and cruelty, are just background to another story she's writing where I'll feature as the torturer or the victim. They're meaningless now, nothing to do with her disappearance.

I don't realize I am dozing off until a sound makes me startle. I drop my phone, knocking over the empty bottle.

The doorbell rings again, and I leap to my feet. For a moment I think about Glenn's warning, about Ava and kidnappers. Then someone knocks on the door and there's an echo, a smaller knock. The sound of a child knocking. My heart leaps with hope.

I race to unlock the door. When it swings open, Andrew is standing there, an overnight bag over his shoulder. At his side is Emma.

I can't move.

"Lizzie!" and she is in my arms. This is all I have wanted to feel complete. I inhale deeply the sweet smell of her baby-fine hair, keeping my eyes on Andrew.

"We didn't have a way to reach you." He doesn't put down his bag, instead standing back, like he is dropping Emma off at day care. "You left your phone with the police, and your parents have an unlisted number."

"I'm sorry." My arms tighten around Emma until she squeaks in protest. "I bought a disposable phone today. I tried to call you from the house phone. I was going to call you again." I should have called him yesterday, when I actually bought the phone. I was afraid.

Now his eyes are kind. "I know this is earlier than we discussed. I've booked a hotel, but we thought we'd stop by here first."

Will he invite me to stay with them? My pulse leaps with the desire to be forgiven.

"I want to see your room!" Lizzie lets her body go limp and swings in my arms. She trusts me so much right now. Someday she will know better, and I want to squeeze her close while I still can.

I glance up at Andrew, and something has softened in his expression. I decide to take a chance.

"Come in. My parents aren't home yet, but I can make you a cup of coffee and we can wait for them."

Everything holds still for a second; then he says, "That's really why we came. To meet your family, I mean." Something heavy in my chest warms and starts to melt. Despite everything being so strange, he is willing to try. He wants us to be together. Why else put himself and Emma through this?

As we step into the foyer, I remember all the times he and Emma and I walked through our own front door, back from afternoons at the park or dinners out. Did I value them enough, each one another moment that proved we were a family? I would give anything to relive even one of those mundane arrivals again.

Now Andrew looks past me, right at the chaise lounge, the empty bottle of wine. Oh God. It's not even five o'clock.

"Actually." He takes pity on me. "Where's the restroom?"

I use those few minutes to toss out the wine bottle and the half-empty container of peanuts. Emma reappears first, since she now enjoys "my own privacy" in the bathroom, even if one of us waits outside the door just in case she does need help. Neither Andrew nor I really want her to grow up.

"Hi, Emma bean. Do you need something to drink?" I take her into the kitchen, where I run my empty wine-glass under the faucet and slip it, dripping, back into a cabinet.

"Can I have a juice box?"

"Sorry, sweetie." I know there's nothing like a juice box in this house, but I open the fridge to confirm. "I can do orange juice in a cup or water."

"Water with ice?"

"Deal." I love this kind of negotiating, seeing her push for an advantage that I don't mind giving. I'd give her all the juice boxes in the world, a thousand glasses of water with ice.

"Lizzie, I'm thirsty now." I realize I have been stand-ing there staring at her, the glass of water with its ice cubes in my hand.

"Sorry." I hand her the glass, and she drinks from it greedily. I have to be careful. Loving someone this much is dangerous. That's why I'm always holding back. I thought I loved Glenn, I think I love Andrew, but there is no doubt how much I love Emma. It's too late. I'm all in. My chest tightens with fear.

Loving is the first step to losing.

As I stand in the kitchen with Emma, my breath comes quickly, but I can't get any oxygen. My lungs seem to be getting smaller and smaller and each inhale hurts. I can hear Emma's voice say my name, coming from far away. The room is rushing around me. I reach out with a hand and clutch at the fridge. I am going down.

Then someone else's arms are under my own. Andrew's voice says, "Easy. Bend your knees."

I sit on the floor. No air. I can't breathe. Through the blur of tears in my eyes, I see Andrew come closer. Then his hands come together over my face.

"Breathe in and out. It's okay now."

His cupped hands catch the air. Each warm breath is a little easier. My panic is ebbing away. I am glad his hands hide my face. I am so glad Andrew is here. All I want is for him to forgive me. I duck my head and kiss his palm. But then he takes his hands away.

Emma's eyes are wide and she clutches her water glass to her stomach. I can't look at her, can't let myself feel that overwhelming, helpless love again. Andrew will have to handle this. I rest my head on my knees, in the circle of my own arms.

I can hear him whisper and her overly loud whisper back. Without raising my head, I say automatically, "There isn't a television here. There might be paper in the drawer by the phone."

I'm doing a crappy job of being Emma's mom right now. Moms suck it up. They solve the problem, stop the tears, find the fun. They always come second. I knew when I met Andrew that Emma would be the top priority. That was always the deal. And I loved her right away. Now I feel scooped out and broken. Emma is not safe with me. I am not her mom. I don't know how to be. And the thought of poor motherless Emma brings tears to my eyes again.

Andrew has gotten Emma squared away with something—his phone or pen and paper—at the kitchen table. If we were at home, we could go into another room and chat. But here, in a strange place, Emma will follow us. He must know this too.

Awkwardly he lowers himself to the floor in front of me. That's another difference between moms and dads. I have sat on the floor with Emma at library story times and preschool picnics, at playgroup outings to the fire station and at the park with Bethany and Felicia.

But we are on the floor of my parents' kitchen and Andrew is sitting next to me.

"How is the investigation?" he asks. "Is there any word on your sister?"

"No. I think the police might believe me, that I wasn't involved."

"Where are your parents?"

"They went to work." He lifts an eyebrow, and I answer, "Even with Ava missing. I know, Andrew. They're not like other parents."

"Isn't there anyone here for you?" Things would be different for me as Lizzie in Sugar Land. Death or illness or loss brings cards and casseroles. There is nothing here in my parents' house. Not even a note from a neighbor.

"Just you." I watch Emma, the kitchen light shining against her hair. "I should have called and told you. You didn't need to come all this way."

Andrew gently touches my face, bringing my gaze back to him. "I did need to come. If this is real, I need to know the real you. Where you came from, who you are. I needed to meet your parents."

"But Emma . . . this is so confusing for her."

Now he looks uncertain. "I just thought . . . she should have a chance to meet her grandparents. And I didn't know who . . . I couldn't leave her."

Andrew is never uncertain, never makes a move without considering all the logistics first. If this were business or home maintenance or even a weather emergency, he'd know just what to do. But this is his weakness: family. When I met him, his wife had been dead less than two years, his mother five. Andrew's only living family is his father, and every day Alzheimer's steals a little more from him. Now he is on the verge of losing me, a wife and mother.

"I wish I had a different family," I tell him, humiliated at how little I can offer. "I wish I was a different person."

Andrew's eyes are the same shape as Emma's, but his are a pure, rich brown, undiluted by the flecks of gold and green in hers. He takes my hand. "I've been thinking a lot about that. You're not who I thought you were. But how you are with me and Emma, that can't be a lie, can it? Not every day of the past two years. It has to mean something."

Anything I could say will sound like an excuse. "That's who I wanted to be. The person I am with you."

He sighs. "It doesn't work like that, though. You have a family. You have a past. You can't just erase them. You can't just choose what to tell me."

"I'm sorry, I'm so sorry. I didn't want to spoil what we had."

Andrew's eyes are so sad as he says, "Lying spoils everything."

My tears do spill over, hot on my cheeks. "I know. I won't ever lie again. I swear."

He kisses me on the forehead. "Deal." That's dependable-man-speak for "I love you."

And I feel forgiven, a little bit.

Emma notices our embrace, and then she's in the middle of it, and I have everything I ever wanted, everything I don't deserve. I just want this moment to last forever.

Of course it can't. The doorbell rings, again and again. We separate, and I open the door to a delivery man needing a signature. When I turn back, Andrew's getting Emma's shoes back on while she tells me all about the television and the pool and the tiny soap in the hotel room. She wants me to come back there with them. I want to with every fiber of my being, but I can't tell from Andrew's face if now is the right time.

I tell her I might, but I'll have to ask my mom first.

We arrange to meet for dinner. And I will bring my parents. I use the house phone to call my mother's cell. There are times at work when she has it turned off, but today she picks up on the first ring. At least that's normal. Maybe she is anxious about Ava.

"Yes?"

"Mom, my husband is here. And our daughter."

"You have a child." This ought to be a question, but my mother doesn't ask.

"She's my stepdaughter."

"Ah." I can't tell what she means.

"They'd like to have dinner with you and Dad."

My mother seems nonplussed. "Dinner?"

"At a restaurant. So you could meet them."

There's only silence as my mother calculates the appropriate action.

"So will you and Dad meet us for dinner?"

"Yes. That would be fine."

"You pick the place and time."

"Well, where are they staying? The little girl and her father?"

My daughter. My husband. But I swallow down my anger and name the hotel instead.

She is silent for a moment. "We'll do Portofino at seven. That's close. Be ready fifteen minutes before and we'll pick you up."

"Have you heard anything about Ava?" I remember the picture of the smiling woman on her honeymoon. The longer she is gone, the more I start to worry. But it's hard to maintain that worry when my parents appear so calm.

"Nothing from the police. Glenn left a message. Something about a press event tomorrow."

Before I can ask if I'm expected to come, she hangs up.

Relief that our awkward conversation is over gives way quickly to the reality of our impending family dinner.

Andrew and Emma will be in the lion's den tonight, all because of me.

CHAPTER

21

ZOE

THE RESTAURANT IS a mistake. I can tell the minute I walk through the door. It's got a hushed ambience that my parents will use to discourage intimacy. Exactly the kind of place that makes me want to disturb the peace.

Andrew is standing to one side of the foyer. He is wearing a tie and a sport coat. Seeing him there, so solid and dependable, unafraid of all my shit, tugs at my heart. My jeans and off-brand T-shirt make me feel even worse.

"Lizzie!" Emma is practically dancing in her favorite outfit, a sparkly pink skirt perfect for twirling and a black T-shirt that proclaims "Self-Rescuing Princess."

In this setting, my mother is imperious, quite the grande dame. Her hair shines silver in the dim restaurant.

She steps in front of my father and offers Andrew her hand. "Nancy Renscoe-Hallett. Doctor."

"Andrew McPhee. And this is Emma." His face is neutral and his tone pleasant, even as she's piled on the formal titles.

My mother glances down at Emma, who has stopped dancing and is frankly staring. "Five years old?"

"Not yet." Andrew smiles, obviously trying to translate this clinical observation into an emotional connection. "She turned four last month. Lizz—Zoe threw her a rainbow-themed birthday. We'll never get rid of all the glitter."

My mother smiles correctly, and her blue eyes are as cold as a fjord. I bristle. Emma is beautiful, perfect. She doesn't deserve to be examined.

My father might never introduce himself, but Andrew takes the initiative. "And you must be Zoe's father." He takes my dad's hand for a brisk shake. "Nice to meet you, sir."

"Yes." My father's mind is clearly working, but all he says is "Also Dr. Hallett. Walter."

Emma's voice cuts through the soft murmur of the restaurant. "Who is Zoe?"

I wince. This night will be excruciating.

The hostess shows us to a table, and then there's an awkward dance. The hostess pulls out a chair for my mother, who sinks gracefully into it; then she pulls out the one next to it and looks at me. I can't help myself, I step back. I can't sit next to my mother. I just can't.

I bump into Andrew, who puts his hands on my shoulders, their weight giving me strength to say, "I better sit by Emma. Could we get a booster seat?"

And that's the excuse needed to make our final arrangement—my parents on one side of the table, Andrew and me with Emma between us on the other.

We're still unfolding napkins when Andrew asks, "Any more word about Ava?"

My father literally rolls his eyes. "Nothing new. The police are having trouble finding any evidence that she was taken."

Andrew frowns. "Is there a chance she's at a retreat or something? Off the grid, writing?"

"That's certainly possible." My mother smiles up at my father. "We know what it's like to get wrapped up in work and lose track of time. But I can understand why other people might be worried."

People who aren't deep thinkers or high achievers. People who aren't special. People like me.

Dinner is all fits and starts. Andrew is used to business meals. In the oil industry, he deals with the gregarious landmen and also the introverted engineers. But I can tell he's never met mind benders like my parents. They speak their own language, they are not interested in social niceties, and they have no obvious affection for me. I am so grateful to be sitting next to Emma.

My mother's gaze is on us as I help Emma color the pictures on the children's menu, cut her spaghetti into bites, and give her my garlic bread. Taking care of my daughter gives me such comfort, comfort that Emma doesn't even know I need. I brush her hair away from her cheek and she shakes me off, busy with her crayon. I'm probably annoying her, but she's the only thing that's going to save me.

Andrew has been gamely interrogating my father. "What do you do, sir?"

"I am a clinical neuroanalyst."

"And the two of you work together?"

My father nods briskly and takes a bite of his pasta.

"Do you enjoy working together?"

Now both of my parents look surprised, as though the thought had never occurred to them.

My mother speaks first. "I suppose we do."

Lowering his fork, my father adds, "It makes things so much easier when you have a partner who understands things."

That's as good an opening as he's going to get. Panic fills me as Andrew puts his hand on mine and says, "I completely agree."

No, I want to tell Andrew, but I choke back the words. *Don't show them you have feelings. They'll think you're an easy target.*

My father raises his eyebrows, and my mother looks away with a little smirk.

I wince and he lets go, withdrawing.

I'm not like my mother and father. I want your love. I recapture his hand. "We had a lovely wedding."

And it was.

Just Andrew and Emma and me. I wore a white summer sundress and gold strappy sandals and so did Emma. I had painted our toenails so they sparkled silver, and we spun and twirled to make our skirts flare. Andrew wore a suit, but he had a boutonniere of white clover blossoms and a fading sunburn across his nose from the day trip to Galveston where he'd proposed. Less than a week later we were married at a walk-up wedding chapel in downtown Houston. I twined my fingers with Andrew's, certain I had found my real family at last. I know it's a cliché co-opted by every Hallmark anniversary card and date-night romcom, but that was the happiest day of my life.

Maybe Andrew isn't appalled by who my parents are, because he gives my hand a squeeze, leans in, and kisses my temple.

Emma has been concentrating on her cut-up buttered linguine, chasing each diced pasta piece one by one around her plate. Now she looks up. "I threw the flowers."

"The flower girl." My mother nods slowly. "And Zoe is your new mama?"

Now Emma looks uncertain. "Who's Zoe?"

"Right there." My mother points at me.

The look on Emma's face breaks my heart. She is lost and I am turning into a stranger in front of her.

I want to throw myself between her and my mother. Instead I put my arm around her, pulling her close into my side to whisper, "My mother calls me Zoe, but you call me Lizzie." She ducks her head against me.

"Ah." My mother nods as if she is just remembering. "Lizzie. So Lizzie is your mother now." *Bitch.* She turns her attention to Andrew. "How did she find you?"

"*We* met each other online. A dating site." Andrew emphasizes the "we," and I feel renewed hope. Maybe just this once, my mother won't make everything worse. Maybe this will make Andrew forgive me, even if I don't deserve it. He is too smart to volunteer information, but he is also too polite to end the conversation.

Mom is undeterred. "What happened with your wife? Emma's mother, I mean."

"Preeclampsia."

My mother nods thoughtfully, then glances at my father. He stops the mechanical rise and fall of his fork.

"That must have left you very vulnerable. How long after her passing did Zoe meet you?"

My chest constricts, and rage starts bubbling inside me.

"Two years," Andrew tells him. Actually, a year and a half, but I have my lips pressed tightly together. Andrew can do all the talking. Anything I say will definitely be used against me.

My parents look at each other. "Textbook," my mother says.

And I can feel my husband pull away from me slightly.

As we get up from the table to go home, Andrew and I fall back a few steps.

I have to tell him I love him, that meeting him wasn't a trick or a trap. I push down the frantic need to make sure he still loves me after all. After them.

Instead I say, "I'm sorry you had to go through that." All the things I am afraid to add run through my head. *Please don't leave me. Please forgive me. I'll be good, I swear.*

Ahead of us, Emma is twirling around, her skirt a pink-and-silver blur. My father gives her a wide berth. My mother doesn't veer aside, striding closer and closer until Emma stumbles and stops.

Andrew doesn't see this. His eyes search my face. "Well, you're a lot like them, aren't you? It's not easy for you to talk about your feelings."

The pain is as strong as a physical punch. How can he think that? I love him. I love Emma. My parents love nothing, maybe not even each other. "I'm nothing like them."

"Hey." He reaches out for me, pulls me close. "I'm on your side. You don't have to be so careful."

I don't understand.

He kisses my forehead and pulls back to look into my eyes. "That conversation at dinner was intense. But you don't have to be on your guard with me. I love you. We're a team, no matter what your parents try to do."

I let out a breath I didn't know I was holding, and with it goes the tension from my muscles, braced for impact, now flooded with warm relief.

My mother pulls the heavy restaurant door open and looks back. "Are you coming, Zoe?"

And Emma stops her twirling and stares at me imperiously. "Are you coming, Zoe?"

The words fall out. "I'm staying with Andrew tonight." I glance up at him, and thank God he's smiling.

He reaches out a hand for our daughter as he says, "Come on, Emma. Lizzie will sing your bedtime song tonight."

In the rental car, the darkened streets and Emma's presence in the back seat keep me quiet. Andrew navigates the roads as though he's done it a million times. No GPS. He seems to have an internal navigation system. "Is there anyone you want to see while you're here?" he asks. "Any friends? Any friends of Ava's?"

"No. Not now." I am not finished mulling over the dinner. My frustration, my anger, and my fear make it hard to remember every detail clearly. I lean my forehead against the window.

No friends in my own hometown. That's strange. I cast my mind back and dredge up a few faces, a few names. The guy I went to prom with. Tom? A girl with spiky blue hair from drama class. And did I ever see Ava with friends? We never had people over to our house.

As we pause at a traffic light, I try harder, and something surfaces in my memory. A table in our high school library. Before homeroom, all the students milled around the cafeteria, filling that holding pen with noise and stink and shoving. A few of us who didn't have anyone to sit with at lunch learned to slip up the back stairs, and the librarian would let us in, as long as we were quiet. The faces are blurry now and the names are lost, but that was the place I felt safest.

Now Andrew is passing me the ticket from the parking garage, and we pull into a spot and pile into the hotel. With three of us in the one room, especially with Emma, there is blessedly little space for thinking or remembering or wondering. Andrew plugs in his phone and brushes his teeth, while I sing Emma "Here Comes the Sun." As I croon, I wish fiercely, desperately for the words to come true. *Just let everything be all right now.*

This feeling of family, right after the meal with my parents, is making me feel very homesick. When Andrew stood by me, when he acknowledged that my parents were aggressively insensitive, I felt the loss of something I never realized they owed me. Now I put a name to it.

My sister. Ava and I should have had friends. More than that, we should have *been* friends. But they treated us like rival nations. There was no "teamwork," no "our girls," no "you kids." It was always me against her, not us against them.

So years later, when Andrew mentioned us maybe trying for a child, I felt my whole body recoil. Of course he noticed. "Don't you want more children?" he asked. And I covered. "No, no, I want more children. I just want to make sure Emma is ready. We don't want to move too quickly." And that seemed to be the right answer.

But the truth is, I would never do that to Emma. Better for her to be our "one and only" than for me to make her an "either/or." Now I wonder if I could change. If I could still have a family, a real one.

I spend the night with Andrew and Emma in the hotel. And lying in the king-sized bed in that anonymous room without a single personal belonging except my shoulder bag, I still feel more at home than I ever have at my parents' house.

Fuck where Ava is.

In the morning, I'm going home.

ZOE

I WAKE WITH A start. Emma is practically nose to nose with me and her eyes are open, as if she has been waiting for just this moment. Loudly she whispers, "I'm hungry, Lizzie. And Daddy is sleeping."

Andrew answers from deep in his pillow. "Not anymore."

In the hallway I can hear other hotel guests—families like us—making their way to the elevator, their voices hushed and cheerful, their luggage bumping along. I am full of good feelings—love and gratitude for Andrew's forgiveness. "Go back to sleep," I tell him. "Emma and I can find breakfast."

Giggling and whispering, Emma and I get dressed, she in a fresh outfit, me in yesterday's clothes.

As Emma punches the elevator button, it occurs to me that there might be a television in the lobby. I don't want to see more about Ava on the news. But the doors are sliding closed and Emma grabs my hand, bracing herself for the downward motion.

In the breakfast area, my eyes go right to the television in the corner of the room. By the grace of God it's set on the Weather Channel. If we eat and get out quickly, all will be well.

Between the canisters of bright-colored cereal, the breakfast pastries, and the industrial-sized toaster, Emma is in heaven. We never buy sugary cereal or doughnuts, and she's so excited that she doesn't know what to choose. I get her settled with a bowl of neon crunchies and a banana, which she manages to eat in a way that suggests she's just humoring me.

I make sure she sits with her back to the television. Just in case.

The entire room has only five small tables, so I'm just two steps away from her, making my own breakfast. I send a bagel through the toaster while filling a paper cup with coffee.

When I turn back to check on Emma, there's a woman standing by our table, whispering in her ear. A young woman with a sleek black ponytail and wire-framed glasses. Too close to my Emma. Her counterpart, a hipster guy with a bushy beard and seventies-style plaid jacket, waits by the doorway. *Strangers.* They could be saying anything, they could be ready to snatch her.

My bagel drops onto the toaster's metal tray, but I ignore it in my haste. *No one will take her away.*

Leaning over Emma, I set my coffee down forcefully. "What do you want?"

The woman straightens up. "Hi, you must be Zoe." She makes the "hi" into two syllables and my name into one that rhymes with "go."

I ignore her and reach my hand out for Emma. "All done, baby?"

Emma protests. "No, I'm not finished." One hand clenches her cereal bowl, and I can see she won't leave without a fuss.

Undeterred, the woman continues, "I'm Sue Solcedo. Maybe you've heard my podcast, *Real Time Mysteries*?"

I pull Emma closer to me. This bitch needs to stay away from my kid. Glancing around the breakfast room, I note that the only witnesses are an old guy hunched over a paper and Sue's backup in the doorway.

"Look, we're just trying to eat breakfast. Leave us alone." As I talk, my voice gets thinner and higher. I wish I hadn't put milk in Emma's cereal, wish I could scoop her up with her breakfast and flee back to the hotel room.

Sue doesn't give up. "I'm just looking into the disappearance of your sister, and I wanted to talk to you. Give you a chance to get on the record."

"Leave us alone. I'll call the manager."

"Given what's been reported in the news today, you can see why people might think you were involved." And she pulls out a folded section of newspaper from her shoulder bag and sets it on the table in front of me.

I can't help it—I look at the newspaper. There in print are the emails. The threatening emails from my computer. From my account. Right there for everyone to read.

My hand moves convulsively and I spill my coffee. Not over Sue, unfortunately, but across the table. Emma cries out and I stagger to my feet. But before I can grab more napkins or ice water, the bearded guy is there with a handkerchief. I snatch it from him and mop Emma off. Thankfully, the coffee hit only her sleeve, not her bare skin. She isn't burned. She will be fine. But my stomach keeps pitching and rolling. Where did these come from? Why haven't the police called me again?

Sue seizes her moment, unfolding the paper and holding it out to me. "You can see how bad this looks for you. Don't you want to tell your side?"

I hear the unspoken warning: *while you still can.*

I look closer. There's a photo, right below the crease of the paper. A picture of me. And Glenn. In front of the house. Yesterday.

He's holding me by the shoulders, and his back is to the camera. I know he's shouting at me, but from my expression in the picture he could be pleading with me, promising things to me, threatening me. I feel dizzy. We look like coconspirators. And someone was secretly filming us. Filming me. The hairs on the back of my neck prickle.

I have to get back to the room. I have to talk to Andrew. "Okay, baby, two-minute warning. Choose a special doughnut," I tell Emma. While she races to the breakfast table, I stand up.

Sue stands too. Her makeup is carefully applied, from her crimson lips to mascara that makes her eyes look wide, trustworthy. But I'm from Texas. I know makeup is an art designed to help you project an image. She may look professional and approachable, but I notice that nothing about her is out of place. Small, tasteful silver hoops in her ears, crisp shirt, trim blazer. She's all about the details, and now she's using them against me.

She keeps her eyes on my face, like she's trying to will me into talking to her. "Please, I just want the truth. Anything you can tell me. Your story."

Emma comes back with a pink frosted doughnut in one hand, and I grab her by the other, striding to the door. The bearded guy and Sue are following me, but I refuse to look back.

All the things I want to say bubble up. *Bitch says she wants my story. Like hell she does. She just wants the story Ava created. My sister dropped off the radar and I get to be the villain. If Sue needs a bad guy, why not Glenn? He looks like the cheating husband.* But I'm not going to say that. I don't owe anyone an explanation. Not Ava, not this Sarah Koenig wannabe.

We're storming through the hotel now, a strange little parade. At the end of the hallway, a woman waits outside the elevator with a toddler in her arms while her husband wrestles with the luggage.

Sue shouts, "Is it true that you and Glenn—"

"Fuck off!"

The couple at the end of the hall whip around like they've heard a gunshot. Even their little boy is bug-eyed.

Emma gives a cry of pain, and I realize I've clenched her hand so tightly that I'm hurting her. She can't keep up and she can't pull free.

I scoop Emma up into my arms, whispering, "I'm sorry, baby. I'm so sorry," and break into a run. Pushing through the family, ignoring their gasps, I barrel into the elevator with Emma just as the doors close.

I set her down and sink to my knees. "Let me see your arm, honey. Are you all right?"

There are tears in her eyes and she is holding one shoulder protectively. "You hurt me. And you yelled."

"Not at you, baby. Not at you." I run my shaking hands from her neck over her shoulders and down her arms. She doesn't protest, and I am almost certain she was hurt but not injured.

She looks down, and I see that her doughnut has been squished, the frosting oozing out from between her fingers. A lesser child would have wailed again, louder, but Emma raises her hand to her lips and eats the sugary mess anyway.

My rib cage is like a corset squeezing tighter and tighter. I hurt Emma. I scared her, I cursed in front of her, I ruined her breakfast, I made her cry. Now there are tears in my eyes. I am choking on self-hatred.

All too quickly the doors ding open, but not at our floor. And of course there are people in the hallway waiting for the elevator. An older man with a tweedy sport jacket and a folded-up newspaper in one hand. He doesn't look pleased to find Emma and me hunched on the floor of the elevator. He is followed by a trio of teenage girls in pastel sweat pants and athletic T-shirts.

My heart pounds as I scan the hall, but there is no sign of Sue or the guy with the beard. The elderly man gives me a sharp look and pulls the newspaper out from under his arm. He's recognized me. I know it.

One of the girls asks Emma, "Did you get that doughnut downstairs? I want a pink one too."

As we get out and the elevator doors slide shut, I hear the girls teasing each other about rainbow doughnuts. Emma would be better off with any one of those cheerful teens than she is with me.

My private emails and my personal history are in the paper. Someone wants to frame me. And judging by that photo, I've been helping them right along.

CHAPTER

23

ZOE

I WAVE THE KEY card and push the door open. Andrew is sitting on the end of the bed, watching television, a news channel with a red banner running across the bottom. And the photo, the one of me and Glenn.

He looks up as we enter, his eyes wide with disbelief. My stomach drops. He knows. About the emails, the affair with Glenn, everything. I'm a lying liar who stole my sister's husband.

Softly, too softly, my husband says, "You were really involved with him. It was serious."

There's an ache in my throat. I want to deny it, but I can't. What could I say? I told Andrew about the emails and my old identity, I even told him I "dated" Glenn, but I never told him everything.

How could I tell him? Glenn and I never dated, not really. There were no ice cream floats or shared popcorn at the movies. All we had was sex. How could I tell Andrew about the first time Glenn and I were alone in my crappy little apartment? He had one foot out the door until I untied the straps of my sundress and let it fall. Then he looked at me, came close, and put his arms around me. I felt powerful, desired. I felt like Ava. But I didn't have the kind of relationship with Glenn that she must have had. He and I never really talked. No shared secrets, no plans for the future. Just sweat and teeth and sex. I marked him as mine, over and over.

Three years ago, that's all I wanted, but it's not true now. It was a hollow victory. And even if he'd never gone back to Ava, it wouldn't have lasted. I know that.

I'd give anything to erase every moment with Glenn. Why can't I just be ordinary, reliable Lizzie? All this happened before I even knew Andrew. It's not like I cheated on him, but I still have to tell him something. The news can't be the only version of my story he hears.

"Lizzie?" Emma is standing in the doorway, her face sticky and pink. Maybe Andrew will put this off. We can't fight in front of Emma.

He says, "Go wash up, sweetie. You're covered in doughnut." I can hear the strain in his voice, how it's pitched higher than usual.

I turn to follow Emma, but he says, "You stay here. Just shut the bathroom door. Emma doesn't need your help."

I freeze, stricken. That's how easy it would be. One word from him and I'd be out of Emma's life forever.

As she turns the water on, he asks, "Did you arrange to meet him yesterday?" All the lightness I saw in his face last night is gone. His mouth is a tense line, his eyes are narrowed.

"No! I just saw him at the police station. We were all there." My insides are liquid with fear and my words are coming out with too much force.

"This picture wasn't taken at the police station." He holds up his phone like an accusation, and I see the same picture there, Glenn and me. We're on the internet, on the news blogs and social media sites. The whole world knows what a monster I am, how Glenn and I are clearly having an affair and plotted together to murder a beloved author.

And Andrew believes it too.

Unless I can change his mind. "He was worried about Ava, and—"

"And you were what . . . comforting him?" Andrew raises an eyebrow, and his mouth twists in disgust.

If Andrew really thinks I am involved with Glenn, if he doesn't trust me to be faithful, what can I do? There's no way for me to crawl back from this. My face is hot, burning. "No, that's not what happened. I went to Ava's house—"

"To meet him?"

"No, I broke in!"

"You . . . what?" His mouth opens in shock.

"I broke in, okay? I lied to you about who I was to get away from Ava, and I broke in to find her. I thought she'd done it to herself. You don't know my sister. She's—"

"You lied and lied and lied." Andrew stands, his hands balled into fists by his sides.

"Not about you!" My voice is way too loud. Distantly I realize the water isn't running in the bathroom anymore. I love him, totally and completely, but he doesn't see it. "I love you. I've been a good wife, a good mother."

He turns his back on me, shaking his head. But it's true. I cleaned the house and fed them home-cooked meals and was perfect. I did everything right for two whole years. And now it counts for nothing?

The bathroom door swings open, and Emma stands there, her face and hands dripping, her eyes bewildered. She's never heard us argue. "You're yelling," she says, like she can't believe it.

Andrew turns to face us like he's facing a firing squad. He never knew Zoe, always angry and mouthy and spoiling for a fight. I was always so damn grateful for his love that I never disagreed with anything he said. He can't just throw that away.

I sink to my knees beside Emma and pull her close to me. She still smells like sugar. "Daddy doesn't know how much I love you," I say loud enough for Andrew to hear. "I love you and Daddy more than the moon and stars."

This is a familiar game, and she pulls back to look me in the eyes. "I love you and Daddy more than the sun and sky."

Then she turns her trusting face to Andrew.

He closes his eyes as if he can't even look at us. *Good.* He needs to feel it, the full weight of our family. "This isn't fair, Zoe."

"Don't call me that." I kiss Emma's head. "My name is Lizzie."

On some level, Emma must know she's being used, because she pulls away from me and runs to Andrew, leaving me kneeling by myself. "Say it, Daddy. Say it."

He bends and scoops her up, whispering into her hair, "I love you more than yesterday, today, and tomorrow."

Not "you and Mommy." Not even "you and Lizzie." He's left me out, and the omission is a knife in my heart. It takes all my strength to stand up. I love him, totally and completely. And it feels like I've lost him.

"Let's go home," I say quickly. "We'll just leave. The police will find Ava; nobody needs me here. We'll go home and everything will be—"

"No." Andrew's voice is soft but firm. He sets Emma down, but he doesn't walk over to me. "No. I need some time to think."

I hesitate, looking at Emma nestled close against him. I can't tell him everything, but I can't seem like I'm holding anything back. "I don't even know him now. It was three years ago. Three *years*. Back then you were married—" I break off. I don't want to bring up Andrew's first wife, the one who died when Emma was born. I've kept all her china, her furniture and linens, because I was so grateful I got to keep her family. But I knew I didn't deserve them.

"I know." A shadow crosses Andrew's face. Is he thinking about what my mother said, about how I found him when he was grieving? Emma swings around his legs like an orbiting planet.

"Let me come home, *please*." That last word is a whispered plea. I can't cry, not here in front of Emma; I can't lose myself in this panic and grief.

Andrew hates causing pain. Even if he's angry at me, even if he doesn't love me anymore, he doesn't want to hurt me. But I almost wish he would. If he shouted at me, really lost his temper, I would forgive him. But he's so controlled, almost like he hates me.

He shoos Emma toward the bed and flips the channel to a cartoon. Then he's finally standing right in front of me, his eyes searching my face. "You can't lie to me anymore. Not now. Not ever."

Hope rushes through me, and I try to temper the desperation in my voice. "I won't, I swear. And I didn't do this. I didn't do anything to Ava. Once we get home . . ."

But he shakes his head once. *No.* "I'll take Emma home, but you stay here. You can go back to your parents' house or I'll extend the hotel reservation. At least until the investigation is over." He pauses, then takes a deep breath. "I need that time to think things over."

His words are a shot to my gut. I can't process the impact; I just feel it sucking all the air from my lungs. *Time to think.* Think about a time before he knew me, a life after me. I gasp, unable to speak. I'm drowning.

My hands reach out for him, but he's already turning away. He pulls the suitcase onto the bed beside Emma. Slowly he scoops up her discarded pajamas from the floor, folding and tucking them into place.

Then the hotel phone rings.

Andrew picks it up cautiously. "Yes? Yes, this is he."

I reach for my bag, but my fingers refuse to grasp the strap. My body is not my own. If I can get away, I can think of a way to make him love me again. But every cell of my body yearns to stay.

Then my husband says, "She's right here." Something in the formal way he's speaking cuts right through me. It's the police. He must be talking to the police, and they want to confirm my whereabouts before they drag me off to jail.

I have to leave. I have to go somewhere, anywhere away from here.

The door is closing behind me when I hear Emma call, "Lizzie?"

If I turn back, I won't be strong enough to leave.

My vision is blurry with tears as I run down the hall, but there's a group waiting for the elevator. I can't handle being with all those strangers, not when I'm falling apart.

I veer down another hallway and lean against the wall beside a fire extinguisher. Closing my eyes, I take a breath and let it fill all the emptiness inside me. But instead of calming me down, it illuminates the magnitude of my loss. Every memory of Emma's face, every echo of Andrew saying "think things over," ignites pain throughout my body.

I know what the police have. The emails, plus the prior relationship with Glenn, plus the incident. The last time I saw Ava. She must have told Glenn. No wonder they think I'm guilty. It will all come out and everyone will hate me. I'll be handcuffed and convicted. I'll never be free again.

My breath hitches, like I'm having an asthma attack. What if they find Ava and it's too late? There's not a single thought that can calm this storm. Losing Andrew and Emma hurts too much to think about, but I can't take refuge in my hatred of Ava. She really might be in danger, someone might have taken her, and I'm scared for her, surprisingly. But there's no time to worry about my sister, because the police are coming for me and I have to run.

But I have no idea where to go. Just away from the police.

I duck into a stairwell and take the stairs at top speed. Panic makes me careless and I stumble, banging my shoulder against the wall. It barely registers.

There's a gray exit door and I bolt through it. I'm at one side of the hotel by a dumpster. The parking lot is small, not busy. As far as I can see, there's the divided highway, other parking lots, tall buildings and hotels, and a few little islands of landscaping. Nowhere to blend in. Nowhere to hide.

I hear distant shouting, and I don't stop to see if it's the police or hotel staff or reporters. Running at an angle, I dart across the little alley that separates one hotel from another. There's a group of people boarding a shuttle bus, and on instinct I beeline for them.

My future has tunneled down to a single point: *get on that bus.* I have no idea where I'll go after this. Every place I can think of—Texas, my parents' house, that hotel room—is closed to me. After I met Andrew, I hoped I'd never be this alone again.

I keep my head down, let my hair swing over my face, and join the group, waiting my turn to climb aboard. I could be a tourist, a student, a wife. The driver doesn't ask for identification. I'm just another hotel guest going from point A to point B.

I don't sit by the window. There's an empty seat next to a woman in a pantsuit, and I collapse on it just before she can set her laptop bag down. I'm trembling. Sweat dampens my hairline. I catch a glimpse of two police cars outside the hotel as we pass. I was right, but there's no triumph in it, only terror. Leaning back to obscure my face, I hope I'm not considered armed and dangerous. Just a flight risk.

It doesn't matter where we're headed. The airport, the historic district, the Metro. It doesn't even matter how long it takes. Andrew and Emma will be getting into a car, heading back to the airport. They're moving farther and farther away from me. Maybe if I can solve this mystery, maybe if I can find Ava, I can follow them.

I just need time to think and plan. But memory is swamping all my thoughts. The look on Andrew's face when he realized I'd lied again. The last time I saw Ava. The reason the police think I'm guilty.

I shut my eyes, but still I see Ava staring at me, blood running down her face.

*   *   *

It was the end of summer, and the air was so thick I wasn't sure I could breathe. I had driven my crappy hatchback the seven hours from Providence past New York and Philadelphia. At the time, Ava was living in Maryland, right on the border. She had a fairy-tale cottage in a little town. The whole thing was so charming and sweet, it made me sick.

The end of a love affair is never easy, especially because Glenn wasn't the love of my life. But I'd thought we had something separate from Ava. That we could have found each other without her. The dedication in her book had exposed that lie. We were together because each of us was at odds with her. He'd slept with me to get back at her. I'd slept with him to prove I was better than her. We were with each other, but it was always about my sister.

I scratched his chest and nipped his shoulder, constantly demanding his attention, trying to exorcise the ghost of her memory. But when we were lying together afterward, my head on his arm, his eyes were closed. I couldn't help wondering if he was still, always, only thinking about her.

For a full week after Glenn disappeared, I woke up angry and went to bed angry. My jaw clenched until my muscles were taut with pain. My stomach was too knotted for food, my nerves too wired for sleep.

At the bookstore I saw an entire window filled with Ava's new book. It was displayed on the wall of best sellers. Glossy, shiny, menacingly bright letters. And inside every book the same message.

When I passed the dump display with the blown-up picture of Ava herself, I couldn't hold back my poisonous rage. I grabbed the flimsy cardboard edge of her cute choppy haircut and yanked the whole thing to one side. Books scattered as the honeycomb shelf came away from its base. I put a foot on Ava's black leather jacket and pulled her cardboard head from her shoulders.

I didn't stay to find out I was fired.

I left my adviser, left school, dropped everything. I didn't pay my rent or my utilities or pick up my paycheck. I didn't give two weeks' notice anywhere. My anger was driving me and I let it gather my things and hit the road.

Done. Gone. Over.

I didn't know I was going to her house, I swear. I didn't have a plan. I almost never do, at first. But when I passed into Delaware, I knew where I was heading. Ava had been living here since her divorce from Beckett. I'd been to the house only once with my parents, but my clenched hands turned the wheel as if on automatic. I hated Ava. I hated her and I was going to hurt her like she'd hurt me.

There had been plenty of chances to turn around. When I think about it now, even when I'm angry, part of me wishes I could change the story. There were so many moments I could have chosen a different path.

There. When I drove past the English Department without a good-bye to my graduate studies. I should have stopped and gone inside to breathe the heavy smell of paper and hear the rolling laugh of Peggy, our office manager. I should have gone into the main office and asked what she was reading. She would have given me a sticky toffee and told me about the professor who'd called her at two AM with a printing problem. I could have let Ava go and finished my degree.

But I was spoiling for a fight, so I went to find one.

I could have stopped *there.* When I pulled off for gas at a Jersey Turnpike service plaza. There was a woman with a golden retriever whose wide doggy smile could have diffused me. I should have knelt in front of that dog and stroked his ears and kissed his silky head. I should have remembered that Glenn wasn't the only good thing in the world and I was worthy of more love than he could give.

But instead I replaced the pump and pulled away, anger and gasoline fumes burning my lungs.

Even *there,* as I pulled into Ava's subdivision. *It's not too late,* I want to tell myself. But it was too late. Years too late. The sun had set an hour ago, but in this neighborhood front walks were lined with lights and front porches glowed.

And in front of Ava's house, Glenn's car.

I felt the sight like a physical punch to the gut. He had left me for Ava exactly a week ago. Before I knew it, my seat belt was off, my door was open, and I was standing on the pavement. My heart felt like a rotting boil. I don't remember walking to the front door, but I do remember the path was lined with the same four-by-four blocks of natural stone that circled the tree in the front yard. They looked like little cobblestones; I'll never forget that.

I rang the bell. I banged and shouted. But no one answered.

There were lights on inside. I pressed my face against the window next to the door, trying to see. The polished entryway was empty, but I could detect movement farther back. I grabbed a stone block from the line edging the front path. The cold weight felt good in my hand.

I hurled the stone through her front window. The crash sounded exactly the way I felt. I grabbed another and hurled it through the window on the other side of the front door.

Now I could hear voices in the back of the house. I scooped up two more, one in each hand.

Come out, Ava.

My fingers clenched the rough stone. More than throwing it, I pushed it. I put everything I had behind that throw. Sent it as high and as far as I could, all the way into the house.

The rock was falling, just losing its momentum, as Ava came out of the kitchen.

And it hit her in the head. She staggered back against the wall, her eyes wide and shocked.

But I was frozen in place. Staring at my bloodied sister through a halo of broken glass.

Behind her, I could hear Glenn's voice. "The police are on their way."

I couldn't let him catch me here, couldn't stand watching his eyes turn cold and disdainful.

Then I saw myself as he would, as Ava must. Disheveled hair, wild expression, rock in hand. And I couldn't stand the picture I made.

I dropped the stone and ran.

CHAPTER

24

AVA

Ruthless self-loathing floods my body along with my choking fear for Beckett. I've been left alone with Cristina, who is obsessed with my mother—she's always addressed me instead of him, always looked at me first, and she seems to think Beckett is expendable. Now he's in the belly of the beast and I can't do a damned thing to help him.

I spent so much time despising him, but all my reasons are insubstantial chaff scattered in the gale force of my regret. He was weak, he wasn't the right husband for me, but he doesn't deserve to be here, afraid and in pain. If he'd never met me, his story could have been so different. Maybe he would have married some nice woman, taken pride in his writing, been happy. If he hadn't met me, he wouldn't be here—I feel the truth of that even without all the facts. I wanted him dead, I hated him, but now I realize how little it all mattered. If he dies here, I deserve blame.

Meanwhile, Cristina is realigning the medical equipment, pulling out a few more empty vials, and replacing the needle on the syringe. It must be my turn for the checkup. *Absolutely not.*

Then Cristina unplugs the laptop, picks it up, and carries it over to me.

She holds it up to the gate, and I see Beckett on the screen, bound in a chair, shirtless and shaking, while Phil tapes wires and electrodes all over his body. I can't blink, can't breathe as I watch. Then the screen goes dark.

Cristina says, "You and I both know you can't get out of here, but you could run around and throw things, waste my time and yours. And you'll just end up on the floor again." Her brown eyes lock on mine, but there's not so much as a flicker in her expression.

In her steady gaze, I see myself shuddering after a blast from the cattle prod, my arm in Zeus's mouth, my throat under Cristina's boot. We both remember. I don't say anything, but she knows I understand.

"I'm going to unlock this gate, and you'll walk across the room and sit down in that chair." She jerks her head at the folding chair where Beckett sat to have his blood drawn. The chair he sat in before they took him away. Not me. I step back, my lips pressed tightly together. Not me.

"You're going to walk calmly across the room and sit down," she repeats, "and let me draw some blood and get some readings."

She can say the words, but she can't force me to accept them, and I tally up the moving pieces. First, Zeus still sitting at attention, but second, Phil's out of the picture. If Cristina wants my blood, she's going to have to shed some of her own to get it.

But I look again at the computer screen, no longer dark. Beckett is the final piece—alone, still bound to the chair, with the black cloth hood over his slightly bowed head. His chest rises and falls normally under the electrodes. He looks so thin, all alone on the screen, but he's alive, not in pain. Not yet. There's an implicit threat, a reason Cristina is holding this up to show me. Beckett's well-being depends on my compliance.

Even though my body's wound so tight that it's painful to move, I shuffle to the gate.

Cristina nods, like this is exactly what she expected. She sets the laptop back on the desk and unlocks the padlocks from top to bottom. The key glitters in her hand. With a tug, there's a gap between the two sections of the fence, and I walk through from one trap into another. My flesh crawls as I pass her.

There's no ambient noise in this room, so far below the surface of the earth, and each step reverberates against the high ceiling.

I sit in the chair, and she sets the laptop on the desk next to the medical equipment. On the screen, Beckett's shrouded head lifts, turns right and left as though he's trying to see. He tugs at his hands and shakes the chair, a heavy wooden one. I can't see his surroundings, just the concrete floor beneath him and cinder-block wall behind him.

Without this visual aid, I would attack Cristina, choke her. My hands flex and I can almost feel her throat collapse.

"You understand who that is?" Cristina asks.

"Beckett," I whisper.

She looks pleased, like I'm smarter than she expected. "Keep your eyes on the screen," she says, taking my wrist in her cold hand.

Instinctively, I flinch and pull away.

With a single finger, Cristina jabs the computer touch pad, and Beckett's entire body convulses. There's no sound, but I can see the hollow of his mouth sucking in the hood as he screams. Every muscle of mine contracts in sympathy, and I can't help crying out.

Cristina taps again, and Beckett's body slumps.

"I'm going to take your pulse, your blood pressure, your temperature, and then do a blood draw." She doesn't tell me to cooperate.

She doesn't have to.

*   *   *

Only minutes pass before Cristina takes the last tube off the needle and unties the rubber cord from my bicep. My inner elbow hurts from the needle being jabbed into my tensed arm. A drop of blood swells at the injection site. I press my thumb against it and bend my elbow. Cristina isn't going to give me a Band-Aid and a lollipop. I'm staring at her with so much hatred my eyes sting, but she's too busy arranging the little tubes of blood into their holder to notice.

"Why me?" I spit out. "Why not a stranger? Why not Zoe?"

She turns to me. "You were easier."

"Easier to find? Easier to catch?" Zoe was in Texas; maybe she was just too far away. I wish she were here and I were safe. But I think of the child I know she has, and I'm ashamed.

My agitation seems to amuse Cristina. "All of it. And we needed to make sure no one came looking for you, not too quickly."

"What do you mean?" The pain from my elbow flares. Has she made it look like Beckett and I ran away together? Maybe Glenn will hate me like Zoe does.

But she just smiles and shakes her head, denying me any answers.

"They'll find you." *My husband, the police, maybe even my parents.*

Cristina sets the tray of tubes off to one side. "No, they won't. They're not even looking. They want an easy answer. Most people are stupid, Ava, just like you."

"What do they think happened to me?"

"They think Zoe and Glenn did this, or that you took off on your own. Either way, nobody cares."

I know she's just goading me, but hot rage propels me to my feet.

She turns, her eyes wide, and my hand flies through the air to strike her cheek. Quicker than a thought, Zeus is on me, knocking me down. I crash into the chair as we fall, the table shakes, and Cristina is right over us, reaching across to the laptop. She's going to hurt Beckett again, and I shout, "No! I'm sorry!"

Zeus has one of my arms in his mouth, and she reaches down and yanks on the other. "*Aus*, Zeus, *aus!*"

She hauls me to my feet and shoves me through the gate. I'm panting with fury and regret. There's a smudge of blood on her cheek from my hand. Under the table lies one of my shoes, kicked off in the struggle, and I stumble out of the other as Cristina fastens the gate, slamming each lock with more force than necessary.

"Just like your mother. Emotional. Stupid." Then she wheels around and strides through the same door where Phil took Beckett, slamming it behind her.

For a moment the relief of her absence is overwhelming and I sink to the floor, wrapping my arms around my knees. The strain of holding still has burned out every nerve ending. Tears of humiliation have already dried on my cheeks. I don't understand her words, can't make the connection between my mother, cold and clinical like Cristina, and the word *emotional*.

All I understand is the rising tide of sorrow building within me, pressing against my rib cage. I clamp my mouth shut, but I'm shivering like a child with the force of my longing. I want my mommy, but not my actual mother. A mother warm and comforting and supportive. I want arms around me, stronger than Beckett's. I want Glenn, but not to see me like this, weak and broken. I want someone who has to love me, someone fierce and funny. Someone tougher than Cristina. I never expected this, but I want Zoe.

My body is too tired to shake, my brain too fried to think. I close my eyes, wishing I could just pass out. I need peace, rest, oblivion, but none of that comes.

All I get against my closed eyelids is a sudden overwhelming memory.

Zoe as I saw her last—a madwoman with wild eyes and bared teeth, an avenging angel in a halo of shattered glass, illuminated by my living room light.

At that time I hadn't seen her in over a year, but I had known where she was, who she was with.

I'd sent Glenn away and thought I meant it. I wasn't ready for a forever love, not after Beckett. I thought I wanted solitude, an emotional fortress around which a thousand years of thorns could grow. But when I learned Glenn was with Zoe, I couldn't help myself; I sent him that message in the dedication of my book, believing that with the power of my words I could conjure him home again. And I did.

He dropped everything and returned, just because I asked. Not in a million years would Beckett have come back like that. Glenn reminded me that he'd never wanted anyone else, he never would have left if I hadn't made him. And that Zoe was as close as he could get to me. She was the false princess, the enchantress in disguise, my pale shadow.

So I forgave him. And then I turned all that anger on my sister. She had no excuse for choosing Glenn over anyone else in the world, no reason to pick him except to hurt me.

Now he was back in my house, my kitchen, washing my dishes. I could hear the faucet running, knew he was up to his elbows in soapy water. He might not have heard the window break. Even though the first rock Zoe threw had caught my head, even though I could feel the hot dampness of blood on my forehead, I felt exhilarated.

This was between my sister and me.

Violence was the choice you made when you were defeated, so I didn't need Glenn to come to my rescue.

Eyes wide, Zoe stumbled back, like she was losing her nerve. But instead of leaving, she raised a second stone. A cube of hand-squared Belgian granite, to be precise. I'd chosen them for their old-world look, not their lethal capabilities.

She hefted the stone, so perfectly sized for a human hand, her eyes darting up to my forehead and then back to my face. If that first throw had hit me directly, I might already be bleeding out on the ground. And now I was facing her, stationary, an easy target.

She might kill me. The thought made me bare my teeth. I might be willing to risk everything for this Pyrrhic victory, proving my own control, making her angry enough to lose hers.

And I didn't move. I didn't say a word, just lifted my chin and silently dared her. *This is your chance to be the author. What happens next, Zoe?*

But a police siren sounded in the distance, and she startled, the stone falling from her nerveless fingers.

Then my sister turned and ran.

Now new tears squeeze from my closed eyes and I wrap my arms more tightly around my knees. We wasted so much time telling stories about each other, but I'm starting to believe *storyteller* is just another word for *liar*.

As time went by, my anger began to fade. Glenn is very straightforward. When I said it was over, he believed me. When I decided to forgive him, he was one hundred percent loyal. And the happier I was, the harder it was to stay angry at Zoe. When she "disappeared," I found her. It was pathetically easy. And I learned she had a husband, a child. I wondered who this sister was, the one who was a wife and mother. Was she happy in her marriage like I was in mine? But after all that anger, after I'd deliberately persecuted her in fiction, there was no way to reach out. I had obliterated any chance we might have had at a relationship.

I'd defeated Zoe. I made sure she knew I wasn't afraid of her and I could take and keep anything—any*one*—I wanted. I was just like Cristina, and even if Zoe knew I was in trouble, there's no way on earth my sister would help me now. She'd think I deserve to be helpless and alone.

Maybe I do.

Once, once, once—a drumbeat of regret, our beginning turned to dust.

CHAPTER

25

ZOE

I CAN'T STAY ON this bus forever. We'll reach a destination, everyone will get off, and I'll be alone again. All the passengers bump and sway in unison, but as separate islands. The woman next to me is close enough that I can smell her perfume and the leather of her briefcase. She's looking at her phone, oblivious to my presence.

What will I do next? I'm good at leaving and at becoming someone new. I could disembark at the airport, get onto a bus or a train, end up in a strange city. Start all over again with a bed in a shelter and a crappy job. Look for a lonely person longing for a roommate or a daughter or a lover. I know how to do all that. Shedding Lizzie might be as easy as dropping my wallet in a trash can.

Outside my window the buildings move farther away, replaced by more and more lanes of traffic. We're on the highway, definitely headed to the airport. And I don't want to leave. I want to get home—back to the place where I sang Emma to sleep and woke up in Andrew's arms. My longing hurts like my heart is being squeezed. It hurts enough to make me gasp so that my seatmate turns her head to stare out the window, pointedly away from me. *Asshole.*

That's what I need to remember. This woman is just like everybody else. No one gives a shit about me. Strangers, the police, even my parents would believe I'm responsible for Ava's disappearance. I'm the only one who knows the truth. If I want to clear my name and try to get Andrew and Emma back, it's all on me.

Ava. She would know what to do. She would make a list, examine the evidence, and get the answers. I've been angry at her for so long, but her skills are the ones I need right now. And maybe it's just because I miss Andrew and Emma, but I actually miss my sister too. At least the idea of her.

When I was in fourth grade, I had a report to do on Georgia and was feeling overwhelmed. I could read a page of a book, but I didn't know which parts mattered. I wrote down the titles of all the books in the bright pile I had collected, but that didn't make a report either. What mattered more, history or climate? The state bird or peaches or the Okefenokee Swamp? Ray Charles or Jimmy Carter or *Gone With the Wind*? I couldn't include everything, so I sat there with nothing.

My parents were in the other room, working. They were writing and talking and moving effortlessly among papers and books and the computer screen. I rose and stood in the doorway, watching them, waiting for them to notice me, but they didn't. And if they had, I wouldn't have known what to ask.

Then Ava came up behind me. "Is it your paper?"

I nodded, too choked with my own stupidity to speak.

"Come on." She pulled on my shoulder. "Let me show you how to do it."

And she sat next to me, my smart seventh-grade sister, with a paper and pencil, and talked me through it. "First you write down your topic. Then you choose some subgroups. Then you write a few facts for each. Then you explain why they all matter. And then you're done."

That was such a clear memory, a moment when Ava was the big sister and I was the little sister, a moment when she was my mentor and my guide.

What broke the spell? I remember working with the yellow light of the lamp shining on my books, but not how I finished, or what the final report looked like, or even the grade I received. The moment was so rare that it is enclosed in amber in my memory.

Now it's been three years since I've seen Ava at all. I lost her, and I wonder if I have lost Andrew and Emma too.

No. I have to believe I can get my family back. And this belief, this hope that we can fix everything broken and go back to the way things were, seems to open a window to Ava as well.

I can figure this out. I have to. I open up my shoulder bag. I have a notebook and a pen, the scraps of paper I swiped from Ava's house and a phone. Ava would make a list, a plan. The bus bumps again, hard, and I flip my bag shut before anything bounces out.

Through the windshield I see the signs for long-term parking. We are approaching the airport.

As the other passengers begin sliding across their seats, ready to go, the woman next to me takes a firm grip on her briefcase and actually locks eyes with me. Looks at me. Long enough to make me worried. Does she recognize me? I turn my back to her and busy myself with the strap of my bag until the bus comes to a stop in front of the terminal.

As we all stand together, pressing to get off the bus, I realize the airport is the worst place for me to be. So much security. So many cameras. Even in the innocuous waiting area, so many televisions, all tuned to an endless loop of news.

I need a quiet place to spread my papers and look at the big picture. I need to become Ava—methodical, intelligent, analytical.

Instead I'm a panicked animal, trapped in a crowd of predators, looking for a direction to run.

Thank God this shuttle brought me to Reagan National. If I were out at Dulles or BWI, I don't know where I would have gone. But here I have access to a dozen easy ways to flee. Buses, Amtrak, taxis and Ubers. I choose the Metro. Fast and anonymous. The Blue Line takes me to Crystal City, and this time of day it's not crowded, except for the couple sitting across from me with a little girl about Emma's age between them. A family. My heart gives a sideways lurch. No, I can't think about that.

Right now I need something simpler than Ava's brain or an act of God.

The internet.

This little burner phone had a limited data plan, one I've already used up. But I'm desperate for information.

From the Crystal City Metro station, it's only a few minutes' walk to the closest branch of the public library. Some libraries make you log in with your card and a password, so I'm gearing myself up to lurk around and steal someone else's open computer. But apparently I'm on a long-overdue lucky streak, because I drop into a chair in front of a computer with my bag in my lap, hit the keyboard, and the internet is right there.

Of course, that's the end of my luck. And in only a few minutes it's clear I have neither the skills nor the patience I need to dig for the right information and analyze it.

What I have is a lot of random clues. Or possibly no clues at all. Just random things. The folded blueprint that shows an unidentified building with the word "Spiegler." The notes from Ava's mood board with words like "SERE," which I now know stands for Survival, Evasion, Resistance, and Escape. That sounds like my life. But I have no idea what it has to do with anything else.

I don't know how to identify a building's shape or search using a blueprint. The numbers on it make no sense to me. Spiegler could be the surname of any of a hundred different people or something in a foreign language. There's too much here.

I get tired of scrolling through screen after screen. Fuck it. If I were braver, I would search for my own name and see what the news is reporting now. But I'm not going to do that. Partially because I don't want to know and partially because I'm not sure how surveillance works online. Maybe searching on myself would trigger something and the cops would show up. It's probably just my paranoia—I know it's stupid—but it feels dangerous.

Luckily I'm in a library, the most logical place in the world to do a search on an author.

I look up "Ava Hallett." There's a full list of her novels, the movies and television adaptations, the awards and speaking engagements. She's available to video chat with book clubs and appreciates all her fans. Her personal biography is brief: "Ava Hallett lives in Northern Virginia with her husband." A micro-biography.

Its brevity reminds me of the way Ava used to answer questions from our parents. They'd ask, "How was your day?" and I'd unleash a flood of words, trying to tell them all the things that happened, all the feelings I had. And every single time, I met the stabbing pain of their disinterest. Even if I got angry, they never rose to the bait. The more I spoke, the less I got back.

Ava never made my mistake. "Fine." That was the answer she always gave, and it was all they ever wanted. Her biography on this author page is the professional equivalent of "Fine." But that doesn't mean things didn't happen and she didn't have feelings. I was so busy expressing my own, I never asked about hers.

I switch to an image search, but it's one glossy professional photo after another. Ava at a podium, Ava in a head shot for a book jacket. None of them has the spontaneity of the picture I saw in Glenn's study, where her hair was blowing and her eyes were smiling.

The things I want to know about my sister can't be found on the internet, but I'm still scrolling through pictures. I stop on a close-up of her face. She's staring down the camera, her deep-blue eyes confident. At this remove I can meet her gaze without flinching, even though it's so much like my mother's. Ava doesn't look at people, she appraises them. Her ash-blonde hair hangs perfectly sleek. Nothing fussy or mussed, everything under control. She could navigate online without any trouble. In the time it's taken me to pull up an unnecessary picture of my sister, Ava would have found every answer.

Defiantly I type it all in—"Hallett, Spiegler, SERE, Survival, Evasion, Resistance, Escape"—and I get a hit.

More than one. The names leap out at me from academic papers by N. Hallett, W. Hallett, and J. Spiegler. And the titles all include elements of SERE. I click on "Coordinating the Effects of Psychological Fragility: The Legacy and Implications of Psychiatric Counter-Espionage" and find a summary of the article with the authors' full names. Nancy and Walter Hallett and their coauthor, James Spiegler.

The paper is on some kind of academic database, and I have to log in with my email and confirm my new free subscription. I use my "home" email address, the one I share with Andrew, praying it isn't being monitored by anyone else. Just because he's taken Emma and left doesn't mean he'd turn me in, I have to believe that. And I have to keep moving forward.

When the article comes up, it's a mess of technological jargon, but I think it's an evaluation of the effectiveness of torture in obtaining information. My parents seem to argue that while physical torture doesn't make people tell the truth, psychological torture does. They use a bunch of historical cases to make their point. This is only a paper, based on other people's research. But still. Psychological torture.

There's a case study referenced, one where the subject was questioned while a family member was threatened with torture. It sounds like something out of a spy film. This study was conducted at a university in the sixties, and no actual torture was carried out and no pain was caused. There's a note in the paper suggesting that the controlled environment actually made the questioning less effective.

That sounds like my mother. Cold. Detached. Speculating about the theoretical setting and effects of an experiment without any concern for the human person, terrified into telling secrets, racked with guilt while their loved one screams.

My mind is spinning. My parents study torture. They've studied ways to break people down. This report—dry and detached—is about those techniques. Ava knew it. And now I do too.

I grip the edge of the computer table and close my eyes, as if I can block out what I've read. The most chilling thing is how right, how absolutely in character it seems.

But what do I do with this information?

"Excuse me." Someone touches my shoulder.

I jump, knocking the keyboard aside.

A teenager with frizzy hair and a scowl is standing next to me. "Are you done?" she asks. "Because your eyes were shut, and all the other computers are taken."

Normally I might have snapped back, but I'm too shaken, unsure what to do or where to go next. Without speaking, I push away from the desk and stand up, pausing only to close the browser.

She rolls her eyes at my assumption that she'd care about my internet activity, and her hands are flying over the keyboard before I even turn away.

I'm raw and exposed under the library's fluorescent lights, and a glance at the clock over the checkout desk tells me it's not even noon yet. Although only a few hours have passed, Andrew and Emma seem as far away as if I'd been flying through a dozen time zones.

Now I need a moment to regroup.

I find the bathrooms. Mercifully, the family one is available, and I can have the entire room. There's a strong possibility I'm going to start sobbing, so privacy is crucial. Standing at the sink, I study my face in the mirror. Red-rimmed eyes, unkempt hair. I run my hands under the faucet and slick my hair down, tucking it behind my ears.

My hand shakes as I pass it under the soap dispenser, and it takes me a few tries to get enough foam. Once it's rinsed off, I splash my face, as if I can wash away all the crappy things I've done and the self-loathing too. I need someone to talk to, someone with good, clear-headed advice. Someone I can trust.

I wipe my hands on my jeans and dig into my bag for my phone.

There's only one person I want to call.

Before I can think about all the reasons not to, I rapidly dial the area code, then hesitate. I'm solid on the last four digits, but the ones in the middle are just a blur. I take a guess, but the number I dial is "not in service."

I feel so stupid, and so alone.

Almost a year ago I locked myself out of the house . . . with Emma inside. I was too scared to think, rattling the knobs, ringing the doorbell, checking under the mat, although I knew there wasn't a key there. Why did we have the stupid child-safety locks on the inside knobs of the doors? I might have broken a window if Felicia hadn't called at just that moment. And before I could think, I was telling her everything, in a rushed jumble of words.

"Take a breath," she told me. "What's Emma doing now?"

Squinting through the beveled glass in the front door, I could see Emma, still sitting on the sofa watching *Dora*.

Calmly and without making me feel bad, Felicia told me to call a locksmith and gave me a number. And she didn't bring it up or tease me about it later. I was dumbstruck, not just by the relief of being back in the house with Emma in my arms, but because someone else had actually helped me.

Now I shiver, my hands resting on the cool porcelain of the sink. The gentle murmur of library patrons outside the door makes me feel even more alone. I want to talk to Felicia. I *know* the area code; I'm almost sure of the last four digits. How hard can this be? I try again, and get a stranger's voice mail. Everything in me wants to panic, punch numbers wildly, hurl this stupid phone at the wall.

What did Felicia say? "Just breathe."

How many times have I written her number down as Emma's alternate emergency contact or as my own? Somewhere in my mind those numbers exist; they have to. I close my eyes, slow my breathing, visualize those emergency-contact lines on a form. First Andrew's work and cell numbers, and then below, Felicia's. Before I can second-guess myself, I dial a number.

Someone picks up, and my heart leaps. Then I remember caller ID can't rat me out, not with this anonymous burner phone. Maybe the only reason she didn't screen me is because she doesn't know it *is* me.

"Hello?" I ask. But there's only silence. This is a mistake. "Felicia?"

Only heavy breathing, but not the creepy kind. The kind that happens when a four-year-old picks up the phone.

"Sam." I speak firmly. "Sam, go get your mom."

"I want Emma to come play." He recognizes me. He knows I'm Emma's mom. I picture his serious little round face and soft spiky brown hair and wish I could scoop him up and hug him. Even though I hate it when kids answer the phone, I can't hate Sam, not even a little bit. Not ever.

"I know, buddy. We'll work it out soon."

He breathes wetly into the phone again until I hear quick footsteps, followed by Felicia's voice. "Hello? Who is this?"

I don't want to have to choose between Lizzie the lie and Zoe the liar. "It's me."

"Shit." Behind her I hear his little cry of indignation at the expletive. "Sam, you can watch *Thomas*. Just turn it on."

Then the background sounds become muffled, and I know she's stepped into the laundry room and pulled the door shut behind her. I know because that's what she did when we wanted to talk about the mean moms or the fight she had with her husband or nursery school politics. She hasn't hung up on me yet, and I feel a cautious leap of gratitude.

We say nothing for a few seconds, then speak at the same time. I don't even know what words are coming out of my mouth, because I cut them off as soon as I hear her voice. But she does too.

I wait, holding my breath, until she tells me, "You first."

"I fucked up." I am surprised by my own words. They are so inadequate.

"You think?" Felicia's reply is fast, but there is a smile in her tone, and the enormity of all the things that have happened since I last saw her hits me.

"So, how was book club?"

She gasps, and we are both laughing so hard that my chest hurts and it's tough to breath. "Get your ass back here and I'll tell you all about it."

I wish fiercely I were home with my own family or bringing Emma over to Felicia's house for a playdate with Sam, knowing Andrew would be home in time for dinner. I was building more than a family there; I was building a new me, one with friends and connections and a real life.

"I will. I swear. Call you soon." The words come out automatically, but I mean them. "Please don't give up on me."

Felicia says, "Stay safe," and I know she means it too. I'd give anything to have her explain how to fix all this. Of course she can't do that. But what she has shown me, just in the tone of her voice, is that we are still friends.

As we hang up, relief floods me. I'm not alone.

I press my fingertips against my forehead. That warm glow of someone understanding and supporting, that's what a sister should be. The way I felt all those years ago when Ava told me stories, when she talked me through my homework, when she was the only one awake with me in the night. Those memories are from so long ago, I forgot I used to trust Ava.

Could I ever get those feelings back again?

But Ava's not the one I have to trust right now. There's only one person in the world who wants her back more than me. Her husband. Glenn and Ava have been married three years. I know marriage now, how deep it runs. I've been married to Andrew barely a year, and losing him could break me. Now that Glenn's anger isn't in the room with me, I can see it as terror. Maybe, if I really want to find my sister, I should ask the person she loves and trusts most to help me.

Someone rattles the handle of the bathroom door, startling my eyes open. A woman asks, "Are you okay?"

Automatically, I answer, "Sorry, just a minute."

I'll go outside to call Glenn and hope he doesn't notify the police.

Maybe trust is a decision you make. You reach out a hand for the other person and hope they pull you across that line.

Until you try, you can't know.

26

ZOE

OUTSIDE THE LIBRARY, the world seems so ordinary. The quiet suburban neighborhood surrounding the parking lot is full of houses with people living normal lives. And here I am, sitting on a stone bench, completely alone, my phone in one hand, the business card I swiped from Glenn's study in the other.

Making this call is even harder than I thought it would be.

After that night of shattered windows, I ran from the memory of my sister's bloody face. I could have killed her. I *know* that.

Glenn was the most awful thing I'd done, one sin for which there was no atonement. It was months before I called my parents, and my mother told me Ava and

Glenn were married. She delivered the news in the same tone as a comment on the weather, but it splintered me like a lightning strike. They were *married*. Now it would always be the two of them on one side, me alone on the other.

Unless I took myself out of the picture forever.

I moved to Louisiana, where I changed my name and tried to obliterate the woman I'd been. Then I found Andrew on the Texas dating site and moved again, with a new identity and a clean slate.

I look at the business card and rub my thumb over Glenn's phone number.

When our relationship ended, I couldn't have imagined finding Andrew and Emma.

And now I've lost them. Was there anything I could have said to make Andrew take me in his arms? All I want is to be back in my family again. But a deeper pain needles at my heart. He wouldn't even hear me out. After the sweetness of our wedding, all the time I spent taking care of Emma on my own, how clean I kept the house. Even after he met my parents, when he knew I didn't have any role models or support, he still rejected me. And I told him the truth.

I wrap my arms around myself and hold on. Mostly. I told the truth mostly.

That's what made the difference. I edited out anything inconvenient. Now I'm paying the price. I earned this pain. It's exactly what I deserve.

How much worse can one phone call make things?

I do it. I dial. At least Glenn won't recognize the number of this phone, and it's local, so it won't look like a telemarketer. By some miracle, he answers.

Then I blow it. "Don't hang up."

The phone goes dead.

Frantically, I text: *I want to find Ava. Call me.*

A slow second passes, then another. And my phone buzzes with his incoming call.

He says, "I can't talk long. You know they're monitoring everything."

"Meet me. We'll find Ava."

"Where are you?"

I hesitate. If I tell him, will the police show up here instead of Glenn? But my choices are stark. Run and lose my family forever, or take this chance.

"The library by the Crystal City Metro."

And he clicks off.

Now all I have to do is wait. Wait, and try not to look suspicious. I turn the phone over in my hands and shift uneasily on the stone bench.

A car pulls into the parking lot and approaches the front of the library slowly. I hunch my shoulders until it angles into a parking space. A woman about my age gets out the driver's side and opens the back door, and then I know who she is. She's a mom, just like Felicia and Bethany, just like I used to be. She's unbuckling a child from a car seat and gathering a shoulder bag of books, and I wish I could trade places with her. Maybe her shoulders hurt with the weight of all those bags, maybe lifting a kid out of the car is hard on her back, maybe she's in a hurry or sleep deprived or irritated. But there's nothing in the world I want as much as her life.

Holding the hand of a sturdy toddler, she comes toward me. Her hair is cut in a swingy bob, and she wears capri workout pants and a fitted T-shirt. Her son has a bowl cut and round cheeks like a kid on a soup can.

He stops abruptly right next to me, staring at me until I meet his eyes. And then he grins.

"I'm sorry. He's such a flirt," his mom says, with the indulgent tone of a mother who knows her child hung the moon. The way I feel about Emma.

"It's okay. I mean, he's adorable."

"He's not bad." She runs a hand over his little head. "Come on, bub. We're going to be late for story time."

Is it my imagination, or does she give me a penetrating look as she leads him through the library doors? Maybe I should have searched on myself online. What other pictures and gossip are out there? I might be more recognizable than I ever imagined I could be.

Now that the woman has gone and I'm alone again, my eyes follow every car that drives past the library. The longer I wait, the more certain I am that Glenn has called the police. But my body is clenched, frozen, as I force myself to wait. I won't run anymore.

When his black Lexus sedan turns into the parking lot, I run to it, pulling on the door handle before the car even comes to a full stop. He's wearing Ray-Ban Predators that hide his eyes like a secret agent in a movie.

"Where have you been?" I ask him, my seat belt not even snapped as he starts driving.

He doesn't look at me. "I've spent the day being interrogated, that's where I've been. They've always thought it was me."

"Then why'd they let you go?"

"I have a solid alibi, a great lawyer, and I opened up my finances. I didn't do this. They'll figure it out."

"Well, I didn't either. But that picture—"

"That fucking picture. There's no way I can go home. Too much press. All the news sites, the Reddit feeds, it's all speculation about us. That we did this together. What's Ava going to think . . ." He doesn't finish, but I know what he means.

Worse than rumors online or the police thinking we're coconspirators, worse than all of it is the look I saw on Andrew's face. Hurt and doubt. None of the lies I told him shook his belief that I loved him—not before that picture.

"She won't think anything, she'll just be glad to see you. We're going to find her. We have to."

Glenn's staring ahead at the road like I don't even exist. And that's what he wishes, I know it. All I am is a regret, the thing that almost cost him his wife. If we're going to find her, he needs to see me as more than a mistake. "Glenn," I say sharply, "I can't go home until she's back. Andrew won't . . ." But I can't finish the sentence.

"So why call me? Because if we're caught together now, it'll look even worse."

"In Ava's study, I found some words: 'SERE,' 'Spiegler,' 'MK-ULTRA.' My parents were working with a James Spiegler on psychological torture techniques."

"Your sister was always researching something. She toured a crematorium and read transcripts of interviews with serial killers. That's not a clue."

"Okay. Someone called me in Texas, threatened me. And then knocked on my parents' door and used my daughter's voice. That's when I found Ava's watch."

"And the photo," he says slowly. "That's what I want to know. Who took it, who sent it to the news?"

"So how do we find out?"

Glenn changes lanes smoothly, and it's crazy how controlled he is. I would be speeding and weaving, desperate to get ahead. With his sunglasses blocking the top half of his face, I have to watch his mouth for any hint of expression. Now his lips are tense. "I already called someone. I'm waiting to hear back."

Right. He probably knows all sorts of secret back channels, stuff the police couldn't get to. I'm almost grateful the government ate our right to privacy and picked its teeth with our personal freedoms. For once in my life, exposing secrets might work in my favor.

"So what do we do until we hear from your contact?"

He doesn't answer. Mentally I run through our options. There's no way I want to sit and wait somewhere with Glenn until some mysterious guy I don't even know finally calls. I can't go where I really want to be, back to Texas, and I won't go to my parents, not unless I'm desperate. I want to find Ava or learn more about her, but we can't show up at her house again, not with the press out in force. There's only one name I've come across that might bring me closer to what she was doing before her disappearance.

"Let's find this Spiegler. Maybe Ava talked to him." She was investigating our parents and their past. That is the only thing I've uncovered about my sister, but maybe it's enough to start.

Glenn nods. "Address?"

I borrow his phone to search, since mine is out of data, but the first thing that pops up is an old obituary. James Spiegler is dead. My stomach drops, but I click on the link and read that he's survived by a son and daughter, both unnamed. What would *Ava* do next?

Pulling up a directory, I search for any Spieglers in Virginia, but the nearest one is way south in Mechanicsville and the internet gives his age as sixty-eight. Too old to be James Spiegler's son. I search again, this time for the District of Columbia. And there's an address for a Steven Spiegler, age thirty-five. "Georgetown," I tell Glenn. "I think I found his son."

We get on the beltway. The traffic thickens around us as we approach downtown. At least half my friends' parents worked for the government, just like Glenn does. From the Senate to the Pentagon to Embassy Row, parents from just about every center of power had children in my neighborhood, trading proximity to downtown DC for larger houses, bigger backyards, and the landed-gentry feel of the Northern Virginia suburbs.

When my friends and I used to go to Georgetown, it was for the trendy little shops or the funky bars. I never met anyone who actually lived there. In my head I imagine Spiegler, young, maybe married but without any kids, maybe a scientist like his father or a psychiatrist like my parents. Georgetown would be a great place to have a home/office combo. All those crazy politicians could see him on their lunch break.

As we close in on the address, the streets get narrow and crowded. And of course, there's no parking.

My stomach tightens. Garages mean security cameras. "There." I point to a tiny pay lot, really just a few spaces wedged between a building and a dumpster. A guy with a puffy jacket and knit hat stands at the entrance.

As we pull in and Glenn hands over cash, I fight the urge to sink down in the seat. Police, federal agents, the government, they are all headquartered in DC, surrounding us. I should have run someplace anonymous. Kansas or Alaska or somewhere overseas.

Once he cuts the engine, Glenn says what I've been thinking. "We're more recognizable together. The last thing we need is to attract attention."

One tweet, a single photo, and any suspicion that we've been collaborating will be confirmed in public opinion, in the eyes of the police, and most importantly to Andrew. But I'm not staying behind in the car. "You're waiting for a call. I'll go talk to Spiegler."

I'm braced for Glenn to argue, but he just nods. He probably thinks talking to Spiegler is a waste of time anyway and he'll be the one to find Ava and save the day, thanks to his secret contact. He says, "Keep your phone out. I'll text if I hear anything."

Walking out of the parking lot, I duck my head, but the attendant doesn't pay me any attention. Guess I'm not that infamous. Not yet.

As I round the corner, my body buzzes with adrenaline. Not knowing is scary. A faceless, nameless omnipotence is scary. But in this house is a person. I can deal with a person.

More than some generic person. Steven Spiegler. A son, about my age, with an academic father. One who used to research torture. So we have that in common. I wonder if he's closer to his sister than I am to mine.

The house is a narrow, detached Victorian with whitewashed brickwork and wrought-iron railings framing the steps leading to the front door. Next to it is a brass intercom set into the wall. All I have to do is press the buzzer.

But I hesitate.

What will I say? If Spiegler doesn't recognize me from the news, telling him I'm Ava's sister will snap it all into context. And although I've been lying for three years about who I am, it's not like I'm some master of disguise.

Glancing down, I confirm my outfit isn't business casual but straight-up casual-casual and my shoulder bag in no way resembles a briefcase. I can't pretend to be anyone official or imposing. I can't pass for police or a professional reporter. But I need an excuse to ask questions about Spiegler's father, just like Ava might have done.

I can feel the bulge of the phone in my hip pocket, but I'm not going to text Glenn for advice. Instead a memory surfaces, triggered by the phone. After dropping Emma at school, I would put on my headphones and take long walks, listening to podcasts. I favored ones about "living your best life," but Felicia was always trying to get me to listen to true crime. The only podcaster I've ever seen in person is that bitch who ambushed me at the hotel. There's no dress code—a podcaster could look like anyone; that's the whole point.

I push the buzzer. All I need to find out is whether he knows anything about his father's research and if Ava came here to ask any questions.

No immediate answer, so I buzz again, then bang the heavy door knocker.

Finally, a faint voice comes through the intercom. "Hello?"

"Can I speak to you for a few minutes?"

"No solicitors." The speaker goes silent.

"It's about Spiegler. James Spiegler. Your father?" I don't think anyone is listening anymore.

Stepping forward, I bang on the door with a clenched fist, finding some relief for my nerves in the action, the pounding, the pain. "Mr. Spiegler, I have to talk to you."

The silence could be rejection, but I hope it's consideration. Maybe the person on the other side is like me, unable to resist curiosity.

And then the door swings open. The guy standing there looks younger than thirty-five. He's wearing those wire-rimmed glasses that look smart or ironic, depending on the rest of the outfit. Given his canvas shoes and the sixties color palette of his burnt-sienna corduroys and the mustard-and-olive paisley shirt he's rocking, I'm thinking ironic.

"Steven Spiegler?" Without waiting for an answer, I start lying my ass off. "I represent *Behind the Crime*, a podcast from the Chasm Network."

Bemused, he says, "I thought you had questions about my dad?"

I'm going to have to tell him some truth, because everything's happening too quickly for my brain to generate lies. "We've been looking into the disappearance of the author Ava Hallett. Did you know she was researching your late father's work?"

"*That* writer, the missing one? No, I had no idea. Why?"

He doesn't seem defensive, mostly curious. I don't think he's acting guilty, but maybe his nonchalance is all an act. I have to hook him.

"I'd love to tell you more, but . . . can I come in so we can really talk?"

There's a second, just a flash, where he's appraising me, and I feel a flutter of danger. Behind the lenses of his glasses, his eyes are sharp, the corners crinkled with something approaching suspicion. But then with a stylized flourish that breaks the tension, he beckons me into a pocket-sized sitting room just off the entryway.

I perch on a supremely uncomfortable velvet settee, while Spiegler folds himself into a wicker chair facing me.

What would a real investigator do? I pull out my phone and set it on an ornately carved end table. "It would be best if I could record our conversation. Would you mind?" Although I don't have any recording apps, Spiegler doesn't have to know that. And this way I can keep an eye out for any messages from Glenn.

A smirk plays around Spiegler's lips, and he pulls out his own phone. "Not at all. In fact, why don't we both record?"

Of course I agree. But once these preliminaries are over comes the real test. I have to think of questions, professional questions. Stammering a little, I ask, "So, about your father. What kind of work did he do?"

"Something for the government, very hush-hush. We weren't close."

"And Ava Hallett, the author, did she contact you about your family?"

He shakes his head. "Why would she? Do you know something about my father, something a mystery writer would find interesting?" I don't like him asking me questions. Lying is easier if the other person isn't already suspicious. Not that Spiegler is calling me on my story, but he's acting like this entire interview is some kind of game, a joke we're both in on.

"Would you mind telling me a little about yourself? Did you grow up in this area?" I need to focus everything I have on the man in front of me. I'm trying to feel the conversation, sense when Spiegler's about to stop speaking so I can slide a question into each gap to make a gentle bridge to the next answer. It makes it really hard to actually hear what he's saying—that he did grow up here, but moved to this house a few years ago.

Stifling the internal panic that insists I'm learning nothing, I ask, "And do you work for the government like your dad?"

He laughs with a surprised bark. "God, no. I do system designs and integration."

I must look as lost as I feel, because he adds, "First I figure out what a company needs, then I design a custom computer program and make it work with any systems they already have."

I should be in the flow, letting the conversation unfold, but I can't shake how icky this makes me feel, trying to draw him out while hiding who I really am. And then I realize exactly why this feels so awful. It's like my first date with Andrew. Creating a false history was easy on the dating app, but not in person. When I sat opposite him over sliders and microbrews on a patio, the fading sunlight fell on his face like a sign from heaven. I couldn't lie, so I had to encourage him to do all the talking. Just like now.

And I can't stand it. There's only so long you can keep a foot on the neck of your true self before it breaks free. I ask point-blank, "Did you know your father was studying torture?"

Spiegler stiffens for a mere blink, then laughs. "You're kidding? *My* father? That's the most interesting thing anyone's ever said about him. Is that what the mystery writer was into?"

"Maybe." Any minute now he might kick me out, and there won't be a thing I can do. "Do you know anything about her? The writer, I mean. Anything at all?"

He wrinkles his forehead, his eyes still amused, like he's doing a bad impression of a person thinking. "Never read anything by her. I've seen a couple of the movies, I think. When I'm working or traveling, I usually have something playing in the background. This whole disappearance . . . it's just crazy."

His phone vibrates with an incoming call, and both of us look at it. Spiegler reaches out to pick it up, but before he does, I can see the number on the screen. Glenn's number. *Shit.*

I grab my own, like maybe it's a mistake, maybe Glenn's trying to warn me. But it's just an inert lump in my hand. Glenn's calling Spiegler, and I don't know why, but it can't be good. Every instinct tells me to run before I'm busted. I'm already on my feet when I ask, "If you had to guess, what do you think happened to her?"

Spiegler holds the phone in his hand, watching the call go to voice mail. Without raising his head, he says, "At first I thought it was a publicity thing. On the news they said something about Agatha Christie having a lost weekend. But if not . . ."

He looks at me and grins. "Well, isn't it always the husband?"

* * *

I come out of Spiegler's house at a run, and I'm breathless by the time I reach the parking lot.

Glenn is pacing beside the car, and he starts talking when I'm still a few yards away. "I got the number, but I don't have a name."

"You called Spiegler." Between my panic and the sprinting, I don't have the oxygen to say more.

"What?" He's staring at me, and his gaze isn't just uncomprehending, it's impatient. Because if he doesn't understand, it's definitely my fault.

"The number you called, it's Spiegler. I saw your number come up. You called twice just now."

"That was the number that texted our photo to the news. The number my contact gave me."

"Spiegler? Spiegler did that?"

"You were talking to him. What did he say?"

"Nothing." Nothing that matters. Nothing that could help us find Ava.

"But you asked him about the picture? You confronted him?"

I shake my head. "I didn't know that's why you were calling him."

"Why did you think I was calling? I would have told you if I knew him. Come on."

And Glenn's striding back to Spiegler's house.

"Wait!" I scramble to catch up, but he's already rounded the corner. By the time I can see him again, he's banging on Spiegler's front door.

"Open up!" He puts his thumb on the intercom speaker and mashes it down. "Open the damn door." Then he grips the handle and shakes it.

Spiegler would have to be dumber than I think he is to come out now. There has to be a better way. The street is lined with houses full of listening neighbors. Even the parking lot attendant can probably hear the din. It's only a matter of time before someone calls the police.

But even as my mind is telling me our time is running out, my blood is running hot. Spiegler is the one who sent that picture. He's the reason Andrew left. And I was in the same room with him. I could have confronted him, found out why he did it and what he knows about Ava. *Stupid.* Why didn't I put it together faster?

Instead of hitting the door or shouting for Spiegler, I turn and punch Glenn in the arm. "Glenn, stop it!"

"What?" he hisses, wheeling around so fiercely that despite myself, I fall back a step.

"Calm down. People are going to call the police."

"Good idea." He mashes down the intercom button again and shouts, "Do you hear that, you prick? I'm calling the cops."

Without waiting for an answer, he pulls his phone out, but I knock it out of his hand. "Are you crazy? You think they'll believe us?"

Glenn swears and bends to retrieve his phone. I'm not hanging around to be scooped up by the cops, especially not with this asshole. Andrew doesn't need any more reasons to doubt me.

But Glenn is right behind me, grabbing my shoulder and yanking me backward. I stagger, trying to keep my footing. His hand feels like iron and he spins me around, gripping me by both shoulders. Then he shakes me. I can't breathe, I can't focus, I can't break free. The world narrows around me, until he lets go and I run.

The only thing that matters is *moving*, getting off this street. Now I remember all the bad parts of being with Glenn. Not just the horrid mix of guilt and spite I felt whenever Ava crossed my mind, but the way the qualities that seemed sexy—decisive, strong, intense—so easily turned dark. Bossy, aggressive, moody. Everything Andrew would never be.

When I hear Glenn behind me, I speed up, but I'm not fast enough. He catches up to me, but before I can scream, he passes me. As we enter the parking lot, I'm practically chasing him.

The lot attendant in his puffy jacket watches us with an impassive face. Maybe he thinks this is some kind of lovers' spat. Maybe he thinks Glenn was making a ruckus out of jealousy. Or maybe he's already called the cops, he's got our license plate number, and he figures his job is done.

Glenn unlocks the car, but he doesn't get in. He wheels around, his face still contorted with fury. "What's the matter with you? The guy was right there and you did nothing!"

"I didn't know—"

"Don't you want to find her? We need to report this guy."

"Stop!" This time I push him hard, right in the chest. He doesn't budge. "We don't know *anything*."

"We know Ava was researching the stuff your parents worked on with Spiegler's father."

"And?" I ask. He's too close, too loud, but even a step back might look like fear. And I'm not afraid of Glenn. Not now. I need to keep him from calling the police, to make him *think*.

"And he sent the picture of us to the news."

"But why?" I insist. "Why would this guy care about Ava?"

"I don't know. His father was studying torture and he wants to keep it secret? No." Glenn shakes his head and slumps. "His dad is dead. And that's on the internet anyway. Maybe he's a deranged fan? She gets crazy letters sometimes. The publisher doesn't forward all of them."

"Maybe they were having an affair." Hearing the words makes me flinch, and I can't believe I said them.

After our time together, he must have wondered if Ava fully forgave him, if she'd ever try to get even. I thought I'd left all this spite behind, but Glenn brings out the worst in me.

His mouth twists. "Bitch." Turning away, he wrenches the car door open. I'm still standing, frozen by my own callousness, as he slides into the driver's seat. "Get in."

I'm so relieved he's not ditching me that I don't care when he adds, "I'm not getting caught here with you."

CHAPTER

27

ZOE

I CAN TELL HOW angry Glenn is when he, the world's
most careful driver, peels rubber out of the parking
lot. There's only one place we can go now, and it's scarcely
preferable to the cops. My parents' house.

They're our only other lead. Ava was investigating
their research. They worked with the father of the man
who sent our picture to the police. And the article they
wrote together was about SERE, the same word I found
pinned up in Ava's study. The best way to learn if there's
a connection is to interview my parents. Or we could just
beat our heads against a brick wall. Ultimately, that
might be as profitable and hurt less.

As we pull onto the Key Bridge, heading from Georgetown to Arlington, rust and gold trees with flashes of

green line the Potomac. I can imagine how lush they were in the spring and how bare they'll be in a few months, but these autumn trees are somewhere in between. Staring out the window as Glenn drives makes me dizzy. I settle back against my seat. I can still hear the way Spiegler tossed out the words: "It's always the husband."

If Ava were ever done with him, there'd be no marriage counseling, no second chances, not a cent of alimony. She would annihilate Glenn, just like she did Beckett. Who cheated on her. Which I know Glenn is capable of, because he slept with me. But surely if Glenn knew what happened to Ava, we wouldn't be running around investigating as a team. Every second we spend together makes him look more guilty. And if he really is guilty, he ought to be acting innocent.

By the time we reach my parents' neighborhood, my whole body is tense, like every nerve has been replaced with metallic wires, and yet my heart is open and raw. It was so much easier to be angry with Ava than it is to worry about her, or worse, to be afraid for her.

I glance at Glenn. From what I saw back in the police station, his relationship with my parents is not much better than mine. This encounter will be easier if we remember we're on the same side. But the longer we continue without speaking, the harder it is to say anything.

He turns onto my parents' street, but then we drive right past their house. "Smarter to park around the corner." Glenn offers the explanation like an olive branch. Good enough for now.

We get out of the car. Our shadows are long on the sidewalk, arms and legs stretched like aliens. By this time of day, my parents should be home from work. What will we do if they aren't?

Without realizing it, I've stopped moving. The fear is back in my stomach, drumming its heels, stirring up all my insecurities. What if they are home? What will I say? Will they answer me? Dismiss me? Call the police?

Glenn's almost two houses ahead before he notices and turns around. "What's wrong?"

If I admit my weakness, even a little bit, Glenn will leave me and keep going by himself. But it's my responsibility too. I owe this to Andrew and to Ava. "Nothing," I tell him. Nothing but my personal issues.

As I hurry to catch up, I swear to myself I'll stay focused. In my head I've gone over and over the information we need: SERE, Spiegler, an unidentified blueprint. I cannot be distracted by questions like *Why did you even have children? Did you ever love us at all?*

Finally, my insides churning, I stand beside Glenn on the front step. My father answers the door so quickly, I know he must have been in his study. He has his reading glasses on, and he squints at Glenn.

Neither of them speaks, so I push forward. "Dad. We need to come in."

My mother approaches the door. Her glasses are on her head and there is a smudge of ink on her cheek. She puts a hand on my father's arm and draws him back into the hallway. "Walter, get out of the way."

Once we are in the living room, I sit on the love seat opposite my parents, each in their leather club chairs. I study their faces, but I've never been able to read their expressions well. Are they curious, worried, bored? It all looks the same from here.

Glenn stands at an angle where my parents will have to crane their necks to see him, in a corner by the crazy modern sculpture. Even the metal angles and spikes seem unthreatening next to his bulk.

For once, my parents' lack of interest in small talk is a relief. I leap right in. "Mom, Dad, we're looking for Ava, and I need to ask you some questions about your work."

"Our work?" My mother sounds astonished. "What does our work have to do with anything?"

"I found some clues in Ava's office—"

"Glenn told us about the break-in." My father taps my mother's knee. "He thought the two of us should be aware."

Glenn gives me a half shrug, a kind of apology, but it doesn't matter. Too much has happened since then.

"Just telling us about your experience with SERE or a man named Spiegler would be helpful." If I admit how little we know, they'll lose all respect for me. And I can't get sucked into answering their questions or defending my intellectual position.

My parents share a long look. Considering whether to answer, or whether to trust me? My heart seems to beat higher and higher in my chest, until my throat is choked as I ask, "You know I'm not involved with Ava's disappearance, don't you?"

My father says, "Of course," and my mother waves a hand dismissively.

"Why are you so sure?" Glenn asks, and I kind of hope my parents won't answer.

"Planning," my mom says. "Although I suppose maybe in a fit of passion . . ."

"Not a chance," says my dad. "No organization. No follow-through."

Only my parents could make innocence sound like a character flaw. "What do you think happened to her?" I ask.

"Well . . ." My mother speaks slowly, as if plucking each word and examining it first. "Initially we thought this might be a misunderstanding."

"Misunderstanding?" That's a dirty word in this family.

She nods. "It wouldn't be inconceivable that Ava decided to take an unannounced sabbatical, a break."

My father waves the idea away. "Speculation. Then we did think that her husband—"

Leaning over, my mother shakes her head at Glenn. "But there wasn't any money for you. She left it all to various charities. And, as far as we could tell, you both seemed . . ." She searches and falls short.

"Happy," Glenn snaps. "We're happy together."

My parents consider the word and nod, at a loss for any other.

Only a few days ago, knowing Glenn and Ava have a happy marriage would have pierced me with jealousy and grief. But to my surprise, I really have changed, and it's easy to stay focused. Leaning closer, as if I can peer past my father's cool exterior, I ask, "What kind of things did you and Spiegler work on?"

My dad answers simply. "We studied the most efficient ways to get accurate information from enemy combatants."

Sucking in a deep breath, I ask the question: "You tortured people?"

He shakes his head before he even starts speaking. "Absolutely not. We never physically harmed anyone. We worked with volunteers who understood the importance of the work they were asked to do. And we never caused them physical pain." There's a sharp edge to his words. Have I hurt his feelings?

"But that's what the government wanted. To break people down." I study the gray at his temples, the vertical lines between his brows. Lines of concentration.

Now he purses his mouth. More lines, and not the smiling kind. "In World War II, the fascist French police force, the *Milice*, found that threats to family could extract information from a resistance fighter who might never break under torture. Physical torture is ineffective."

"And cruel," I insist. "All torture is cruel."

"Of course." But the dismissive way he answers makes me wince. He doesn't understand that psychological suffering is real pain too.

My mother leaps to his defense in her own way. "This should all be done in a professional setting. One has to be certain that the subject believes loved ones are actually in danger, and it helps if the subject is already stressed by discomfort—no more than might be experienced by a delayed meal or sleepless night. This method gets information without actually causing pain or violating ethical guidelines. Any emotional distress is an unfortunate side effect of gathering information."

If I ever needed proof that my parents prioritize intellect over emotions, this is it. But I don't feel vindicated, I feel heartbroken.

My dad is talking past me, like he's trying to get Glenn to understand. "We needed a means to produce information without violating ethical concerns. What? There was no actual torture. Theoretically, our experiments were humane."

Mom puts a hand on his arm. "And efficient. What we study, it's about understanding all the stimuli that

affect neural stability. We found interpersonal relationships were the best way to extract actionable intel."

Dad looks at her, and the lines in his face relax. "We
never tortured people. We tortured a visual representa-
tion of a social relationship, the idea of a person."

They are falling back into their private conversations,
their life of the mind. A glance at Glenn tells me he's as
lost as I am. "I don't understand."

Mom turns to me, her blue eyes so much like my sister's. "The government project we worked on with Spiegler was designed to get reliable, actionable intel from
prisoners of war without violating the Geneva Conven-
tion. Subjects who believed their loved ones were sub-
jected to physical distress were more compliant than
those who underwent the same distress themselves."

"You tortured their families?" I feel sick and confused. Dad explicitly said they didn't torture anyone, but
I'm not sure he understands what torture means.

"No!" My mother's voice is strong. "Subjects suffered
mild disorientation due to lack of sleep or erratic meals,
then watched videos of a hooded figure undergoing sim-
ulated torture. The greater the disorientation, the more a
subject believed the torture was real and personal. We
were trying to help our country without hurting
people."

My father braces his hands on his knees, leaning in
like he's willing me to understand. "But none of this has
any bearing on Ava. She was never involved with our
research. We kept both of you isolated from it."

I can't even imagine he wanted to protect us. It sounds
like he wanted to keep "feelings" from contaminating his
work. The same work that twisted a person's love of

family into an instrument of torture. Now, more than ever, I wish Ava were here, sitting beside me, confirming how crazy it all sounds. All I say is, "Ava was investigating your work. She knew about SERE and about Spiegler."

At the same time my father says, "James is dead," my mother says, "Cristina?" He frowns at her. "You didn't tell me Cristina ever worked with you."

My mother presses her lips together and doesn't answer. I always thought they were a team. How often does Mom keep secrets from Dad?

Glenn asks, "Who is Cristina?"

My father answers, but it is my mother he addresses. "Cristina is the daughter of our former collaborator, James Spiegler. Twenty years ago, our research was more . . . involved. James was instrumental in designing the framework of the experiments we used. When he passed away, we had to scale back."

Twenty years ago, Ava and I were latchkey kids, doing homework at the kitchen table in an empty house. Maybe every teenager feels awkward, like an experiment gone wrong, but our parents really were running experiments, straight-up studying psychological torture techniques. And they worked. All these years later, I'm still doubting myself, still an outsider, and still searching for something my parents are incapable of giving.

Dad continues, "Your mother ran a streamlined version of our previous research while I handled the clinical side. Several years afterwards, we were approached by James' daughter. I didn't think she had the necessary experience or the temperament. I thought that was the end of it."

My mother's voice is tight. "If I ran all my hiring choices by you, I'd have a cadre of white rats in lab coats twitching every time I spoke to them. I needed someone strong enough to do the work, and smart enough to know I was the boss."

"Oh, she was smart enough." My father laughs, but there's no humor in it. "She knew how to be just the thing you wanted. But stable? That girl had a perfect Electra complex."

"You think I didn't see that? There are no humans without clinical issues. This was one I could use. She believed in her father's work, and so she believed in me. Transference served my purposes."

I almost feel sorry for this mysterious woman, a pseudo-daughter vying for my mother's attention. And with a pang of jealousy, I wonder if her skill as a scientist earned her some love Ava and I never merited.

My father sits forward in his chair, but he doesn't stand up or raise his voice. "You were reckless, inviting someone so volatile into the lab." He must think he's demonstrating control over his emotions, but I know anger. I see it now.

"No." My mother's thin hand trembles. "No. She was intelligent and driven."

"You were looking for a protégée. You were blind."

I've never seen my parents argue like this; it's something that must have happened behind closed doors. Even now, it's the quietest argument I've ever heard. Maybe the more heated my parents become, the better our chances of getting to the truth.

But while they bicker with each other, Ava's in real danger. I ask sharply, "Are you still in touch with Cristina?"

My parents turn their heads in unison, even when they disagree. My mother says, "No. The funding dried up, and we—I'd had enough. It was time for a change."

"What happened to her?" I ask, my fingers laced together because I have to hold on to something, even if it's just myself.

My mother gives a little shrug. "We didn't need a team anymore."

"How did she feel about that?" My eyes are fixed on my mother's face.

"I have no idea." She's incredibly still, her lips hardly moving as she speaks. The more she shuts down, the more I can see how truly agitated she is becoming.

My father says, "That girl was unstable, fixated on the research and on you."

"You don't know that," my mother says tersely.

I pull out the piece of paper from Ava's study, the one with the blueprint of a building. "How about this location? Does it look familiar?"

My mother starts shaking her head, but my father pulls the paper closer. "Where is this?" he asks.

"Do you recognize it?"

"It's just a floor plan, but . . ." His voice trails off as he rotates the scrap one way and another. "This part." He indicates the large circle off to one side. "It reminds me of a place James owned. He must have put a couple million into it."

My mother reaches over and takes the paper from him. "The missile silo?"

"What missile silo? Where is it?" I ask, with an urgency that makes both my parents study me with piercing intensity.

"You're worried." My mother sounds surprised. "You think all this has something to do with Ava, that she might be here?"

My father squints at me. "That is what she thinks. Look at the micro-expressions."

I glance at Glenn for confirmation. My parents' reaction isn't normal. It's somewhere between a hole in my gut and a relief to see him meet my eyes with pity and understanding. There's no point in expecting human behavior from them. They study it like it's an alien response. But now I need more from them, even if it's only more information. "We just spoke to Steven Spiegler, and it was his phone that texted our photo to the news. He's been watching us, watching me, and now you're saying his sister is obsessive and you worked with their father on torture? There's too much going on to be a coincidence."

Glenn leaves the corner by the sculpture, coming to stand behind me. "Do you know where this building is?" he asks, and I add, "Please."

My father answers. "Somewhere in West Virginia?" He eyes my mother for confirmation, and she nods. "We drove about an hour and a half, but I couldn't tell you the way."

"James was driving," my mother explains. "He always drove. He liked the control."

"We certainly couldn't leave until he was ready." My father's expression darkens. "A ridiculous place for a research facility."

An isolated lab. Owned by a straight-up evil scientist. Whose daughter is fixated on my mother and obsessed with research on torture. Whose son has been stalking me, photographing me, framing me for the disappearance of my sister. My missing sister, who was investigating these torture-based experiments.

I'm ready to leap into action, to leave this awkward conversation behind and rush out to find Ava. But I let the silence draw out a little longer. My parents are good at silence, and it fills the room with a weight I still find suffocating. That heaviness contains all my unanswered questions about their culpability, their lack of love, why we still pretend to be a family.

Then Glenn puts his hand on my shoulder, as if to bolster me. "One last question," he asks. "If Cristina's involved, what do you think is going on?"

My father looks at my mother, and I think there's blame in that gaze. "If your speculation is correct, I would assume Cristina is continuing her research."

"But why would she take Ava?"

My mother blanches, whispering, "Because she's angry."

Glenn leans down. "What's she going to do?"

But my mother only shakes her head.

Standing up, my father says, "I think we should share this information with the authorities. Cristina had a tendency to be . . . overzealous."

I'm still reeling. Ava could be afraid, tortured, in danger. Then I realize what he said. He wants to talk to the police.

My mother looks as skeptical as I feel. "What information? That Zoe—their primary suspect—broke into a home, stole evidence, evaded arrest, and thinks that maybe there might be a slight connection to work we did decades ago . . . all based on a few scraps of paper and an interview that—I'm guessing—would be inadmissible in court?"

With a small nod to acknowledge her point—because after all, they're just positing and testing a theory—my father says, "Understood. But what's the alternative? Zoe and Glenn go off on a wild-goose chase? Even if they were to find Ava, even if she's being held against her will, how are they equipped to bring her back?"

I say, "That's the time we'd call the police. Once we know where she is."

My parents lean toward each other as if I hadn't even spoken. "Perhaps," my mother says, "this is the time to hire a professional. I think we both agree that the police are ill equipped to—"

A knock at the door cuts her short.

My breath catches. Another delivery person? Other than that, no one comes to my parents' house. Did they call the police somehow? But no, they appear just as startled as I am.

"Don't answer it," my father says decisively. "We're not expecting anyone."

As if to argue, the pounding gets louder, and the doorbell buzzes.

"Ava." My mother stands up, letting her glasses fall to the floor. "It's about Ava."

It's the cops. They've found me. Or—and my buzz of adrenaline runs cold—it's a death notification. They've found my sister too late. I barely register rising to my feet.

My mother hurries to the door in an awkward gait, almost a run. My father stands, but he doesn't follow her. His hands clutch at each other and he looks at me. "Zoe," he says, "you should go into the kitchen. Just in case."

He's saying that I'm wanted by the police, but he's implying he wouldn't turn me in. This is the first time I've felt like my dad's protecting me, that he might actually care.

Shaking off Glenn's hand, I shrink back so I won't be visible from the hallway, but not before I see my mother is opening the door to two figures silhouetted against the fading daylight.

"Mrs. Hallett? Did you know your son-in-law was involved with both your daughters?"

Reporters. Did a neighbor call them when we showed up, or is this just terrible luck?

They're still shouting—"Do you know where Zoe is? Do you think Ava's alive?"—when my mother slams the door shut with more force than I thought possible.

She pivots to face me. She's ghastly pale and the corners of her eyes are drooping. "Are you okay?"

I don't know how to answer. The reporters are just on the other side of the door, ready to strip my bones and declare me the villain. And if they know Glenn's here, they'll never leave. They can't get a picture of us. Not another one.

Glenn says, "I'm going to check the back of the house." He disappears into the kitchen.

I join Mom in the entryway and Dad comes with me, his breathing as rapid as if he'd been running. Something else I never imagined seeing. He pulls a handkerchief from his pocket, one of the cotton ones he sends out with his shirts every week to be cleaned and pressed, and dabs his forehead. "This isn't what I expected."

Does he mean from me? Or to happen this afternoon? But whatever he meant doesn't matter, because he sticks out a hand and, like someone touching an exotic animal, pats me twice on my arm.

He clears his throat and then says, "So, you have some sort of plan?"

I'm still reeling from his attempt to express concern. "Yes. I mean, sort of."

My mother says, "If they think Ava's being held in James' old cabin, the logical way to find it would be to ask his son. The one they just interviewed."

And she's right. "That's the plan," I agree. We'll track down Steven Spiegler again. And this time I won't be stupid or blow my chance. I'll get every answer we need.

Mom studies my face, and I see unfamiliar uncertainty in her gaze. "Zoe, if your theory is correct, if Cristina has anything to do with this, it could be said that my actions contributed . . ."

Does my mother feel guilty? If so, it's the first emotion we've ever shared. But I have to be honest, and there's no way Dad or Mom would have hurt us on purpose. Even after my years of rage, even after I ran away, they still took me home. Because as awful as they are at parenting, they have always tried to follow the letter of the law, if not the spirit. "No, Mom, this isn't your fault."

She shakes her head a little, unconvinced, and her eyes don't leave mine. "I can't . . . I mean, it's such a loaded word, with cultural associations and . . ."

I don't understand what she's trying to say, but this time I don't feel stupid. She's not being clear or precise like usual. She's struggling.

Moving as stiffly as a marionette, my mother gives me a swift hug. It's unyielding, but her gray bob brushes my cheek like a kiss. "I'm your mother," she whispers, over-enunciating the word. "I'm trying."

And before I can recover, my father steps in and I'm pulled close and then released, the scent of soap and starch lingering longer than the hug itself lasted.

Glenn calls, "If we run, maybe we can get out through the back."

"Be careful," my mom says. "Your father and I will make a distraction."

I say, "I'll call you with the address, when we get it. Then you can send the police after us. They might not believe what we think happened, but maybe they'll come after me and Glenn."

My mother nods. "Please be careful."

I nod, hesitating in front of these strange new parents.

And then I run.

28

ZOE

I CAN'T EVEN IMAGINE what my mother means by "a distraction," but Glenn and I creep out through the back door. Unlike Ava, my parents haven't planted a charming herb garden or arranged wrought-iron furniture and glass gazing balls. This backyard is a boring rectangle of green grass, and we're trapped here by an eight-foot red-cedar privacy fence.

We can't just burst through and sprint down the block to Glenn's car, because the gate opens on the front lawn. *Hello, reporters.* Our only chance is to jump the fence into the yard behind us. Then we'll be one street over, and if we run, we might just get away. But climbing the fence will make us visible. We don't even want to speak, because the reporters might hear us.

Glenn meets my eye and indicates with a jerk of his head that he's ready.

The fence has only two horizontal rails, one right at the bottom and one at the top, nothing we can use to scale it, but at least there aren't any points or spikes. Through two of the slats, I can make out something in the yard behind us . . . a trash can.

Glenn sees it too. "If one of us got over and threw that back . . ."

But how can we do that without drawing any attention?

Then the world fills with sound. The initial blare of the siren terrifies me. Is it the police? But no, it's coming from my parents' house. They've triggered the security system. And there's a secondary sound, a car alarm. On top of that, I hear my mother's stern voice, not shouting, not exactly, but cutting through the din around her. "Go on! Get off my property! Do you hear me?"

Glenn makes a stirrup with his hands, and I step into it without hesitation. As he raises me up, the sprinkler system hisses on, and sprays of water rise while I scramble over the top of the fence.

I land heavily, but immediately wrap my arms around the trash can, using my knees to lift it up. Struggling, I push it up the fence, using my shoulder when I can, pressing it up and up until the weight is gone and it falls into my parents' yard. From the shouting, I guess the reporters are too busy trying to stay dry to notice.

In a breath, Glenn is up and over, hitting the ground with a grunt. And we are off, sprinting to the gate. I barely notice the elderly woman opening her back door, her gaping mouth already a fading memory as we hit the street, Glenn's car in our sights.

Once we're safe inside, we both start laughing, all the fear and the tension spilling out in near hysteria. Glenn passes me his phone. "Guess you better search for Spiegler again."

"Spiegler Junior." My giggles subside as Glenn starts the car, carefully heading away from my parents' house and the mob of reporters. "Hey," I say to him. "Thanks."

He squints at me from the corner of his eye. "Just trying to find my wife."

"Me too." I lean over the phone. What I want to say is that I forgive him for not choosing me. Hell, I'm kind of grateful. If Glenn and I had stayed together, there would have been no Andrew for me, no Emma. I would always have been angry and guilty, the girl who'd stolen her sister's man. That guilt would have poisoned my future. And I didn't love Glenn, not the kind of healing, supportive, forever love I feel for Andrew. The only thing I was good at was self-sabotage, and Glenn was just another example.

"I need her to be okay," he says softly.

"Me too." Ava is my way out from under the mess I've made. She's my chance at a fresh start with Andrew and Emma, if I can convince him to give me one. But despite the terror and longing of that desire, I know finding Ava is about even more than my future. It's about our past.

No matter how far apart we've grown, no matter how different I thought we were, she and I are bonded, the only two creatures in the world raised in an environment created by my parents. We share more than blood. We share a history of nights huddled under the same blanket, whispered stories and secret glances, an understanding that the world shouldn't be like this.

And maybe it's good she knows I made it out. That piece of paper with my Texas address on it could be a sign she still cares somehow. I want to show her my life is different, and to know hers is too. We were formed by where we came from, but it doesn't have to determine our future.

Not if I find her in time.

* * *

AVA

I'm all alone. No one's coming. There's no one to see me release my grip on the metal cage, my fingers cold and sore from gripping it so tightly. No one sees me sink down to the floor, wrap my arms around my knees, and sob. This is not who I am, not someone I'd let anyone see. I cry to myself, I hug myself. And the whole time I know Beckett's even worse off. Against my closed eyelids I can see him bound to the chair, writhing in pain.

Time passes in a haze of fear and regret. Maybe I should have spent the hours making peace with my past, but all I can think is that I need more time. Time to embrace Glenn, time to forgive Beckett, time to learn who Zoe is now and what being sisters could really mean. *Once there were two sisters, separated from each other by a vast and thorny wilderness, who were never reunited.*

I'm still groggy when Phil comes back into the room, the cattle prod in his hand. Something inside whispers to me *You're getting what you deserve* as he pulls me back out of the cage and zip-ties my hands behind me. "Can I put my shoes on?" I ask, and then, "Where's Cristina?" but he acts like I've said nothing.

When he shoves me through the door into a narrow stairwell, he keeps a firm grip on my two hands bound together behind my back. While it's true I could wriggle out of these bonds, I can't very well do it while being shocked by a cattle prod.

I might have earned everything that's happening, but I'm no martyr either, walking placidly to my doom—no, resistance keeps building and building inside me. Every time my shoulders strain or I feel discomfort in my wrists, I want to step through the loop of my arms and snap the zip ties like I did before.

Then I remember Beckett, and I choke that desire back down.

Phil opens another door and shoves me through; then I understand why he's holding so tightly to me. We're in the hollow shaft for the missile. I'm standing on a metal walkway edged with a thin railing that encircles a terrifying abyss, a column of pure nothingness. The light from the room behind us isn't bright enough to see the opposite wall, so all I can see is the railing and darkness. My feet make the metal grating groan, and it echoes again and again above and below us.

He moves me along the metal walk, away from the doorway. "Keep going."

I shake him off. "Where's Beckett?" On the screen he'd been in a small room, nothing like this.

The cattle prod pokes me hard, but Phil hasn't powered it up. I slip in my stockinged feet, stumbling forward until I feel the railing press under my ribs like a Heimlich before he yanks me back by my bound hands. "Just go slowly."

My whole body is humming with the shock of cold air rushing up and over my face. Phil gives me a little shake, his nails digging into my arms. "Move."

I slide my feet out one at a time, waiting for my eyes to adjust to the darkness, but they never do.

We go only a few feet before he stops me. "Right here."

Phil releases me, and for a moment I stand alone in the dark. I know I could rush at the railing and throw myself over. I could, but that's how stubborn hope is. Even when it's clear I can't escape any other way, I just can't force myself to die.

Suddenly harsh light floods over me, and I flinch, unable to tell if it's a spotlight or a desk lamp, but blinding white is all I can see and my assaulted eyes sting.

After the seconds it takes for my vision to adjust, I see the railing runs in a circle around a shaft about fifty feet across, and on the opposite side is a hooded figure who looks like he's standing in space. Squinting against the harsh light, I see that the figure is tied to the outside of the railing, hanging over the abyss.

All the terror I couldn't feel for myself swamps my senses. My head and stomach spin as though I were the one hanging there, helpless. All at once I know this is what they're going to do to me. "Beckett," I whisper, and the hooded head jerks upright, as if looking for me. Maybe this figure is too short to be Beckett, maybe my desperate mind is grasping for nonexistent proof it isn't, couldn't be, him, but between the darkness of the abyss and my own panic, I can't tell.

"Why are you doing this?" I choke.

Phil grabs the back of my neck. "Forward," he says.

We start walking again, making our way around the perimeter. I swear I can feel a breeze rising up from the darkness that laps at the edge of the metal walkway, and a chill tendril snakes around my ankles.

As we approach the hooded figure, I want to break free and rush to help. Now that I'm closer, the figure does look smaller than Beckett, and the clothes, silky black trousers and a fitted T-shirt, look feminine. They look, I realize with a chill, like my own.

"You feel sorry for him?" Phil sounds mildly curious. "You want to save him?"

Even through my confusion, I can't control the "Yes" that escapes my lips like a sigh.

"Would you take his place?"

I stumble, my feet giving the answer I'm too proud to say. I do feel sorry for Beckett or whoever this figure is, but I would do anything not to hang over that abyss. Even falling into it would be preferable to being suspended, helpless.

We are standing a couple of feet away now, and I have just enough time to notice how thin the figure seems, much smaller than Beckett, surely, before a chill needle pierces my neck. I sink to my knees, reaching for anything to hold me up, but darkness overwhelms my consciousness.

*   *   *

I snap from oblivion to discomfort in the same second. My arms are now fastened separately, one out to each side, my shoulders pulled backward.

Against my face I can feel a dank updraft, and I'm afraid to open my eyes, afraid I won't see anything. I am standing on a surface and my ankles are also bound to something behind me, a cold metal rod. My eyes are still squeezed shut, like a child afraid of the dark. I am not a child, but I am afraid, so afraid. When I open my eyes, I see the infinite open space before me. No railing, no wall.

I try to back up, to scramble away from the edge, but I am bound too tightly. The same restraints that keep me from falling to my death also keep me from retreating to safety. The void below me fills my head with a rush of vertigo. I wish I were unconscious again.

From behind me, Cristina says, "I'm going to ask you some questions."

"Why are you doing this?" I cry.

There is a light shining on the opposite wall, like the light from a projector without film. Craning my neck, I can see the beam comes from somewhere above me, but I can't make out its point of origin. I catch Cristina's movement in the edges of my vision, but I can't really see her either.

When she speaks, her voice is completely devoid of emotion. "Remember what I showed you on the computer? Now look straight ahead."

My whole body is shaking, shuddering, and only the bonds on my wrists and ankles hold me upright.

A film suddenly appears projected in the square of light on the wall, like some kind of documentary made with a handheld camera. The image judders before settling down, so I can see Beckett sitting shirtless in a wooden chair, electrodes taped to his bare skin.

The last time I resisted Cristina, I saw Beckett get shocked. Now I'm even less able to help him, but I'm so scared and disoriented, I forget to be smart. Horrified, I hear the words coming out of my mouth. "Your dad, he studied psychological interrogation, not torture. This isn't real."

Cristina laughs, thin and cold. "My father isn't here. Neither are your parents. This is real. Look at the wall. Do you believe that's really Beckett?"

Panting, I stare at my ex-husband, his eyes wide with fear. It is Beckett, no question. "But the hood . . ." When I saw him jolted with electrical shocks, there was a hood over his head; maybe that wasn't him. Or maybe this is my storytelling instinct, my liar's mind, warping the truth, trying to escape this grim reality.

"For the connectivity." Cristina sounds like she might be smiling. "Would you gamble with his life? What would you tell me to save him?"

The screen flickers and the image of Beckett in a chair is replaced with one of the hooded man. Is his chest too thin? Are his trousers, his hands, his arms the same as my ex-husband's? How could I have been married to Beckett, known him so well, and still be unsure now? It's a damning indictment of our relationship, of all my relationships.

I wish I could believe this is footage of someone else, that Beckett is okay, he has to be okay, but then the light goes off again and a soundtrack comes on.

There is no mistaking the voice I hear in the darkness. It's completely recognizable. Beckett is pleading. It's hard to make out individual words, but I hear my own name, over and over again.

Cristina says, "What would you tell me, what would you give to save him? Would you transfer your money? Give me all your passwords? Power of attorney?"

If I give her that information, she'll clean out all my accounts and escape, just leave us here forever—I know this—but nothing I know matters while Beckett's cries are ringing in my ears. Then they stop, abruptly cut short.

Before I can draw a breath, Cristina continues, almost like she's reading from a script. "To save him, would you tell me everything about your parents, your sister, her daughter?"

Her daughter, Emma. My niece.

And that's the cost of compliance. Maybe I can spare Beckett pain, but there's nothing to stop Cristina from coming after the rest of my family—Glenn, my parents, even Zoe and her new family, the one I've never even met, her happy ending.

"I can't," I whisper.

Something strikes the metal fence next to me, sending reverberations through my body and echoing through the hollow missile shaft.

"Don't be stupid." Now Cristina's words are fluid, full of passion. "Imagine a world without torture. The atrocities of Abu Ghraib never repeated. A library of images we could use, footage to get real answers. That's what I'm working toward, a secret only those in power will know, a tool to make the world safer. And you, you selfish bitch, you can make it happen. The key to the whole thing is belief. Do you believe I will hurt Beckett?"

The screen in front of me flips back to show my ex-husband, tied to the chair. He's crying now, something I've only seen him do once, when I told him I was leaving. Answering tears well in my own eyes. "Yes," I whisper. She will hurt Beckett, and my words are all I have to save him.

"Then give me your answers. Tell me everything."

29

ZOE

Now Glenn and I are headed for Spiegler, and this time I won't let him get away. He took the picture that wrecked my marriage and made it look like I was plotting with Glenn, like we were guilty of murdering Ava. If his sister is our villain, he's definitely her accomplice.

Our plan is simple. Find him. Grab him. Make him talk. The first part was easier than I thought, thanks to the internet. Spiegler's listed as a panelist for a cybersecurity workshop at a tech conference downtown. Cybersecurity. I think again about my hacked email. *Asshole.*

I-66 is a river of red lights, cars bumper-to-bumper. My body is full of adrenaline with nowhere to go, and my mind is still processing what just happened at my parents' house. They embraced me, like they were being directed in a play about loving parents, but those brief moments of physical closeness made my eyes sting with unshed tears.

I will hug you twenty times a day, I promise Emma. My hugs will feel as familiar to her as her own skin and she will never have to doubt for a moment the vastness of my love for her.

And even though my parents' embraces were stiff, there wasn't anyone watching. There was no need for them at all. We could just call it quits and admit we're strangers to each other, but we aren't. We're family. Whatever they feel for me is the palest shadow of what I feel for Emma, and that makes me pity them.

Outside the car window, the sky is turning the deep indigo that precedes sunset. Ava and I used to play in the front yard of our old house on evenings like this. Lying on our bellies, we created worlds for our dolls in the grass. And I remember looking up from a handful of sticks to see my mother watching us from the doorway. Maybe her expression wasn't clinical. Maybe she really did want to understand the feeling of connection, but she was always on the other side of the glass.

Glenn and I are surrounded by cars, all going home to neighborhoods winding down, getting ready for evening. The air is cooler here than in Texas, but the sky Andrew and Emma are seeing from their car window on the drive home from the airport is the same. They'll see the same crescent moon, Saturn still shining brightly to one side, the "star" upon which Emma will make a wish. I squeeze my eyes shut and fiercely make my own. *Home.*

Finally we reach the exit for downtown Arlington, and it's lit up like Times Square. Especially in the business district, where streetlights illuminate pedestrians, store windows and upscale restaurants.

We pull up to a traffic light in front of the conference center. The scheduled parts of the event must be over, because the steps are littered with clusters of twenty-somethings and thirtysomethings, all wearing some variation of khakis and buttoned-down shirts with lanyards and name badges. It's an unbroken panorama of tech people with phones in their hands and laptop bags on their shoulders.

At the apex, right in front of the open double doors, I see Spiegler. In a sea of navy blazers, he's wearing lime sherbet. "There." I tap Glenn on the shoulder and point.

There's nowhere to park, not on this street, so when the light changes, Glenn joins the traffic creeping forward. He cranes his neck to look out the window. "Lot of camera phones on those steps. That's the wrong place to make a move. I'm going to go around the block."

As the car slows down, I catch a glimpse of a bar, surprisingly run-down for this part of town. I get the impression of a dark space, a tatty awning, and the neon silhouette of a horse; then we make a left turn down a little side street.

Glenn whips the car out onto the next street to a cacophony of horns. As we drive back toward the other side of the conference center, it seems like the whole block is under construction.

We can't snatch a man with a hundred witnesses around. There has to be another way to get him. I remember the way Spiegler seemed so amused by my questions at his house. He must have known Glenn was the one calling when he said to me, "It's always the husband." The taunting calls in Texas, the creepy game of hide-and-seek outside my parents' house when I heard Emma's voice—this guy likes to play games. Maybe we can lure him into a trap.

Anticipation flutters in my chest, the kind of buzz I used to get from sneaking out as a teenager. Glenn has Spiegler's phone number, but I'll use my phone, the anonymous burner to contact him. I don't know what will happen if I text Spiegler, I don't know if he'll believe my blackmail threat, but I need him to take the bait. *I can do this*, I tell myself. Lying is easier when it isn't face-to-face.

Quickly, before I can second-guess the plan, I compose a text message. *I know about Cristina and Ava. Do a job 4 me & I won't tell . . .*

As we pull up to another red light, I turn the screen toward Glenn, and after a quick glance, he nods.

If we can find out where the cabin is, if Ava's really there, I stand a chance of getting my life back, and it all comes down to Spiegler. Even if he knows this text is a trap, I just hope his arrogance makes him take the bait.

Glenn makes another turn, and I keep my head bent as we drive pass the conference center. As we approach the bar on the corner again, I confirm what I thought I saw. There's an alley beside it. The perfect place for an ambush.

I compose a second text without waiting for Spiegler to respond. *PaleHorseBar in 20 min.*

I watch Glenn scan the text, and with his nod of approval, I send this one too.

As we drive past the tech conference, I risk looking out the window and catch a glimpse of the lime-green jacket and Spiegler's head bent over his phone. Then it slides behind us again, as my phone chimes with an incoming text. A thumbs-up emoji.

That terseness makes my skin prickle with doubt. Everything seems to be going right, but I don't know what I'm doing. Not really. Spiegler does. He knows not to waste time asking who I am or how I got his number or any of the things that might prolong our interaction. He doesn't trust the person who sent the text, but I bet he thinks he understands. At least, he ought to understand the kind of person who would take advantage of criminal behavior to enact a little criminal behavior of his own.

That's the kind of person I need to be, at least for now. He has to tell me where his father's old house is. Ava has to be there.

I can't bear the alternative.

But in a flash, we are at the corner again and Glenn has turned left. "What's he say?"

"He'll meet us at that bar we just passed. Go around again and pull into the alley next to it."

As we circle the block, I see Spiegler striding along the sidewalk, his former insouciance gone. Now he looks like an extremely overdressed delinquent, the kind of wannabe tough who'd steal a laptop but run away from a Chihuahua. He glances to the side and I duck involuntarily. Did he recognize us?

Then we pass him, and with a bump, Glenn drives up and into the alley, all the way to the dead end where a dumpster sits. The brick walls of the two buildings on either side press in, framing a space so narrow I don't know if we'll be able to exit the car. Glenn rolls down his window, folds in the side mirror, and pulls almost flush to the wall; then we squeeze out.

We're standing on bricks covered with such a thick layer of dirt that you can't see the separation between them. On one side, the building has a low basement window with a grate over it, and then three more windows higher up, dark behind their wrought-iron security bars. It's not hard to imagine this building as an old factory or warehouse, back when barges still traveled on the Washington City Canal. On our right is the barroom, also in an old brick building. There aren't any visible security bars, but the windows facing the alley are darkened. The only light is a dim yellow bulb next to a service door. And the end of the alley is blocked by a gate, and the massive dumpster.

Heat is rising in my body, a righteous thirst for revenge. I wish we had timed it to herd Spiegler into the alley in front of our car, to chase him to the end, pin him against the dumpster, and make him scream.

But we don't want to kill him. We need information. We need to find Ava. That's the path to everything else I want. My nostrils fill with the smell of damp stone, the faint undercurrent of cigarette smoke, and the tang of exhaust. I hate waiting. I hate Spiegler.

Glenn stands at the entrance to the alley, waiting, but after ten minutes, our target still hasn't appeared. Spiegler must have seen me. My plan has failed. Maybe he's called the police.

I look down at my phone and type out another message. *Where r u?*

Almost immediately it lights up with a response. *@bar*

"He's already in there." I wheel around, ready to go charging after him, but Glenn grabs my arm.

"Wait, are you nuts? I'll bring him out."

The hell, I think, angry he's holding me back. But he might be right. Thinking about the picture Spiegler captured reminds me of the vicious emails, the threatening calls, standing in front of Emma's school feeling exposed and vulnerable. Everything I've lost. All that fear has curdled into something bloodthirsty in my gut. *It's not about you*, I remind myself. Glenn has tactical experience. At least, I think he does. "Okay," I say. "You do it. But I need your car keys."

He doesn't hesitate, reaching into his pocket and tossing them to me. "We'll get him," he promises, before making a crisp about-face and heading into the bar.

Some clenched fist in my heart releases. I didn't realize how much I needed Glenn not to hate me. Now he's actually treating me like we're on the same team.

Music and laughter spill from the front entrance of the bar as I climb into the car and sit on the edge of the driver's seat. Without taking time to adjust anything or turn on the lights, I let it roll backward until it's at the very front of the alley. I've turned it into a trap.

I slide back out between the car and the side of the building. I'm coiled with rising excitement, swamping my fear. This is the moment we might make Spiegler pay and get the information we need. But I'll never forget what he cost me.

And the door flies open. Spiegler stumbles down the steps. No, not stumbles. Glenn has a grip on the neck and hem of Spiegler's stupid green jacket and is giving him the bum's rush into the alley. My pulse leaps. Through the open doorway come the clanging of pots and shouting, then someone slams the door.

Glenn shoves Spiegler, who stumbles, before regaining his balance. He stands and looks around in the dim light. When he sees me, his eyes widen.

I ask, "Where are they?"

With the sly glimmer of a smile on his lips, Spiegler says, "Who?"

Glenn's hands form tight fists, and I reach out to grab his arm.

"Ava and Cristina," I tell Spiegler. "Don't be an idiot."

Spiegler's eyes dart from one of us to another. I can practically see his mind calculating the odds. He thinks he's the smartest person here, but he's never imagined a scenario where he couldn't escape. *If there are only two of them and the car is there and this is a dead-end alley . . .*

He answers mildly, but there's no color in his face. "I don't know. Haven't seen Crissy in a couple of weeks."

I can't hold Glenn back now; maybe I don't want to. He grabs Spiegler by the already rumpled lapels of his blazer. "Where. Is. She?"

Spiegler's not strong enough to break free of Glenn's grip, but he draws himself as far back as his jacket will allow. "I. Don't. Know. Beat me up if you want to. Won't change my answer."

"Then how have you been communicating with her?" I demand.

His eyes crinkle, like he's amused at a precocious child. "That's a good question. She's been calling me from a burner. Or so she says. The number changes every time. And there's usually no reception."

"She has Ava." I'm not asking. Saying those words makes me realize the truth. Ava could be alone, scared, hungry, in pain. I feel the echo of those things in my own body, and I wrap my arms around myself as though I could give my sister, wherever she is, comfort too.

"I thought she was going to take the husband," Spiegler says, arching an eyebrow at Glenn, who sets him down. Spiegler thinks he can finesse this, just like he's probably always talked or paid his way out of trouble. "Imagine my surprise when she told me about the change in plans." He straightens the sleeves of his rumpled blazer. "Guess you were a little too hard to grab."

"Are they in your dad's old cabin?" I ask again, trying to keep my voice as calm as his, trying not to show how angry he is making me.

Spiegler shakes his head, his bright eyes on mine. With a chill, I remember the tapping on the door, Ava's broken wristwatch, the sound of Emma's voice outside my parents' house. He knows all my vulnerabilities, and he's used them against me. "Cristina's too smart to tell me. This is her little game, not mine."

"But you helped her. You framed me. What did you get out of it?"

"She paid me."

But that wasn't the only reason. It couldn't have been. If he had Ava's watch, he'd gotten it from Cristina or he'd help her snatch my sister. And money wasn't motivation enough for the rest of it either. The photo, maybe. The emails. But the whispered threats, recording Emma, making me run out panicked in the night—these are the kinds of mind games you play for fun. "You got off on harassing and stalking me. What kind of person does that?"

"Did I scare you?" He actually looks hopeful, and anger swamps me. I stomp on his foot. Hard. His gasp of pain is worth it.

Glenn pulls me back and holds out the slip of paper with the blueprint of Spiegler's dad's house. "Tell us how to get to the cabin," he demands.

"And then what? You'll turn me in? Beat me up? Pay me? I think not." Spiegler crosses his arms. He really doesn't believe he's in any danger.

I pull the phone out of my pocket and hold it up. "Got your confession. Accomplice to kidnapping and accessory after the fact. And my parents—you know, Cristina's former employers—know everything too. If you don't help us, we're taking you straight to the police. Tell us where Cristina and Ava are, and we'll let you go."

"For how long?" Spiegler runs a hand over his hair, but it springs back into place as though untouched. He's considering it, though. I can almost see Spiegler's mind working, weighing his culpability and his chances of get- ting away scot-free. Now that we know what he did, the fun of tormenting me is over. He's the kind of guy who gets off on the anonymity, savoring his victim's fear and panic, and feeling superior, safe behind a wall of technol- ogy. And I bet he's got all kinds of money squirreled away.

As long as he stays ahead of the police, this cockroach will survive.

Go on, I silently will him. *Take our offer.*

With a sigh, he says, "Fine. I'll give you directions to the cabin."

"And any security codes," Glenn adds. I pull out a pen and hold it with the blueprint of the missile silo in front of Spiegler. When his hand closes on them, I don't let go. "If you lie to us, if for any reason we don't find my sister alive, you're taking the blame for all of it."

I let go suddenly and he takes a step back, before recovering. He drawls deliberately slowly, "So dramatic. Very impressive." But I can tell he's shaken. Asshole's used to tormenting people from behind a computer screen. Has he ever been held accountable face-to-face?

Spiegler scrawls a rough map and a few notes, then holds the paper out. "That's as close as I can get you. The last three turns don't have any road signs or markings, so I don't think you can make it in the dark."

I snatch the paper and pull up a map on Glenn's phone, glancing back and forth at the instructions and zooming in on the screen until finally I see it, a cleared space in the middle of the woods roughly the shape of the building on the blueprint. Is that where Ava is? I set it as our destination and nod to Glenn.

Spiegler starts inching away from us, edging himself closer to the street, and Glenn's hand shoots out, grabbing him by the upper arm. "Any security we need? Any codes or hidden keys? Remember, you only go free if we find her."

Spiegler's not scared enough for me, not half as scared as I was, standing in that parking lot, sure I was going to lose everything. He holds out a hand for the paper and adds a series of numbers before giving it back to me. "I can't swear she hasn't changed the code. She's not stupid."

I just want my sister back so I can go home. My whole life is there—my husband, my daughter, my friends. I have to believe I can rebuild everything my lies have shattered, and I won't let Spiegler make me lose sight of that goal.

But there's a furtive gleam in his eyes, like he still has the upper hand. He knows something more, something about what Cristina's done to Ava. He's amused at the thought of what we'll find after racing through the wilderness.

Glenn doesn't let go. "What if he contacts Cristina? The minute we're gone, he could warn her."

I study Spiegler, his brown hair in a styled pompadour, his eyes wide in false innocence. He did say Cristina called from burners, implying he didn't have her number. But he's also a lying liar. I should demand his phone, but instead I ask, "Why? Why's Cristina doing this? Why take Ava? What does she want?"

Surprise flickers through his eyes before he says simply, "Your mother. Cristina wants to be her daughter. Her *only* daughter."

"But they haven't worked together in years."

"Three years, almost to the day. That's how long she's been planning this."

"Why didn't she just kill us? Why is she playing games?"

Any hint of a smile is gone from Spiegler's face. "This isn't a game to Cristina. The science is her mission, and she thinks you and Ava are emotional distractions for your mother."

A familiar pang hits my breastbone and I feel unwanted, insignificant. A week ago I would have mocked the idea that my sister and I mattered at all to our parents. But that was before they distracted the reporters, before their awkward expressions of love. Now I think Cristina must understand my mother better than I ever have. I can't linger on this regret. "Why would she take Ava? Why not me?"

"Ava was easier to find, and you were easy to frame. Using Ava as her guinea pig just makes her lab work that much more fun."

Something in his expression makes me think he's been on the receiving end of Cristina's crazy in the past. Maybe money and sadism weren't the only reasons he helped his sister.

"How do we know she's still alive?"

"Until Cristina finishes her experiment, your sister will be fine. How strong is Ava, mentally?"

Glenn's face has been getting grimmer as Spiegler has been speaking. Roughly he yanks at Spiegler's blazer. "Give me your phone. And turn out your pockets."

Spiegler pulls out his phone and holds it up, allowing Glenn to take it. He digs into the pockets of his trousers, pulling out a slim black wallet and the off-white pocket linings. Nothing else. Not a tissue, not a breath mint. From his blazer pocket he produces a name tag with a tangled-up lanyard.

"Anything else?" Glenn gives him a shake.

"That's everything, officer. Let me go."

"If you warn her, if you've lied about anything . . ."

"You'll do what?" Spiegler puffs his chest, and I can't help myself. He knew Cristina took Ava, he helped frame me, and now if anything happens, if we get to the woods and Ava's already dead, he'll have escaped without any penalty.

I get in his face, close enough to smell his licorice breath freshener. "Put him in the trunk. If there's a problem, we can pull him out. Hell, maybe we can trade him for Ava."

Now Spiegler can't get away from me, not with Glenn holding his arm, holding it so hard it probably hurts. He looks at me with fear crinkling the corners of his eyes.

But he addresses me as if we were the only two people here. "What do you really want? Revenge on me, or your bitch of a sister back?"

My hands draw into fists, my nails cutting into my palms. It's like he's in my head, calling Ava a bitch like I have so many times before. But she's alone and afraid. And my anger at Spiegler almost made me forget how much she needs me. "Let him go, Glenn," I say. "He'll just slow us down."

Glenn doesn't let go. "I could knock him out, or we could tie him up, or—"

Then the door from the bar's kitchen opens, the light temporarily blinding in the dark alley.

With a quick twist Spiegler breaks free and is gone, leaving his empty blazer hanging from Glenn's fist.

We can't stop him from warning Cristina, we can't guarantee Ava will be at the cabin or that she'll even be alive.

But I have to go after her.

And pray we're not too late.

CHAPTER

30

AVA

I DON'T KNOW HOW long I've been hanging over the edge of the abyss, my feet perched on a tiny platform, my head tied into one position, facing the place where the movie plays.

My bound hands are now so numb I can't feel them at all. Layers of tears have dried on my cheeks and caked my eyelashes. Still the cycle continues—a video of Beckett, bound and terrified, then Cristina reappears with new threats, demanding more answers. "What if I told you that we've framed your husband for your disappearance, that he'll be arrested for your murder? Now will you tell me everything?"

Whenever I balk, the screen shifts to show the hooded man, his body spasming with electric shocks. After the second time, I don't argue or resist. I tell her everything she asks, anything I can think of. My social security number, my kindergarten teacher's name, the alarm code to my house, my first memory of my mother, a stream of unconnected answers, every scrap of information I've ever known.

Maybe a few days ago I would have lied, spun some kind of tale, but today I am powerless, physically and emotionally. I care about Beckett more than I care about my money, my information, my own pride. I didn't know I had this much caring in me.

Only when Cristina leaves and I'm alone in the vault am I free.

"Please," I cry to the darkness. "Please let him be."

I scream until my voice fails completely.

But no one is listening.

I am helpless to save myself or Beckett or anyone.

Not every story has a happy ending.

* * *

ZOE

As Glenn drives us through the woods at night, I feel like anything could happen. I've sent the map to my parents and told them we are on our way. The police might show up to help us or arrest us. We could find Ava. Or we'll find her remains. Maybe we'll save her, or maybe we'll all be captured and tortured too. This is the moment when all endings are still possible.

The darkness seals us into the car, and the tiny light from the map on Glenn's phone seems disproportionately bright. It highlights his lower jaw and the hard set of his mouth. If we're too late to save Ava and the two of us are the ones who find her . . . No. I can't even think it. Nothing Glenn and I shared before means anything compared to this moment. We both love Ava, more than proving our innocence, more than our own safety.

I know he must have regretted our affair—especially now—but the thought doesn't bring the stabbing pain it once did. It's diluted like a childhood memory of a broken limb. I remember the events leading up to our breakup, I remember the aftermath, but the poison has drained from it.

But the memory of Andrew packing his bag, his hunched shoulders, his grim mouth, is agony. I didn't know what loss was when Glenn left me. All I lost was him. Losing Andrew means losing an entire life—taking Emma to her first day of kindergarten, a thousand mornings kissing him as he leaves for work, making plans for our future. Year after year after year watching Emma grow and loving Andrew more. When I threw that rock at Ava, I didn't know what losing was. Three years won't be long enough to recover from this loss. Three lifetimes won't heal me.

I'd sell my soul for more time, but who knows if we'll even survive this night.

I tilt my head back against the seat. This is my only shot at earning back everything I've lost. My family and my sister.

We're hurtling along a road that's rutted and rough. The car bounces, almost skidding, and my breath catches. "Don't wreck us before we get there."

Glenn doesn't answer. I can't tell if he's slowed down at all between the blur of shadowy trees, the bumpy road, and the rising acid in my stomach.

This is exactly how I used to feel on our way back from the boarding camp my parents sent us to every summer. For reasons known only to them, they'd chosen one in the Catskills. Each July we made the seven-hour trip in a single shot, Ava and me together in the back seat. And I was usually the one who got carsick. No music, no radio, just my parents in a conversation we couldn't quite hear for hours. Ava had an iron stomach, and she would read out loud to me while I closed my eyes and tried to forget my queasiness. Her voice made the stories come alive. The thing that differentiated each year was not what happened on the drive—nothing ever happened—but what she read to me.

Now the only way I can quell my nausea is by thinking of her clear, precise voice. And suddenly it occurs to me that maybe she has been trying to talk to me, all these years, through those goddamn books.

I look over to where Glenn is just a shadow hunched over the steering wheel. "Did she ever write about you the way she did about me?"

I can't make out his expression in the dark. The silence stretches between us, and I let it bloom, giving him space to answer. Finally, after a long sigh, he says, "Not directly."

"Why was she doing it? I mean, she was never interested in my life for real, just in her books."

"I don't know, Zoe. I'm not much for fiction. I'll tell you one thing. Your sister does not waste her time writing about anything that doesn't interest her."

I sit with that for a minute, letting it sink in. "What about when she wrote about us? Right after . . ." No need to finish. He knows which book I mean.

"The way I see it, writing is the way she works out how she feels. It's like putting the situation into Bizarro-world and running through her emotional options."

"I thought she was messing with me. When I was in culinary school, she wrote *Santoku*, about a serial killer who fillets her victims with a santoku chef's knife."

And with certainty I know that if I told Andrew this story, he would laugh. Hard. And none of the things Ava wrote would matter then, because they aren't real. All those years she drove me crazy because the words felt like an indictment. Sometimes it was subtle, a crazy detective mispronouncing a word like I did; or creepy, like the time I got pulled over for speeding, and even though she couldn't have known about it, her next thriller featured a woman killing traffic cops; or really personal, like with me and Glenn. But it was all bullshit. Just fiction. Not true.

We drive in silence a few more minutes, until watching the road disappear under the hood of the car starts to make me even dizzier. Then Glenn says, "If she wrote a book about your life right now, I mean back in Texas, would you bail on it for something new?"

"Of course not." I've never been so instantly sure of anything.

"Then maybe all those other things were wrong choices in the first place."

He's right. My life in Texas is the one thing I'm not willing to give up. Lying about my identity brought me to the core of my true self. Ava couldn't ever take this from me. If I lose Andrew and Emma, it's because of the choices I made. And just like that, all the nausea, the fear, and the adrenaline rush back, pulsing through me with nowhere to go.

"Wait." I squint at the phone, the light leaving dim halos in my vision when I look up. "There's a turn."

Without answering, Glenn wrenches the wheel and we take a sharp angle. I'm thrown against the door. Then the trees begin to thin out, and the pale light of a full moon filters through.

Finally we bump out into an open clearing and come to a stop.

Through the windshield, I see a house, a sort of fancy hunting lodge with huge glass windows. A faint glow shines from an interior room; the porch lights are unlit. I don't see any other cars parked out front.

I suck in a hard breath. This is the house in the horror movie, and we're the sacrifices headed straight inside. No, I can't think like that. Not a horror movie, a fairy tale, just like Ava used to tell, where two sisters defeat the evil witch. But in the chill air, happily-ever-after seems like fantasy.

Glenn turns off the ignition. Before he opens the door, I blurt out, "Wait, do you have a gun or something? Because of work?"

He looks back at me, surprised and a little defensive. "I'm an analyst. I sit at a desk."

"But the government—"

"You know," he says, opening the glove box, "owning a gun increases your risk of being a victim of gun violence."

He pulls out something small and presses it into my hand. "It's a multipurpose tool," he says. "Big knife blade, also a screwdriver, pliers, and a corkscrew. Just in case."

"Don't you want it?" If I take this, Glenn won't have any defense. I don't care what he says; I'd feel safer with a gun.

"I'll be fine." He gets out of the car, and I follow.

In the autumn night, a chill breeze raises goose bumps on my arms. Spiegler gave us the right directions, but did he somehow warn his sister? It's hard to imagine he wouldn't have.

The house looks bigger here, looming above us, limned by the moonlight. Anything, anyone could be waiting inside. And it's quiet, quiet as death. Behind it I can see more branches stretching out, and above that, stars glow sharply against the inky sky. There's a faint milky spot I recognize as the Pleiades, the Seven Sisters. *Let it be a sign.*

But with the whispering forest stretching for miles around us and the menacing hunting cabin before us, hope seems very far away.

CHAPTER

31

ZOE

WE APPROACH THE house in silence. Without a keypad, the code Spiegler gave us is no good. I see the
bubble of a security camera affixed to the wall and put
my hand directly on top of it. Even if someone is watching, they won't know who we are.

Glenn tries the knob, and the door is locked. If Ava
weren't in danger, we could just knock, bluff our way
in, but I can't forget the word SERE and my father's
description of Cristina as "overzealous." Glenn steps
back as if he's thinking about breaking a window, then
rushes forward, throwing his shoulder against the
door. It shivers but doesn't break. He pulls back, considering, and this time he kicks it hard, right by the

knob. Once, twice, and the door flies open, a small piece of metal—the strike plate—hitting the ground at my feet.

And we are inside, with an open kitchen to the right and a large living area to the left. Both dark and quiet. I run straight ahead to a back hallway, flinging open one door and then another, checking behind a shower curtain, under a bed, calling my sister's name. After all, we broke in the front door, so there's no point in being quiet anymore.

This isn't the slow, methodical search I did of Ava's house. I don't care about the prim suitcase standing in a corner or the contact lens solution on the bathroom sink. Cristina Spiegler isn't an enigma I want to unravel. I'm looking for my sister, and everything else is just visual clutter. *Not* in the closet. *Not* behind that door. *Not* here. *Not* there.

What if I find Ava's body? My heart grows cold. *Not* Ava. Our past, our future gone. I hurry, as if I can outrun my thoughts. I hear a panting, whimpering noise, but it's me, struggling to suck in air and expelling little sobs at the same time.

Nothing. I find nothing, and it's like a nightmare of an abandoned world. Bedrooms empty, bathrooms and laundry room and closets all empty. I'm alone in the hallway; in the front room Glenn's shoving furniture around, stomping on the floor and listening after each thump.

My puzzlement must show on my face, because he says, "There's got to be a way underground to get to the missile silo. I've already been through the kitchen, and you opened the doors in the back, right?"

I did, I know I did, but fluttery panic rises again. Turning, I see a rustic staircase leading to a loft. Even though the loft itself is visible from here, with plush leather furniture and bookshelves, I have to make sure Ava isn't lying helpless just feet above us. I take the steps two at a time, heaving myself over the last one onto the wide planks of the floor.

There's a rug the color of dried blood and windows reflecting the interior lights so completely that they seem to close the room off from the outside world. Below me I can still see Glenn looking for an entrance or trapdoor. Ava's not here. But there is another room that opens off to the side, an open doorway through which I cannot see.

It's so quiet up here, I falter. Ava could be behind any corner in this house, just out of sight. I might find her, save her, and a future of possibilities would open. Andrew and Emma and a life of reconciliation and joy.

Or I might be too late. I can't imagine anything beyond that. Every surge of hope is met with biting fear.

Quietly I approach the doorway, the open-floor-plan type without a door, and slip through it.

There's a dead deer mounted on a plaque above a large wooden desk. The deer's black nose is huge and lined with white, its mouth a harsh bitter line, its antlers soaring up into sharp points. But the worst thing is the pair of glasses jauntily perched on its nose. They are grotesque, an insult. Stepping closer, I reach up to flick them off, and when they fall onto the desk, I see they are a woman's reading glasses.

There's a tremor in my hand as I pick them up. Are they Ava's glasses? I can't tell, because I haven't seen her in so long. The impassive glass eyes of the deer judge me. *This is how it is*, they seem to say. *You ran away. You didn't want a sister. You don't deserve one.*

I slip the glasses into my pocket like a good-luck charm. The surface of the desk is covered with papers. I pick up one packet, the manuscript of a book, and read the title: *New Directions in Information Acquisition: Solving the Human Problem.* Ava's the problem, the human problem. The dead deer, the lab rat, she's the one they're torturing. *Oh God, let her be alive.* I turn, running out of the room, propelling myself down the stairs, promising I'll be a better sister, wife, mother, just *better* if she's okay.

I miss a step at the bottom and pitch forward, but Glenn catches me. His hands on my shoulders, he searches my face. "What happened? Are you all right?"

My heart is pounding so hard, he must feel it shaking my body. "I'm fine."

Behind him I can see the room, its minimalist furniture scattered here and there, the black leather sofas askew, a metal lamp lying on the floor, but the lack of clutter makes even this disarray seem artistically arranged.

"Where else can we look?" I ask. No unopened doors, no furniture against the walls, hiding a secret passage. The only items left untouched are a few framed photographs hanging on the living room walls.

Pulling away, I run toward one, desperately hoping for a clue, a sign, anything. But it's only a black-and-white picture of this house. Behind me I can hear Glenn flipping pictures over, even breaking the frames. This is our last chance. The light gleams off the glass over the photograph until all I can see is my own reflection. I yank it off the wall, but instead of smashing it on the ground, I let it fall.

Behind it is a keypad.

Glenn gives a whoop of triumph and pushes me aside, already holding up the scrap of paper with the security code Spiegler gave us. By the time he types it in, I am vibrating, full of fear-fueled adrenaline.

Somewhere in the depths below us, a piercing alarm sounds, then cuts off. We freeze, looking at each other. Uncertainty flickers across Glenn's face, softening the angles of his brows. Then it settles back into its familiar lines as what seemed to be a panel of the wall slides open. We're at the top of a staircase that leads down into darkness.

Before Glenn can take that first step into this new doorway, a blur rushes past him.

And knocks me to the ground.

Everything is fur and teeth. No growling, no warning bark. A dog is lunging at my face, snapping, held back only by my outstretched arms and my hands clenched in the fur of its neck and chest. Its hot, fetid breath fills my lungs. I hear Glenn cry out, but there's no way for him to help. Everything's too fast.

After its initial lunge, I can tell the animal's smaller than it seems. My grip on its coat is deep, and I throw my body sideways and roll onto the dog, not away from it. Now the dog is on its back, pedaling its legs in a futile attempt to dislodge me. It's making noises, panting little whines.

Somewhere in the edges of my attention, Glenn is shouting, trying to get around me, but all my concentration is focused on making the attack stop. When Glenn disappears, I hardly notice.

The dog and I are at a standoff. It cannot tear out my throat or escape me, but I can't let go or outrun it. My knees are pinning it down. I think I see fear in its flat blue eyes, and it isn't snapping anymore. It's just protecting the house; that's its job. I'm not going to hurt a dog; it's only what people—evil people—have made it.

Then Glenn is back beside me. "Let go."

I push the dog to one side hard and roll away from it. Glenn lunges over me, cloth billowing in his hands. But the dog bursts up, attacking, and seizes him by the forearm, its teeth sinking deeply into his flesh. He's trying to hold it off with his other arm, and the curtain trapped between them is streaked with blood.

Before I can think, I'm on my feet. Glenn staggers under the weight of the dog. He must have raised his arm just in time to keep it from ripping out his throat. Despite the low, desperate growling in its throat and the terror in its eyes, the dog hangs on.

I try to grab the scruff of its neck, but Glenn shakes his head. "The sheet!" he shouts at me. "Wrap it!"

I grip the end of the curtain, but before I can pull it up over the dog's head, the animal moves again, biting swiftly once, twice, three times, moving up Glenn's arm, sending him reeling back against the wall and pulling me with them. I'm too afraid to breathe, but I force my hands forward, lifting the cloth higher than the dog's head. Glenn uses his free hand to pull the wrapping tight. The dog thrashes under the curtain and then the whole bundle falls to the floor. Glenn's arm is free, but his skin is torn and bloody.

We have to get away before the dog untangles itself.

Glenn is already moving through the open door and down the stairs. I follow, slamming the door behind us.

The air temperature seems to drop twenty degrees as I descend.

At the basement is another door with a keypad and a large wheel like a bank vault. Glenn is struggling to open it. His one good arm isn't enough. He calls to me. "Come on!"

"Wait, we have to stop the bleeding."

"There's no time."

But he's pale, so pale, and his mouth is drawn with pain into a tight line, like the deer in the study.

"If you pass out, you won't save her." Where can I find something to stop the bleeding? If I had been smarter or braver, I would have checked the kitchen before we came down the stairs, but I don't know how much time we have before the dog gets loose. My shoulder bag and cardigan are in the car, but I remember the all-purpose tool in my pocket. Quickly, before he can hurt himself anymore, I pull it out. "Give me your socks."

I cut a strip from the bottom of my T-shirt, cropping it, while Glenn slips his feet out of his shoes and struggles to remove his socks. Bracing himself against the door, he cradles his arm against his chest. I take the socks from him and ball them up, but a closer look at Glenn's arm stops me. The swollen skin is streaked with red and already darkening bruises, and the puncture wounds are still oozing. I pick the places where the bleeding seems heaviest and place the socks like pads there, then tie one end of my T-shirt strip around his arm and wrap everything as best I can.

"Keep the pressure on and raise your arm up!" I pull out my phone, frantically dialing 911, but I can't get a signal. Nothing. My whole body is shuddering, racked by the aftereffects of the attack, and I hear myself whispering encouraging lies. *It's going to be okay. You're doing great. Help is coming.*

But it's not enough. This is no skinned knee on a playground or even a sliced finger at a kitchen counter. Blood is everywhere—my hands, the floor, and already seeping through the makeshift bandages. I don't know how to stop it. But the dog is at the top of the stairs, and Ava is somewhere ahead of us.

We have to keep going.

Together, Glenn and I crank the door open, revealing another stretch of stairs. How far under the earth will we have to go? We stagger to the bottom, and opening the next door, we find a large room with a concrete column in the center. No one's here.

"Ava?" I call, but there's no answer. And then I see the two halves of an accordion fence splitting the room in two, creating a giant cage. Three open padlocks dangle from the steel trellis. This cage wasn't for lab rats or even the attack dog. There are folding chairs and bottles of water. *People* were held here. The sight of a lone woman's shoe in the corner feeds my darkest fears. Ava's shoe.

If Ava doesn't need her shoes anymore, if she's not in the cage being tested, we may be too late. My sister may be a bruised and barefoot corpse.

Oh God, she has to be alive. Where is she?

Then from behind a desk, a man in a lab coat rushes at us, his head tucked low. I cry out, throwing my arms up to defend my face, but he's not attacking. He's trying to get around us to the stairs.

Glenn grabs him by the sleeve and swings him away from the door. The guy stumbles back, and he's about my age, very thin, completely ordinary. He could be a delivery man or a bank teller or the manager of my local grocery store. He's nobody I'd look at twice. But now he's in a defensive crouch, his eyes wide with fear. And he's in this secret lair wearing a lab coat. My fear curdles into anger.

"Where's Ava?" I ask at the same time Glenn shouts, "Where's my wife?"

Lab Coat holds his hands up, but we advance on him and he backs away. "I don't know. Wait, just wait."

On the desk behind him I see medical tubing, charts, and a syringe. That's what's so awful about this room: not the things that are here, but the things that used to be—caged victims, medical experiments, and a twisted psychopath.

I'm getting answers. "Where's Cristina?"

Lab Coat flinches. "I don't know." And then he makes a break for the door. Glenn blocks him but cries out, even as he pushes Lab Coat away.

The stranger falls heavily, and faster than I can process the thought that he's inside the cage, my hands are struggling to pull the sides of the fence closed. Desperately I wrench the mesh together as Lab Coat scrambles forward.

Glenn is right behind me, reaching around me to snap the first lock, then the second, and then the gate is secure enough that I can step back while he snaps the third. He fumbles this one, his fingers slipping before he gets it locked.

"We know Cristina did this," I say to the guy in the cage.

At the sound of her name, a shiver ripples over him. "She isn't finished. If you spoil her results, she'll be unhappy." There's a disconnect between the word *unhappy* and the kind of person who keeps a killer dog and humans in cages. The kind of disconnect between action and emotion I've seen in my mother. He backs away from the fence, shaking his head. "I can't help you. I won't."

Then beside me, Glenn sways and drops to the ground.

CHAPTER

32

ZOE

IGNORING THE MAN in the cage, I kneel beside Glenn, placing my fingers on his throat where the pulse beats. His breathing is steady, but his arm is still oozing cherry-bright blood through the crappy bandage I made. It's not gushing, but he's pale, and sweat beads along his hairline.

I rush to the desk with the medical supplies, knocking the syringe and stethoscope to the ground. Under the medical tubing is some tape and a packet of gauze, tiny and useless. I take the tape and kneel beside Glenn.

His eyes flutter open, and to my horror, he starts trying to get up.

"Stay down," I order him. "You'll bleed to death." But as soon as he starts to move, his eyes roll back and his head falls heavily on the concrete floor. I don't know what I'm doing. I've only practiced "mom medicine," patching up invisible scrapes and putting Band-Aids on minor bumps. But I have to do this. I take the tape and wrap it around Glenn's wrist. Maybe if I make it tight enough, it'll supply pressure. That's the only thing I know about wounds. You have to keep them under pressure. So I wrap the tape up his arm and then again back down, crisscrossing it over the sodden T-shirt bandage.

When the tape is gone, I sink back on my heels, my stomach churning with the effort of holding my shit together. I can't fall apart, no matter how frightened I am. I'm all Ava has left.

Glenn's completely vulnerable, but I have to go. We've checked the whole house, the attack dog can't get through the door, Lab Coat is in a cage. Glenn will be fine. He has to be.

Ava's still in danger.

I rise to my feet and realize Lab Coat has been silently watching every move I make.

I step right up to the cage. "If you don't tell me how to find my sister, I will leave you where you are. They'll never find you. You'll never get out."

My voice is low and menacing, and I'm selling it with everything I have. His body collapses inward, just a little bit. He's not a psychopath. The things he was doing down here affected him, even if he didn't know it. And his greatest fear is being the one in the cage, overlooked and alone.

He whispers, "The police—"

"The police will save *you*? They only care about Ava. We'll hide that secret doorway and no one will ever see you again."

"I don't—I can't—I mean, it wasn't me. It was her. This whole plan. It was her. And nobody was hurt, not really. We used old footage and videos. But Cristina took it too far."

"Where is she?" Without Glenn, I'm afraid I'll be lost down here, running through a claustrophobic subterranean maze. But I can only go forward. There's no way to carry Glenn up the stairs, no way to get past the dog, and no future for me unless I find my sister.

"I don't know where Cristina is."

"Ava! Where is Ava!"

"Don't leave me down here. Let me out and I'll show you." But his gaze shifts past me, and I turn to see a door beside a file cabinet.

I hurl myself toward it as Lab Coat shouts behind me, "When Cristina finds you, you'll wish *you* were in this cage!"

I open the door onto a metal stairwell like an indoor fire escape. My hand is already on the knob of the next door when I hear a thump coming over and over from above. *Ava.*

I sprint up the staircase, each step clanging beneath my feet.

Panting, I fling open the door of a room that's completely dark except for a red light shining like an eye. I grope for the light switch, and an overhead bulb illuminates a small room, barely big enough for the wooden chair in the center of it.

The chair with a bound and hooded figure in it. "Please," a man croaks.

And it is a man, slight of build, wearing soiled khaki trousers and a stained pinstriped cotton shirt. Not Ava, but another human guinea pig.

"It's okay, I'm here." Gently I touch the black cloth, rolling the bag over the man's head and exposing the contours of his face, patchy dark stubble over his jawline, the blackened smudge of a bruise on his cheekbone. Only then do I look at his whole face, his brown eyes on mine. *I think I know this man.*

"Beckett?" We are not quite strangers, although we never met. I've seen him in a photo from the wedding I didn't attend, and after the divorce I looked him up online. From his confused expression, I'm thinking he didn't do the same for me. Why is he here?

"Ava's my sister." Clumsy with fear, I pull out the multi-tool and start clipping the duct tape binding his arms and legs to the chair.

"Zoe?" So he does know my name.

"What did they do to you?" I finish slicing his right arm free, but there's something hanging off the duct tape, some kind of wires. Before I can move to the other arm, he says, "No, take it off. Quickly!"

I work my fingers under the edge of the duct tape. It's stuck directly to his arm, so I treat it like a Band-Aid and yank it as hard and fast as I can. I expose more than Beckett's bare arm. On the underside of the duct tape are electrodes, but the wires running from them are taped harmlessly to the back of the chair.

Now that one hand is unbound, Beckett is scrabbling at the duct tape on his other arm, but it's wrapped more than once and his hands are clumsy. This time I cut the wires leading to his arm and legs, then hack through the tape.

"Where is Ava?" I ask, afraid to hear the answer, as I work on his second leg. There's a stench that recalls the animal smell of the cage.

"I don't know." His nerveless hands fumble to peel back the cut tape. "Cristina might have seen us. We have to get out of here."

"Not without my sister." The way he keeps looking behind me to check the door creeps me out. I'm finding it hard to concentrate on clipping the duct tape without hurting him, because I feel like someone's hovering behind me.

As soon as his legs are free from the chair, he stands, then staggers. I jump to my feet in time to keep him from falling.

Beckett leans heavily on me and he tries to steer us both to the door, saying, "We have to go before she comes back."

How did Ava describe him after the divorce? "Weak." I guess that was all it took for her to call it quits. I can't be weak, not now. I have to be strong enough to find her and bring her home.

"I'm not going anywhere without Ava." I speak sharply, but he doesn't even look at me, too lost in his own panic.

"Ava's dead. She has to be. If you saw what I saw—" He pushes away from me, but I grab him, holding his arm as hard as I can.

"What happened?" The torture was supposed to be faked, but Beckett's terror is real.

"I saw it on the screen. They crucified her. And if Cristina finds us, she'll do it to you too!" With desperate strength, he wrenches himself free and stumbles through the door.

Stunned, I follow him down the stairs, unable to process the word. Crucifixion? Like on a cross? The word is so far from anything I expected that it reverberates in my mind.

Beckett lurches down the stairs, faster and faster. "Wait!" I yell after him. He has to help me find Ava. He has to . . .

But he barrels right through the door to the cage room, leaving me alone.

I can't follow him. I can't run, not yet.

Ava's waiting.

CHAPTER

33

ZOE

WHEN THE DOOR shuts, the sounds of Lab Coat shouting and Beckett's retreating footsteps are cut off abruptly. I'm left at the base of the stairs, facing the other door in absolute silence. No keypad on this one. The knob turns easily, but the thick door is hard to push open.

I rush through so quickly I almost plunge headfirst over a metal railing. I catch myself, just in time, but I can't look away from the void in front of me. The darkness has depth; it seems deeper the more I look at it. And there's the rising thrum of animal fear, the fear of falling, the fear of oblivion, the fear of death.

My breath is shallow as I step back, dizzy with the close call and the rising sense of danger.

I call for my sister, overwhelmed by the vastness of the space, and my voice echoes again and again as though the world is crying out Ava's name.

And then I see something, a figure standing on the walkway across the open expanse from me. No, not standing. Hanging out over the void with its arms stretched out to either side and head raised. At the chorus of her name repeating, the head struggles, bound in a fixed position. And it's all I can do not to vault over the space between us.

Ava.

"I'm coming," I shout, and take off running to the left. My footsteps fill the missile silo with sound. Ava is saying something, but her voice is weak, and I'm moving too quickly to hear her. I am running faster than I can control, all my fear and guilt and love making my feet race so fast that when something trips me, I go flying.

I skid along the metal walkway on my belly. One arm ends up underneath the railing, my hand clutching at empty space.

Then a woman's voice cuts through the dark. "Ava, this must be your little sister."

Scrambling to my feet, I scan the silo. There by the door, backlit against it, is a slim figure. She pushes the door closed, and then with a clack that reverberates like a shot, she locks it.

Cristina.

She flips a switch and around the edge of the walkway a few bulbs turn on, driving back small patches of the darkness but intensifying the shadows in the center. Now I can see a woman with short dark hair and a slight, wiry build, holding a stick or something in her hand. She doesn't look like a monster. Just like her accomplice, she looks ordinary, except for the way she's paired silky black trousers with hiking books. She could be a high school science teacher, a financial analyst, an optometrist, a neighbor who signs for your mail. But she is none of those things.

Cristina is the woman who took and tortured my sister.

I have to stall her long enough to get to Ava. "Cristina," I say. "Cristina Spiegler. Steven told us everything. The police are outside."

"Bull-fucking-shit." She strides closer, the heels of her hiking boots booming. "You are such a screw-up, just like my brother. What exactly do you think you can accomplish?"

I match her pace by backing up, a little closer to where Ava is perched, helpless and bound, over the space in the center of the missile silo. Only about six feet more . . . but Cristina is also only six feet away from me, and I've seen how quickly she moves.

She says, "Why are you even here?"

All I can say is, "She's *my sister.*"

"What does that mean?" she scoffs. I could swear her eyes are glowing. "This study was based on relationships, and I knew torturing her ex-husband would get better results than torturing you."

"What did you do to her?"

Cristina ignores my question. "We only needed you to take the fall. But here you are on some kind of rescue mission. Maybe I misread your relationship after all."

"It's over now. You have to let us go."

"What makes you think it's over?" She sounds chillingly indulgent, like she thinks I'm stupid but she's willing to hear my explanation. My mother uses this trick, and it always makes me shrink inside.

"I'm not alone." But my voice doesn't sound convincing. "The police are coming."

And she laughs, a sound pure, clarion, and cruel. "Do you really think *this* was my end game? A sample group of only two subjects? Your mother hasn't even seen my results. And this was just the warm-up."

Then Cristina lunges forward like a fencer, the stick in her outstretched hand.

Instinctively I scramble backward, and it hits the metal railing, sending a shower of sparks into the darkness. I hear Ava's scream, so weak it's mostly air.

Cristina takes a slow, deliberate step closer, her eyes drilling into mine. I think she missed on purpose, because it's more fun now that I know what she's holding. And if I turn to run, she will definitely skewer me with that shock stick.

"Your sister was the basis of my preliminary study. From here I'll go to countries where no law can touch me, places with funding and disposable human subjects."

"Why are you doing this?" I ask, not really caring, determined to creep another step closer to Ava.

Something shifts in Cristina's face, an idea coming to life, and she says, "Now that you're here, it might be fun to run the experiment again. Especially since you do seem to care about her."

I can't help looking at Ava, and the minute I take my eyes off Cristina, she strikes. I catch a glimpse of motion and throw myself forward, closer to Ava, landing on my stomach on the metal railing, but I'm pinned like an insect with Cristina's boot on my back.

"Poor little sister," she croons. The grating of the walkway is icy against my face.

And then I hear Ava's voice again, calling my name.

My love for Andrew and my loyalty to Ava give me strength. I'm not alone, not truly.

Grabbing the railing for extra leverage, I twist out from under the foot holding me down, but it kicks, catching me under the ribs. I'm on my back looking up, so I see the clinical interest she takes as I gasp at the stabbing pain.

"If I let you go, would you leave Ava behind?" She sounds only mildly interested, like this isn't a life-or-death offer.

This question is clearly theoretical, and that's the insult. "Fuck you."

I kick hard at her legs, and when she flinches, I scramble to my feet. Now that I'm standing, she's no taller than I am. Maybe I could take her in a fair fight, but there's no fairness here. Only survival.

For me and for Ava.

Cristina is stalking me now with deliberate steps. Then she lunges again, and I backpedal, staying just out of reach of the electric stick. I need to slow Cristina down, but how? I say, "Scientists are supposed to help people. What's the matter with you?"

She smiles, thin and mean. "I *am* helping people. People who want information."

I'm right beside my sister now. The platform she's standing on is slightly lower than the walkway, so her head is about shoulder height, and she's facing the abyss. I *can't* go any farther around the walkway. I *won't* leave my sister exposed to this vicious woman. Ava is straining to move her head, trying to see what's happening. She's helpless, like I always wanted, but am I strong enough to save her? I think of that stone, throwing it through the window. This is my chance for redemption.

My insides are shredded with terror. I fumble in my pocket for the multi-tool, but there isn't enough time.

Before my fingers find it, Cristina pounces again, the stick buzzing with power.

My back is against the railing; I can't retreat, so I throw myself forward. The edge of the stick grazes me, searing my side, but through some miracle my hands grab right below its handle and yank it forward.

Cristina's momentum from her lunge sends her past me, right up against the railing.

She catches herself and spins to face me, her arm extending so the shock stick is pressed against Ava's neck.

I pull up short. The voltage could hurt Ava, maybe kill her that close to her head. Panic rises like bile in my throat. My sister is so pale that the circles under her eyes turn them into hollows. And for the first time I realize that she and Cristina are wearing the same clothes.

Cristina's panting, but her lips are curving into a smirk. She says, "Back up. Right now."

"Don't hurt her." I draw back, just a little. My big sister, who protected me from the dark and told me bedtime stories, looks like she's already dead.

Then Ava's ashen lips part, and she whispers, "Run, Zoe."

"That's right, Zoe. Run." Cristina raises the shock stick for a second and electrifies it, a blue light sparking at its end.

"Take me. Let her go." I don't know where the words come from, but I've said them.

Cristina looks puzzled for a moment. Then she laughs again. "You'd give me your life, but all I want is data. And you don't have any worth knowing."

Then the smile leaves her lips, and she says, "Climb over the railing."

"What?"

"You want to save your sister? Climb over the railing, or I'll finish her now." Her flinty eyes narrow as she holds the shock stick against Ava's throat.

Behind her on the other side of the missile shaft, the lab door is bolted shut. "Glenn!" I shout, but I don't know if he can even hear me.

Cristina smiles, and her hand on the shock stick is steady. "If you really want to save your sister, climb over the railing."

As slowly as I dare, I inch closer to Cristina, angling my body so I appear to be headed toward the railing. I could swear the abyss is growing darker, opening wider to swallow me up.

When I reach it, the entire missile silo above and below us is silent. If I plunge into the depths, my own screams will be the last thing I ever hear, and my sister, hanging there, will be the last thing I ever see. I put my hands on the top bar.

Cristina watches me, her tongue flicking over her lips in anticipation.

I swing a leg over, holding tightly with my hands, and then I'm standing on the wrong side of the barrier. One foot is still on the catwalk, the other hooked firmly through the railing like that of a child on a climbing frame.

"Go on," Cristina urges.

I turn to face my death. The darkness is velvet, soft shadows that grow thicker, inviting me to look closer, closer. Ava and I are almost in the same position, our arms spread wide, on the edge of oblivion. But I still have one leg painfully twisted through the railing.

And then I let go with one hand and swing out, throwing myself to the side as hard as I can. For a single heartbeat my body is out, over the pit below. Then I'm slamming against the railing. Even instinct says to grab tight, to hold on, to save myself.

Instead I reach for Cristina.

She loses her footing, and my weight tips her over headfirst. Her hands clutch at my face, my legs, even my foot as she goes down, falling with a scream that sounds like a thousand screams. A scream is ripping through me too, vibrating through my entire body.

Then silence.

I'm hanging by one leg, hooked through the railing, cramping with pain. My breath comes in gasps and the darkness looks hungry, ready for me. I feel like I'm falling.

"Zoe," Ava chokes out.

With a sob, I manage to get my hands back around the railing. Struggling, I heave myself over. Then I can't resist. Leaning over the cold railing with a chill draft taking my breath, I look, but I can't see the bottom. Cristina is gone.

I'm shaking as I pull out the pocketknife and kneel to saw through the duct tape around Ava's neck.

"You came," she whispers, like she still can't believe it.

The tape comes loose, and I help her step up and back onto the walkway, but she's still on the wrong side of the railing. Then I start working on the zip ties that link each wrist around a metal pole.

I can't saw through the restraints and hold on to Ava at the same time, and she is weak. I can feel her muscles spasming. What if I free her and she slips and falls?

Then there's an explosive clang and the door bangs open.

Glenn has smashed the handle off. Gasping, he runs around the walkway, reaching us just as the last of the plastic restraints give way. He puts his good arm around Ava, and together we heave her up and over the railing until she's standing beside us.

Then he pulls her close, whispering into her hair, "You're safe."

She is looking over his shoulder at me when she whispers back, "You came for me."

*   *   *

When I step out of the Houston airport, the steamy air envelops me like the warmest hug. I make my way to the car I ordered and slip into the back seat. We enter the swooping overpass, and I lean my head against the window.

I can't begin to process everything that happened to Ava, but the experience changed her. When we sat at the police station, going over the events, her hand found mine. And it felt like it did when we were little, how she used to hold my hand before we crossed the street. But now I was the one giving her safety and strength. It's too early to tell yet, what this means for us. But she's safe with Glenn in her own home.

Now it's time to discover what finding Ava means for me and Andrew.

I've been texting him, just once a day, with updates. And he replied, which filled me with hope. I almost expected an offer to fly back to Virginia until the police wrapped up the part of the investigation that involved me. But he didn't offer. And I didn't ask.

Instead, once all the interviews were over and I wasn't needed anymore, I booked a ticket back home. My mother drove me to the airport, and even hugged me good-bye. It was only marginally awkward.

The car slows, then speeds up, and I open my eyes. We're on I-59, headed for Sugar Land. The buildings on either side have become such a familiar landscape to me, taller than DC, spreading out to the visible horizon. There's the exit for the roller-skating rink where I took Emma for a birthday party, and there's the one for the restaurant where Andrew and I celebrated our six-month anniversary. Being this close makes it real, the scope of my love for my family and the devastation I face if they won't take me back.

I pull my phone out and type *I'm 15 minutes away*, hesitating only a moment before sending it. It's not the clothes in my closet or the whirlpool tub or cooking dinner in the kitchen that makes Texas my home. If Andrew doesn't want me, there's no point in this journey.

But he doesn't answer, not as we exit the highway, not entering the manicured neighborhood, not on the final approach down my very own street. As the car pulls up in front of the house, I drop the phone into my bag, barely registering the buzz of an incoming text.

Our front walk is short, but my heavy feet move so slowly, crushing the fallen blossoms of our crepe myrtles. The front curtains hang undisturbed, and for a panicky moment I wonder if anyone, anything is behind them.

What if Andrew packed up and moved, if the house is abandoned and I am too?

Then I'm standing in front of the door, stretching my shaking hand to try the knob. I have barely touched it when it flies open. Andrew is standing there, love and relief on his face. He takes me in his arms, and in the fierceness of his hug I can feel how afraid he was for me, how much he still loves me. Tears fill my eyes as he kisses my head and then pulls back to kiss me for real.

"Lizzie!" Emma squeezes in between us, her arms around my knees.

And I'm home at last.

EPILOGUE

AVA SITS BESIDE me in the studio of America's biggest morning talk show. If it feels like a million eyes are watching us now, I can only imagine what it will be like when the interview actually starts.

"Just breathe," Ava whispers, and I realize she's talking to herself. Her eyes are closed and her hands are clenched on her knees. All these years I thought she enjoyed the spotlight, but instead it's just the price you pay for being famous.

A best seller. *I'm* a best-selling author. That's something I never imagined.

The PA adjusts a tiny microphone clipped to my collar. As she moves away, I smile at her in thanks. She smiles back and whispers, "I loved the book, but it's so scary. That woman was insane." As the PA heads off to get her next round of instructions from the talk-show host, Ava catches my eye and winces. I put my hand on her arm. It still feels awkward, but my sister seems to relax a little.

I know we're both thinking about Cristina.

She had been obsessed with her father's research, and then with my mother's role in it. As a research assistant she was helpful, creative, the perfect replacement daughter. But she clearly didn't realize that my mother has serious attachment issues. When the project was over, no matter how fond she may have been of Cristina, my mother fired her.

But when you've built your entire world on a delusion, there's nowhere else to go. Cristina found a weak-willed guy who would follow her orders without question and set off to finish the research. What was the bedrock of her life's work? She believed relationships are torture. That a person who believes they are seeing and hearing a loved one in torment will tell you things no amount of personal pain could ever elicit. And the intel will be more accurate. After all, as my mother helpfully pointed out, information extracted by torture is notoriously unreliable.

So Cristina drugged and kidnapped Ava and Beckett, made sure they were stressed and disoriented physically and mentally, and then started her pseudo-experiments. She and her accomplice starred in the "torture videos," Phil playing Beckett and Cristina playing Ava. No control groups, no consistency. Cristina believed she was coldly rational, but she was driven by her desperate longing for my mother's approval. If I hadn't ditched my past and started over, would my anger at Ava and my frustration with my parents have made me crazy too?

After Cristina's death, Steven Spiegler fled the country. I hear there are numerous internet blogs devoted to tracking him down. I'm not giving him any more mental space. He was an enabler, but not the mastermind, and I have better things to think about now.

Poor stupid Phil is the only one left to stand trial, but he pleaded guilty right away.

And finally, I'm arguably as famous as my sister. I just wish I were back inside the four walls of my own home, now that I have it.

Andrew is waiting just off-camera. Beside him, Emma is watching Ava, her new favorite storyteller, with shining eyes. Whenever my sister and I find ourselves at a conversational dead end, Emma bridges the gap. Even in the makeup chair a few minutes ago, I heard Ava whispering, "Once upon a time," and I thrilled just like I had when I was Emma's age.

And we agreed to keep my family, the rest of it, out of the spotlight. There's no way either Andrew or I would show Emma to the world. He really does love me enough to take me back, although he insisted on counseling. We see a nice family counselor who is absolutely not a clinical psychiatrist. We're not back to where we were last year, when I was lying about my past, my parents, even my name, and that's a blessing.

Now that I'm not walking on eggshells, I'm not quite as careful about making the house perfect, and I disagree with Andrew sometimes. And I love him more than I ever thought possible. I think we're actually heading to a better, more authentic future.

Bethany still looks at me like I'm an alien, but Felicia says I'm officially the most interesting person she knows. And she wants a picture, if I can get one, of me behind the news desk in one of the two anchor chairs. She'll photoshop herself into the other.

The host sits down, adjusting her skirt. She leans across me and addresses Ava. "So they're probably going to ask about your next book, the novel. What are you going to say about your inspiration?"

I exchange a wry glance with my sister. "It's me, isn't it?" I ask. "I'm your muse."

She grins, beautiful and brave and vibrant. "This one's about a total badass who saves the day. What do you think?"

Emma waves, and I have the strangest feeling, one that might become familiar. I have a family I love and friends I trust. If things continue like this, if I don't screw anything up, I think I might be . . .

Happy.

ACKNOWLEDGMENTS

I couldn't have written this book without my husband, Tim. I love you every day and always.

One could argue I wrote this book despite our kids, but they definitely added joy to the process. My favorite part of every day is when we gather together around the kitchen table.

My talented agent, Melissa Jeglinski, believed in this book, found it a home, and offered moral support along the way.

I'm thankful for my editor, Terri Bischoff, for her encouragement and insight, and for the talented and dedicated team at Crooked Lane Books, Madeline Rathle, Melissa Rechter, and Ashley Di Dio, as well as Rachel Keith and Melanie Sun.

I'm no solitary writer, so I thank all the friends and writers with whom I've traded pages and critiques, commiserated and rejoiced: Felicia, Barbara, Erin, and Kena; Bill, Chuck, Heather, John, Melissa, Rodney, and Vanessa; Alice, Anne, Betty, Cheryl, Ginger, Grace, Kathy, and Mona; Angélique and David; and my relentless taskmaster Stacey, who repeated "You've got this" until it came true.

As a beneficiary of Ursula DeYoung's mission to celebrate first chapters as well as the ongoing writing journey, I'm thankful to her for including the first chapter of this book in *Embark: A Literary Journal for Novelists*.

My parents have always been encouraging, involved, and very present. I've never doubted your love, and I hope you know how very much I love you.

Finally, my sisters—Rachel, Mary Curtis, and Rebekah. You are my friends, my cheerleaders, and my inspiration. I think you're all intelligent, funny, dedicated, and endlessly amazing women.

And I don't think any of you is the "bad one."